In the Bronx, in other parts of New York City, in other places in the United States, and in some areas of Latin America there exists a religion sometimes known as Santería. It is the legacy of the Yoruba peoples of Africa and their descendants in the New World. Though often hidden, and changed now and then throughout the years —with its drums and its songs, its dancing and its moments of ecstacy, as well as its strong demand for self-control—it commands a vital and alive community wherever it is found.

Raymond was white, but his parents had died helping black revolutionaries in Africa. The heritage they had left him led by devious means to an acquaintance with Santería. And through it with Concha, who finally set his head straight. Though Puerto Rico, Haiti and Cuba, as well as the Bronx, had had a part in making Concha the priestess she was, her practice of Santería was very like modern—and ancient—Yoruba rites.

Concha's road to Santería—and Raymond's —with its mysteries, its power and its gaiety, blend to make a story that belongs especially to today. Though Santería itself comes out of the past, its place in today's world is made by today's problems, attitudes and needs. The story is fiction, but the base is real.

SANTERÍA, BRONX

SANTERÍA, BRONX

JUDITH GLEASON

Atheneum 1975 New York

Library of Congress Cataloging in Publication Data
Gleason, Judith Illsley.
Santería, Bronx.
SUMMARY: An African exhibit at the museum
draws Raymond deeper and deeper into a mystical
and powerful religion based on the beliefs of the
Yoruba people of Africa.
[1. Santería (Cultus)—Fiction. 2. Negroes—Fiction] I. Title.
PZ7.G48145San [Fic] 74-19493
ISBN 0-689-30447-1

Dedication and Acknowledgments

For Maud "grown up and gone away" first and foremost who shall always be daughter, sister, and "mother of all the Orisha"

To Sunta I owe a special debt of gratitude, which this book, whether or not it makes her "famous," attempts in small part affectionately to repay

To Helen Gleason for her wholehearted participation, for her intelligent reading of the manuscript, my fondest appreciation

To Eric Simpson for his wonderful photographs, and

To Cathy White for her research, loving thanks

To all the children who engaged in explorations of the upper and lower regions of the River Bronx during the spring of 1971, dandelion memories

To all the scholars and folklorists upon whose work the island portions of the book float as upon salt seas, I hereby acknowledge not only an obligation but enormous pleasure:
Lydia Cabrera, Fernando Ortiz,

Alfred Metraux, Odette Menesson-Rigaud, Maya Deren, Cayetano Coll y Toste, Carmen Marrero, Walter Fewkes, Cesário Rosa-Nieves, Francisco López Cruz

To all the *santeros*   *salud, tranquilidad y suerte*

Coming Attractions

Cast of Supernatural Characters

Orisha

Agayu	volcano, old, alone
Babalú	Disease
Eshu	messenger, trickster, personification of chance
Obatala	greatest of all the orisha, creator of child in the womb
Ogun	iron, hunter, smith, lover of Oshun and Oya, warrior
Oshun	river goddess of great charm
Oya	tempest, lightning, speaks to the dead, also a river
Shango	thunder, masculine charmer, husband of Oshun, Oya and Oba, who is "mistress of the cemetery"
Ibeji	twins (known as "marassa" in Haiti)
Yemaja	mother of the waters and of all the orisha

Loa

Agwe	master of the sea and ships
Damballah	great serpent

Ghosts, Guardian Angels, and Other Spirits

'yaloko and waka'tu	Taino Indian *Zemis*
Seraphina	An African Princess, formerly called Nafansi
Carabalí	Revolutionary slave hero, later a *Boumba*
Morris, Lewis	A judge
Drake, Joseph Rodman	A poet
Ranaque and Tackamuch	Weckquaesgeek Indian Sachems
Osu	Bird of the Soul, messenger of Obatala

Christian Saints and Sinners

Our Lady of Candlemass (Candelaria)
Saint Michael, archangel
The Devil
Jesus of Nazareth

Raymond Raps

I am sitting on the bed, legs dangling like this participle I'm suspended in this light and airy, this familiar room, looking in on itself as I look out upon the clutter of leaving: satin remnants from Bathgate Street, unhemmed, pins still in; cartons stuffed with borrowed crockery Jamón won't pick up, plus a pile of old clothes for delivery to Manuela's tenants on Hoe Street; jars of unstrung beads, bewilderment of hairpins and foot creams on the dresser, together with flea powder and dog vitamins, plastic crucifix, plaster statuettes of various saints, coconut shells and small paper bags filled with only she knows which dried leaves and powders.

On the wall between windows, see—beads hanging from shower curtain rings hooked into nails driven into the flimsy plaster. That bunch has been newly strengthened: observe bits of dried blood clinging in the cracks between shiny surfaces. In the opposite corner, a cabinet with glass doors painted over so you can't see in—not yet anyway. Nearby on the floor, however, are visible certain containers I know to be empty because she has already put their contents in bright cloth bags and thence into her suitcase. The earthenware saucer, the cast-iron caldron, the red wooden bowl with a lid, the heavy crock: these remain. But anyhow, aren't you worried about overweight, Concha? Not really. She knows how to stare any official out of countenance, how to make any scale go wacky.

Now she packs her Bakelite bag with wash dresses—reserving a couple to stuff neatly around Eshu and the bird of her soul, which she'll carry upright in her hand luggage; and I am thinking it is I who during the days and nights of eclipse to come will be packing my godmother's trunk with all of her saints, the medicine ball from Haiti, which I've never seen, and Seraphina—who is going astrally, while the doll she resembles sits on in the parlor to protect whatever of Concha's soul lingers. I'll be packing the dwarfs (one good-and-bad, one only malicious), while their images continue to teeter on the chiffonier, not forgetting the fearsome Boumba (never dared ask her what happened to it); I'll be taking inventory so as not to forget the contents of my godmother's mind as mine imagines it.

"Don't look so glum, Reymundo," she says. I like it when she calls me king of the world like that in Spanish, for then my face suddenly becomes a mirror pulling all distorted odds and ends together into the one, entire, tranquil reflection that to the initiated Concha is.

"Cheer up," taking her comfortable house slippers off and tucking them in, "I'll be back before Christmas, maybe even in two weeks if we don't hit it off. You got to take care of yourself, hear? Now, there's a little more room. Should I take any food? You think they got rice over there, coffee? Suppose my stomach can't take what theirs do. Maybe I lose weight. A few pounds or so wouldn't be bad for my feet, but I don't want to get run-down. Maybe I should be sending you out to buy me vitamins."

"A better bet would be to take something along in case of

diarrhea. Haven't you got some Kaopectate in the bathroom? My mother always stuck it right in her camera case. As far as food goes, I think they eat cornmeal instead of rice —to which you won't object, and . . . let me think . . . cassava, that's it, cassava. Never tasted it, but it can't be all that bad if it's so widespread. Anyhow, you shouldn't worry about getting sick. They've got fancy modern hospitals over there, seen pictures of. . . . Everyone wearing masks and dressed in green. Besides, the old people will certainly know how to take care of you their way. Don't forget why you're going!"

"You aren't kidding! But what if they have forgotten a few things. And diarrhea, that's Babalu—a very dangerous orisha. Maybe I'll have to get him too."

"I think," continuing pedantically from the memorized explanations accompanying dioramas at the museum, "they take kola nut instead of coffee as a stimulant."

Bitter comfort. Although I know chronologically she's not young, know also that this is unimportant, although I think she is terribly game, even such modest signs of anxiety, of possible frailty make me impatient with Concha. I want her to take it whole, head-on and under the aspect of eternity. Come back and sock it to 'em, Concha! Imagine us, grandly, as planets. Me the impulsive lightweight Mars, she the expansive Jupiter. So Concha and I have been born and reborn ancient friends. I know it. Me the hot line; she the central switch. She the citadel; I the grisly halberd—secretary of defense. While she's off on her state visit, let me not fail to keep the spiders and scorpions from crawling in to ruin her reputation. Since all drains have to stay open for the cockroach dead, I shall have to do battle along pipelines to the infinite . . .

Now it's come to, "Good-bye, good luck, take care, Concha. Hope you'll write me a card when you get there." I'll be thinking of you every step of the way, for we invented this trip together, didn't we? and now that it's actually happening I can't believe I'm not going along to clear the path with my puny penknife. (Thank heaven, anyhow, Thornskyl isn't.) But how could I? Africa is far away, so terribly expensive, and here I've got to sit down at Ferryman's infernal machine and find the right words to pay for my initiation.

She's gone. The Brotherhood from Brooklyn have insisted on driving her to the airport—two cars, in case one breaks down. Ebo Jones kindly asked me to go with them, but I said I'd rather not, meaning I'd rather see her off in her room—as if she were staying as well as leaving—with a final inevitable send-off down on the street, which is where I'm standing now, watching the bumper of the second Oldsmobile recede over the hill that takes St. Anthony to Tremont.

O patron of lost things, I'm crying now that no one but you is around to see. Already the Bronx seems desolate. I turn and go the opposite direction, to the dead end that leads to the ramp above the Expressway they'll be taking out of the city.

CONCHA

Adventure in
La Cueva de los Muertos

So far so good.

I was born in Otoao, up in the mountains; but when I go back to Puerto Rico, I don't bother to visit my hometown anymore—not even the cemetery. Hardly worth the long trip. Some modern people got hold of the church, emptied everything out and painted the walls slick. There used to be statues everywhere and, on the walls, illustrations from the Bible. Hardly anyone's left over from the old days. Only a few familiar faces. Yet the air's the same, the river as sweet. Sometimes I've thought of sending my daughter's kid over there; but where would he stay? With my brother in Rio Pedras? Except for the climate, not much different from Queens. Children ought to grow up in the country. I wish all my godsons could have done the same. . . .

No complaints.

Not that I haven't been in hot water now and again. But once there's an in, there's always a way out the back door. That's Seraphina's expression. But it was Mama Titi helped me out of the trouble I got in when Uncle Jochem took me to visit the Cave of the Dead. He meant the best, and, as it turned out, I've had plenty reason to be grateful for what he showed me there. It's what I found on my own account that like to have drove me crazy.

Uncle Jochem. He used to take me everywhere. Owned a couple of shacks on the south coast between Ponce and Guayama. We'd go rattling over the unpaved roads in his car, sleep overnight in one of his houses, and very early the fishing boat he was expecting put into shore. They'd unload it quick. Morphine, I think—for selling to hospitals. He had contacts all over the island to handle it.

Uncle Jochem took me along because he enjoyed my company, but *he* was the person fun to be with. Listening to him go on. Didn't mind if I said next to nothing. He knew everything that ever happened in Puerto Rico, same with all the islands, and enjoyed telling it. He was a Dutch uncle, really Dutch—with eyes blue green as the sea—but not, strictly speaking, my uncle. Husband of my grandmother's godchild, who died before I was born. Which didn't stop him from coming back to visit the family. His real home, though he couldn't have stayed there much, was in Curaçao—off the coast of Venezuela.

I was twelve or thirteen. We were going along the Arecibo road, that's the way the river runs to the sea. Halfway, he pulled over and said this was the day we were going to visit *La Cueva de los Muertos*. There was something inside he wanted to show me. "You aren't afraid of ghosts, Concha?" I shook my head. "Which you *can* see?" Silly question. Everybody did. It wasn't just me. Our neighborhood was full of them.

Right next door to us, in fact, lived Doña Lucinda, a love-suicide who walked the balcony every night. Wrapped in a sort of glowing *mantilla,* she was forever keeping a missed appointment. She never spoke, maybe because she was a distant relative, and we've never been a talkative people; but others did—in their way. Sometimes before dawn, bells from vanished campaniles rang out, phantom dogs barked, and occasionally, when the wind was right you could hear *Salve Regina* coming from the burned-out hermitage of the Rosario, or drums sounding up Guaonica Ravine.

All sorts of tricky business went on at night, some of which Padre Pepito insisted was on the up-and-up. Certain souls, he taught, granted God's permission, were allowed to leave purgatory to rouse us out of our slothful condition. As if our sins weren't bedsores enough, said my failing grandmother, who didn't believe half of what Padre Pepito said. But whatever they were up to, there was no mistaking those souls from purgatory, clothed as they were in the fires of their torment. Every house had a big rain cistern to catch the runoff from the roof. Out of which the dead swarmed (through cracks in the lid if you covered it) like fireflies in the darkening air—candles with no stems—warning us kids we'd stayed out too long playing hide-and-seek in the orchard. Inside, kerosine lamps had already been lit, and our parents would surely punish us.

So I had seen plenty, but there are ghosts and ghosts, and as I followed Uncle Jochem up the trail, my heart, I must admit, pounded with fear of Carabalí and those who'd escaped to join him; for they were the most dreaded spirits in the neighborhood. In broad daylight a column of smoke was often seen to pour forth from the cave, and this should have been enough to keep everyone away. Not Uncle Jochem! Seen fiery in full moonlight, people said, "Now Carabalí is sacrificing to Luzbel." Whether to the devil, to St. Blas, or to some wild spirit of his own, so long as those spirits all stayed within the cave, you could keep your safe distance. But there was nothing even Padre Pepito could do to prevent their coming out on the Eve of St. Blas, patron saint of the sugar plantation from which Carabalí ran away in the first place.

The Eve of St. Blas happens to coincide with *Candelaria,* and it was timed so that the moment all of us went singing forth from St. Michael's church, each holding a candle to carry round and about the main streets of Otoao, at that very moment from *La Cueva de los Muertos,* Carabalí and his followers set out to curse all remnants of that family dumb enough to entrust their property to the patron saint of torments. For a while, of course, the slaves were the ones who suffered, but as soon as Carabalí was able to make a pact with St. Blas, owners and overseers began to get their comeuppance. And how! By the time I'm speaking of, there weren't many living descendants around anymore; but those that were left, sons of bastards mostly, whatever the color of their skins, whether their hair was straight or nappy, breath of slaves' curses was sure to put their candles out. Some took the humiliation as a bitter joke and survived to walk next year in the procession. Others simply refused to go out that night. No soap. Carabalí and his followers found them out, spent their curses in worse ways—some we'll never know about. But I'll tell you this: every year, on St. Blas Eve, in some forsaken spot, one more unfortunate hung himself. Would leaving town have gotten them out of range? I doubt it.

Having struggled up for about an hour, we burst through thornbush into a grassy clearing where grazed—odd, I re-member thinking—a single goat. There was no place else to go but straight into the face of a black cliff, guarding that little meadow with a scowl. And sure enough, down on his hands and knees went Uncle Jochem, eased his way through a crevice out of sight.

"Here's where we part company," said Seraphina. "Wild dogs wouldn't drive me in there. You go ahead, though. I'll be waiting right here."

"Coward!" I stuck my tongue out at her and followed Uncle Jochem.

Although a dim light was getting in from somewhere

toward the back, it took time for my eyes to get used to so, scrambling up, I stood still awhile listening to the whirr of bats overhead until, at the top of the vault, I began to make them out. And as I took my time, I heard a high-up squeaky voice say (sounded nonsensical, but I was used to that sort of thing) something like:

"*Guacca-iarima,* round me belly legs, squat feet." And another, sharper pitched,

"Shhhh furry brother. She's asleep. Won't you rummage for me?" To which the first,

"Tell us the tic-tac, watchman, is it sun-bake or slither-black?"

"No use," said somebody else. "Macho—hael's stone deaf, outside."

"Say, where's Jobo, do you remember?" piped up another.

"Silly, sun fixed him into a tree."

"And Giahuba?"

"Gone for the cleansing grasses, wind hummed him hurriedly into a bird, can't you hear? *pitirre, pitirre.*"

I thought I could, just outside the entrance, but that was a common enough sound about the island. I must ask waka'tu and 'yaloko if these be distant cousins.

"Concha!" My uncle's shout made the vault reverberate. "Aren't you coming?"

He was standing at the edge of what looked to be a bottomless cut in the floor. "Good girl," he said, "I thought you'd got frightened. Now here's where we jump. Steps have been cut out of the rock, but there's no use taking them down, too slippery. I'll go first so's to catch you coming down. Don't worry, even if I didn't, you'd be perfectly all right. It's high, about six meters I should judge, but the bottom is covered with a deep layer of soft mud all year-round—springs, don't you know."

It occurred to me to ask him why he hadn't brought a lantern or torch along, but then, since he always thought of everything, he must have had a reason. If there was one thing he wanted me to see, maybe there were others he didn't.

When he called out to jump, I did. So far so good. Taking my hand he led me down a narrow corridor in the direction of sunlight.

"Look," he said, "the back door. That's how Carabalí got out the first time. How easy, now, to imagine it . . . He'd gathered all the bush he could find to barricade the entrance, and when he heard dogs snarling at the break, he must in desperation have set fire to it. Smoke drove him back as far as the ledge where he crouched, thinking all was lost. When the fire began to die down, rather than give up any part of himself to them, he jumped—as it turned out—into freedom. One learns to take that sort of risk, Conchita. It *is* possible to get in and out this way, I've done it myself; but without ropes—too dangerous even for me! It took them a long time, down at St. Blas, to admit he was still alive; but dead men don't cut overseers' throats in the cane fields. From here he must have signaled at night to those waiting to join him. See, beyond the ruins of the plantation factory, the far hills where others lay in hiding . . ." He trailed off and we stood awhile, looking.

"Well, I certainly didn't bring you here to talk about Carabalí. He almost made me forget my own purposes." And with that he began trudging back along the corridor, counting his strides as he went. At ten he bent over and thrust his arms elbow-deep in the mud. "Here, you can give me a hand. Feel around till you get a grip on one of the handles. . . . All right? Now pull, I'll push. Don't worry about the weight, just keep her straight and steady." As we worked toward the "back door," the rock bed gradually rose beneath our feet, and with a series of sucking sounds the little chest we were hauling slid onto the slab lip of the opening. "Now, what kind of a mudfish do you think we've caught?"

"A pirate's chest?"

"Smart girl. Almeida's own, as a matter of fact, from *his* hiding place on the *Cueva de los Muertos*—which is why I brought it here; too nice an irony to miss. Yes, Almeida's," he repeated proudly. "Everyone says it was only his wife buried there in the cave on the key; she was from my hometown, by the way, Alida Blanca from Willemstad. But my grandfather was cabin boy on the *Relampago,* and he knew better. Afraid of her ghost, though, as was my father after him. Not me." He winked. "Being unable to see them. Found the chest, though, thanks to those ferns from the river bottom you gave me. Remember? And that business with the thorns kept the eyes of the curious turned aside till I was able to coax a mule up here to the entrance. Now, can you guess what's in it?"

"Gold, I suppose, if it's a real pirate's chest."

"Right again. Old coins—doubloons, guilders, *escudos, réis,* sovereigns and guineas; and before that, *guanin* the Indians called it, a touch of the sun on breast and forehead, beautiful as the princess by that name. . . . 'I know the Spaniards' god,' the Cacíque said, 'and we must gain his power the better to resist his worshipers. I shall bring forth a basket of golden ornaments, all that remain to me, blow the solemn smoke upon them, then we shall sing and dance the night in this god's honor. At sunrise I shall throw the basket into the sea, and they will leave us alone.' But the Spaniards did not, for their weapons were iron, and their kiss that of the Destroyer. Now, Concha, so long as I live, whenever you must have some of this, just ask me and we'll come here together. After I'm gone, you'll have to go to the bank yourself." He laughed. "Ask someone, the only person you really trust, to help you. Take out a bag of coins, polish them up in great secrecy, and sell to a goldsmith in San Juan. If he asks you any questions, say you found them in an old trunk that once belonged to your uncle. Now, shall we open up and have a look?"

That was the last thing I wanted to do. "No, Uncle

Jochem, I believe you; but I'm afraid of their power, of the Indians' and of Almeida's."

"You mustn't be so. I took only what belonged to the sea, and that, dear girl, is my privilege."

But I turned distractedly and wandered off toward the dark end of the corridor. Something else was pulling me. At a certain point, for no reason at all, I plunged my hand in the mud and felt around on the bottom, as if for something I'd lost. What, I couldn't have said, but all at once I came upon it sure as a tooth come loose in a mouthful of porridge. Without telling, I put that thing into my pocket.

Together we got the chest back into place. Then Uncle Jochem helped me up the cliff ahead of him, calling out where every hand and foothold ought to be. This time I crossed the cave ahead of him, for I wanted to take a private look at what it was I'd found down there. The floor, I now noticed, was littered with bones, glowing phosphorescently.

When I crawled out onto the grass, into the sunlight, the goat was gone but there was Seraphina lazily stretched. She looked queer. I had to call her three times to get her attention.

"Where's your hurry, Conchita," said my uncle puffing after. "Ah, what's that you're examining so intently? Did you cut your hand? Let me see."

My fingers closed up reflexively, but then Seraphina gave me a look that said I owed showing what I had to Uncle Jochem—the least thanks I could give him.

"Something I found at the bottom of the cave, a bone of some kind. Here, have a look."

He drew closer, flung his arm over my shoulders and with great solemnity examined my treasure. "A knucklebone, I should guess, in all probability human. What do you think?"

"I don't know, but it's trying to speak—in its way. See, when I hold it up to the sun it gets heavy." I stretched out my palm to show him, and there was a strong tug that made us both lose our balance.

"Now you're in for it, better keep it covered," said Seraphina.

"Odd," said my uncle. "Well, no use fretting over things that can't be explained. Do you want to throw it back?" I shook my head. "All right, let's see how it behaves wrapped up in my handkerchief. May I?"

"Sure, go ahead."

"Now put it in your pocket. Concha, look here, we're covered with mud. Your mother would have a fit to see us this way. Down below." He pointed. "There's the river. What do you say to a swim?"

"That's a great idea, Uncle Jochem; just a moment till I . . ." It was only that I didn't want to move right then. I wanted to stand very still and take it all in. Down and beyond the kinky slope through which an occasional palm head butted, the river appeared a silver snake gliding in easy curves along the 'green path of its own reasoning.' A strange idea, but that's how it came to me, just that way. Behind, all was ugliness and fearful suffering. Glancing over my shoulder I could see how cruelly the midday sun was treating the cliff face, showing it warty, wrinkled, gouged on either side of the entrance with rifts of hate that would not leave him be, so that the wind gave no peace, stinging insults from the rain. Enough was enough.

"All right, Uncle Jochem, ready or not," I announced gaily. "Can't catch a nanny goat, can't catch me!" And I dashed down the trail ahead of him.

There's a song the Puerto Rican children sing that goes something like this, in English:

> *Saint Serenity of the mountains,*
> *Saint Serenity of the plains,*
> *If you can't get me going up,*
> *Catch me coming down again . . .*

That song flew into my head like the pitirre bird as I flung myself, never mind the scratches, down through the under-brush to plunge into that beautiful, reasoning river. Over and over I chanted the words, not to tease Uncle Jochem, but as a charm to prevent what in effect had already happened. Seraphina, Saint Serenity herself, would have a hard time pulling me out this time.

Secrets of the
Rio Grande

I used to wake up every morning to the sound of a cart
lumbering up our cobblestone street on its way, I always
supposed, to the cemetery. For which reason I never got out
of bed to look, but lay holding my breath until it went by,
listening to what that cart said to me, above dull clump of
horse hooves, creak-rumble-lurch of shaft and planking:

> *For the rim, it's begin, begin, begin*
> *For the hub, no trouble . . .*

Whether my grandmother got these words from the wheels
or not, I don't know, but that she heard the cart go by is
certain. I knew without checking that her face would be
open to the dawn, her ears, no longer sharp, to sounds; and
though we never talked of it, I'm sure she had the same idea
about where it was going. At the first rumble of its approach,
her hands closed tight about the crucifix of carnelian that
she wore, and her eyes stared wildly at nothing.

When that awful cart was finally out of earshot, I counted

to ten, just to make sure, then jumped up and opened the long shutters that led out onto our balcony. Craning over flower boxes, I looked first down the street and across the flat tin roofs of the squatters' houses to the mango grove on the dark side of the mountain, then turned the other way and looked over the brow of the hill we lived on to the square below where, at the nearer corner of the raised patio in front of the church, I could just make out the cuttlebone wings and raised right arm of St. Michael. It was seldom possible to see his sword, but my knowing filled it in like a pencil stroke upon the gray stone wall behind him.

"Shadow of St. Michael," I began aloud, signaling to my grandmother inside so she could form her words along with mine:

> *Shadow of St. Michael*
> *evil darkness overcome,*
> *Gather light from every corner*
> *of the distance you call home.*
>
> *As our prayers bring in the morning,*
> *take up your iron sword,*
> *Cut back the torments of the night,*
> *illuminate our road.*

At this moment, always, as if in reply, St. Michael's church bells clattered into sound, the neighbor's fighting cocks crowed for the second time, some wisps of smoke went up from shacks huddled against Mango Mountain. Black turned to heavy green; certain glossy-leaved trees began to pull away from the mass of darker foliage; and it was morning.

My grandmother lived closed up in herself. All day long —she had her own corner in the parlor—her thin, black figure sat hunched over the long-legged bolster upon which she worked the most beautiful lace you ever saw. They don't make it like that now. Grandmother didn't need a pattern drawn, she knew them all by heart. Her yellowed fingers hooked up the clicking bobbins, looped, twined the threads, pinned each waiting strand where it had to go as surely as if that delicate stuff she formed were secretion of her snail-self, or what spiritists call an ectoplasmic emanation of her soul.

Although she prayed, lips moving almost all the time, she hardly ever went to mass, preferred to have Padre Pepito come to her; but when he did, she always gave him a hard time. On the Day of the Dead, though, she made, like everybody else, the long trek to the cemetery. Refusing my father's arm, she picked her way over the cobblestones with her manzanita cane. When she finally got there, she never went in, but hovered nervously on the edge, by the wrought-iron gate, while my father, awkwardly stuffed into his best suit, took both vases of flowers in.

Otherwise, as I have said, she hardly moved anything but her lips and fingers all day long—except in anticipation of thunderstorms, for which she took most severe and spectacular precautions. Even before the obvious signs—hush and heaviness of the air, bird flights across darkening sky, chill come down from the mountains to silver the leaves of pomarrosas in the public square—my grandmother knew. Shivering slightly—for all that the sun through the jalousies still threw bands of light on the polished floor—she would secure all dangling bobbins to the sides of the cushion, then lean against the antimacassar of her chair and run her fingertips across her forehead in fanlike motions. And, as if at the touch of healing wings, her crinkled nutmeg face seemed before my very eyes to grow smooth again, her brow serene; and when she reopened them, her deep-set eyes were fierce with energy.

Suddenly her boots were unhooked, off her feet, and she was over at the Dutch chest pulling out the drawer that contained the silk slippers and other items such occasions warranted. "Hurry, Concha," as I fumbled with my laces, "put these on and alert your mother in the kitchen."

By the time we got back with candles, grandmother had already covered the mirror with a sheet, bolted the jalousies and drawn blinds over the half-moon windows cut in their upper parts—out of reach unless you climbed on something. While my mother went to call the rest of the family in, I "did" the bedrooms; then we closed the door leading out onto the kitchen porch and were all set.

On a small table beneath the framed chromolith of Christ holding the Sacred Heart, most of the candles were set; and at the first roll of thunder, my grandmother went down on her knees before this altar to set off the wordy fireworks with which she never failed to ground real lightning.

"Señor Mío Jesucristo," she always began, "you who purified the waters of the river in which Juan baptized you, purified the air as you grasped the outstretched branches of the holy tree, O Señor Mío I implore your pity, take away from the cloud that lies before me (over my shoulder, above my head, upon my right hand, left hand) all malignity. Untie the winds holding it together, bind the infernal power driving it this way, convert its wrath into beneficial rain that your name continue to be blessed and exalted."

After which she dispatched six *Our Fathers* and one *I Believe,* before continuing: "Hear O Señor, this our prayer, and permit your holy angels, St. Michael in particular, to defend our persons, our houses, the beasts in our fields, yield of our trees, leaves of our tobacco from all peril: *may they dissipate this tempest!*

"Mateo, Marco, Lucas y Juan, four directions, winds of the gospel, let this danger discharge itself upon distant forests, upon mountain peaks where it will do no harm; by the intercession of Santa Barbara, Our Lady of the Candelaria, by St. Blas . . ."

At which point with her left hand she took up the little paper knife, the letter opener she had readied on the table, and, repeatedly making the sign of the cross toward the sound of thunder, spoke right out to the danger itself: "I conjure you Storm, Tornado, if so be your name, or Hurricane as the old ones called you, retire at once to the wilds, get you up the ravines, begone with your hailstones, infernal fire, begone with the four words God spoke to Moses, may your name resound in the heavens far off, forever!"

Then, after a final round of *Our Fathers*, my grandmother, flushed with excitement, got up from her knees and sank into her chair to enjoy the aftermath. I adjusted her shawl, which she hugged close around her (for she was sweating), and so she would sit, tapping her feet and nodding her head to the harmless rat-a-tat-tat of the rain outside. When, after an hour or so even this stopped, the balcony doors she'd so carefully bolted were thrown open again to refresh the house. All silken slippers were put back into the chest, along with mirror cover, paper knife, and my grandmother, before her face had a chance to crinkle again with the old anxieties, shuffled into our bedroom for a nap.

She was great. My father, arrived sheepishly late from the shop, even my mother, had to indulge and admire her then. But her powers, she confided to me, were nothing now compared to what they had once been. When she was a girl, if a thunderstorm rose north along the horizon of hills in the direction of Arecibo, which was where they always did, all grandmother had to do was take paper and scissors from the special box kept on the desk where she learned her lessons. Rapidly rounding the edges off a piece of that paper, she said but one word (never told me what it was) and cut straight through the oncoming tornado.

My father, so far as I could tell, had inherited none of my grandmother's curious talents. He was a shy stocky man with a face swarthy as hers but differently shaped—round, with a drooping moustache; and he had large square hands, fingers pudgy as parsnips. I can see them now on green baize in

the yellow circle of the lamp. He looked, when relaxed at
the kitchen table, rather soft, even flabby when compared to
the laboring men with whom he smoked and played cards of
an evening; but in those hands, as in his arms and chest,
were concealed a massive strength that enabled him to throw
a calf to the ground or butcher a hog with no help from his
squeamish brother.

He and Uncle Beltrán were co-proprietors of a small general store, to which was attached the meat market, owned
by Don Montoya, that my father ran on commission. Meaning he butchered the animals in our backyard, smoked
meat there, sold over the marble counter in the shop, and
also acted as purchasing agent for his boss, which involved
his taking day and sometimes weekend trips back into the
mountains to look over stock. For such business he was
allowed to borrow one of Don Montoya's horses; and if the
distance was fairly short—say up to Señor Salvador's estate
and back—when I was very small he often took me with
him.

Right arm about my waist, he swung me up in front of
him, behind the pommel, to which my hands reached out
and hung on—as to an unfailing promise of excitement.
From the kitchen gallery my mother, arms folded across her
bosom, looked impassively down, those dark eyes fearful
beneath their thick brows' scorn. It was this solid posture of
helpless disapproval that tempted me to cry out, "Let me
down, I'll stay," but instead I responded, as if unaware that
anything was wrong, by kicking my heels against the horse's
shoulder. To which my father, with an exaltation belied by
thc hang of his shoulders, would call "That's my little wife,
aree! aree! See how she sits so fine in the saddle!"

Otoao sprawls in the corner formed by two torrents that
come down from the mountains to join there and become
one peaceful stream we always simply called Rio Grande.

To get to Señor Salvador's, you took the left branch up the ravine my father used to say must have been named for me —Quebrada Conchita—along which climbs the old carriage road from Arecibo across the island's spine to Ponce. Three miles out of town along this road was the Rolvig farm where my father liked to stop for coffee and a piece of that sweet bread those people make. Mr. Rolvig had a tall, blond son, very nice, who, while my father was talking of this and that in the kitchen, used to piggyback me around the place, letting me go wherever I wanted, which was always, by whatever roundabout route, to the edge of their meadow whose drop to the river was marked by an enormous boulder.

The steep side of this was covered with curious little faces carved out long ago, the boy said, holding me out over so's I could see better, by the Indians. They all peered out of that rock at you with the same round, unwinking eyes, but otherwise the creatures looked quite different. One had rabbit ears and a ring nose, no hands, no feet, and wore a striped jacket—or maybe it was ropes he was trying to burst out of. Another looked like an owl with a jaunty plate on his forehead—like a dentist's mirror. Another, poor thing, had no body at all, not much face either, only a long, sad nose. Another was mostly forehead with ears scrolled up on both sides like a telephone receiver—his snout the dial. Still another was heart-shaped, like Erzulie, Haitian Mistress of Love. And the strangest of all had four spidery legs dangling from his chin like a very sparse beard, jug ears and something sprouting from his head like a petalless flower. Only one, the heart-shaped lady, had a mouth. The others spoke through their eyes. Above the roar of the river you could hear them quite plainly, "*Toa, toa, toa.*"

"You hear them, don't you?" I asked the Rolvig boy.

"Not now," he always replied, "but when I was your age, sometimes. I think," he once added, blushing, "they are crying for the milk of their mother."

Higher upstream, about a mile past the farm, is a place they call the "dancing ground," a great circle of cut stones. On the side nearest the road, again you may see the rabbit-eared fellow carved, and the one with the stalk growing up —from his nose, this time, complete with petals. *"Toa-o, toa,"* they croak as we ride by, *"O-toa, toa."*

From the main road, which continues to climb in the midst of an ancient cedar grove, a bypath begins slyly to slip away from the canyon wall, and once out of sight veers quickly down through scrub to meander across mountain pasture. Now for the first time you can hear the roar of El Salto de Merovis.

My father urged the horse on, but the ground was soggy and he balked, so we relaxed and waited for the ground to rise, for the path to harden. At a clump of poplars we forded the river, careful not to let the horse stumble on loose stones, sprinted up to the dung-dry trail that bordered an alfalfa field, loped grandly along a couple of hundred meters more, and arrived.

The hacienda was a busy place: tough-looking cattle drivers striding about or sprawled in the shade of mammee trees that surrounded the main house, scrawny mountain women—heads bound in white rags—crossing the lawn with baskets of laundry, and everywhere small children running —how lucky they were! barefoot. After a cool drink of Mavi and a babble of compliments—my father twisting the toe of his right boot, fidgeting with his moustache, blowing out his cheeks, he and Señor Salvador finally went off to look at the stock while I, obediently, stayed put on the steps of the ve-randa. Too shy to do anything but lower my head when any-one, particularly another child approached, I closed my eyes and pretended to be asleep—all the while feeling the cool wind on my neck and listening to the song of the water-fall . . .

Confined for miles to narrow ravine walls, the river sud-denly, at El Salto de Merovis, is released to plunge hit or miss across an avalanche of boulders. Shouting with spray it leaps and falls flat on face after well-worn face of granite, shoulders with ferocious speed through gaps and crevices, taking time out to rest, occasionally, in deep black pools, attended there by water sprites called *guijes*: "darker thoughts its own eddying leisure breeds," according to one of the silly local poets we had to recite, bringing a wreath, on his anniversary. Along flanks of flat rocks grouped about these pools where the river takes it easy, again curlicues and wistful little faces like the ones down by Rolvig's farm. Here, if anywhere, I thought, they would tell me everything they had to say, if only I could manage . . .

It would be this time, or never, I had decided.

I knew the path from the estate because my father always went out of his way to let me have a good long look at the falls before starting home in earnest. And so—I had never disobeyed my father before—getting up from the stoop, I deliberately crossed the grass, looking to neither left nor right, convinced by so doing I'd not be seen. And I wasn't. Having made it to the edge of the lawn, I slid down the bank, followed the mule trail fifty meters or so upstream, then, using both hands and feet, crawled up over the boulders (white water tearing itself to shreds between) to reach a flat rock that lapses into the pool fed by the great cascade, which there takes its first breathtaking fling, over and over, with the roar of a dragon. There I sat in the shade of jagüey-entangled trees that grow along the bank, with a fine mist dampening my bare arms, my cheeks, forgetful of why I had come, of everything but that shattering leap. Hugging my knees close to my chest, I—every muscle in my body— ached, against all bonds of fear, to climb up and try to claim for one awful second my part in it.

"She's stunned . . ."

"O no you don't, Nafansi would be furious."

"Who cares? That foreigner's got no claim on us. We arrived first, didn't we? Now she can't get through for a long time, toe-hoe!"

"What's that? Who's talking?"

"Hoo-hoo, Concha, tic-tac, you'd better stop looking at that waterfall, big eyes, till you've treated them properly, or whipped what you're sitting on."

I stared at the little faces on the rock. "*Toa, toa*," they all creaked.

"Shut up, porridge-eaters," said a contemptuous voice, first of the speakers, surely the beard-legged creature whose sprout in this place looked more feather than daisy, "If you don't I'll bash your peeper-breathers in."

"Ouch, don't menace me," said the second. It was the rabbit-eared fellow speaking, the striped. "I'm her protector, too, and much more useful, for all that sweat sometimes slackens me. He may be fierce," addressing me, "but then again, he's limited to only one direction. Allow me to introduce ourselves. He's waka'tu, bent on evil. I'm 'yaloko, for both bad and good, depending . . ."

"Why does everyone say, *toa toa*?" I asked.

"Why do you suck your thumb," waka'tu countered.

"I don't anymore. The lady across the street put bitter juice on to cure me."

"Well, there's your answer!"

"You see," 'yaloko attempted, more kindly, "all of us were frogs once, bats before that, but the old ones stranded us where the sea is near and we had to hop up to fresh water hiding somehow, didn't we? Now we're all kinds—sun struck . . ."

"Stones, though," glowered waka'tu, "first and foremost, sons of our mamalith, don't ever forget *that* or we might refuse to serve you. Let's cut the babble, flab-sack," addressing 'yaloko, "now we've lured her up here, we've got to get down to fish-business or miss our catch. Who knows when her father's going to turn back and start thinking her?"

"I told you, pearly-nosed-son-of-an-itch, I'd see to that," said 'yaloko, greatly offended. "Concha, now you've got antiquated, you'll want to keep in touch, won't you? And the only way that can be done is to pocket us home with you, isn't it?"

But how? I didn't see any way to pry them off.

"I said we were stones, didn't I, not faces. For the last time, don't forget it. If you really want our company, you'll have to dive down and get. Frightened?"

"It won't be too difficult," said 'yaloko reassuringly. "After all, we will be protecting you. Better take off your smock first—get advance rid of the evidence. That's a girl. Now slide down and ease in head-first. Don't be afraid; once you're under, jagüey roots and our *guije* friends will help. There you go; now take a deeeep breath . . ."

It was true, just as 'yaloko had predicted: no sooner had my arms and head folded themselves into the water, than certain liquidish creepers gripped me under the armpits and pulled me steadily down till my hands slid along the bottom. Then they held me there while each set of fingers, crablike, groped for exactly what waka'tu and 'yaloko wanted themselves as. Then those roots, currents, whatever gently somersaulted me round and pushed.

When I climbed out, still giddy from the shock of cold water, I lay flat for a few moments thinking of nothing but the warmth of the rock, which I could have fallen asleep into, spinning . . .

"Hurry up, put on your dress," said waka'tu crossly.

"Your father's memory keeps straying back to you, and I'm fit to be tied tethering," gasped 'yaloko.

I jumped up. "Put us down, idiot, can't possibly pick up your clothes with your fists shut."

But I'd been clenching them so hard they refused to open.

"Concentrate!" said waka'tu in an exasperated voice.

I thought them slowly opening, and there in each palm lay a smooth stone of a remarkable shape—flat on the bottom like a three-pointed star (if there be such a thing, with the points softly rounded) and hump-backed on the top. Which was which? The lighter gray was moist. That must be 'yaloko, who sweated. The darker, waka'tu. They weighed the same. I put them down, got dressed, and then, careful to keep them from knocking together, I wrapped the stones in my handkerchief and stuck them in my pocket.

"Now get going," mumbled waka'tu.

A few minutes later I was safely back on the steps of the big house with no one, apparently, the wiser. I had just time enough to set my face into a dozing expression before my father and Señor Salvador strode round the corner. "Concha, we're late," said my father, mopping his brow. "No time to visit the falls this trip, I'm afraid. If we aren't home before dark, we'll catch it from your mother."

As soon as I could manage, I buried the stones at the base of the acacia tree in our backyard. They wouldn't have been safe in the house, what with my mother everywhere cleaning and straightening. Anyhow, it was nice to sit out there under that yellow cloud of blossoms playing with the dwarfs. I say dwarfs for that's what they soon grew into.

I drew their features on the stones with pen and ink. They said that was a good thing. And one day I simply found them sitting on a branch of the acacia—free and easy, looking exactly as they do to this day—small, stocky. Waka'tu has heavy eyebrows that meet and protrude, a thick beard. He wears a single feather flush with his flat nose, carries a club, and over his back is slung a quiver of poison arrows he blows through a bamboo tube. 'Yaloko in some ways is the opposite—no hair at all, sort of like an albino, arms and legs mere stumps. When he walks upside down on squishy ears, he calls it 'moon madness.' His stripes, he says, are from a crueler time; he likes to cover them with his silken cloak, closed at the neck with tassels.

Together in those early days we made a good deal of mischief. Even then they would have done anything I asked, but being ignorant of jinx, I held them down to simple things like breaking plates, stealing papayas from the neighbor's yard, or giving my mother headaches. Sometimes, for no reason I could figure out, they balked, wouldn't appear to me as dwarfs anymore, nor, when I spoke to them, say anything but the sulkiest *toa toa*. Once I got so mad at their stubbornness that I clunked their heads together, after which they uttered no sound at all. This panicked me. Uncle Jochem happened to be visiting, and I thought, if anyone could help me, he could. So, asking him to come out in the backyard where we could be private, I got up nerve enough to say, "Uncle Jochem, you've been lots of places, know a lot, what would you do if you had a couple of . . . sick stones?"

To my great relief he didn't laugh, but put his hand to his beard, closed his eyes and thought. "How sick, in what way?"

"I don't know how to explain. Sometimes I think just stubborn. But then again, I think they must want something. What happens is they won't come out of themselves. Now it's really bad. I'm afraid they're dead or something."

"Aha. Now if they're ordinary stones, I'm afraid there's nothing you can do about them. But, if I had a pair of special stones, and they acted that way, first thing I'd try is a little tobacco. I've seen it done with great success in Guyana," he added with authority.

If he had been mystified in the beginning, so now was I. "Tobacco? How? What kind?"

"Just light a cigar and blow on them like this," he demonstrated with the smoke from his pipe. "Your father has lots lying around. Do you want me to show you the way to get one started?"

"Sure, thanks a lot, Uncle Jochem. You won't tell anyone, will you?"

"Of course not, Concha," looking very solemn.

"How are they?" he asked, a couple of days later.

"How are who?" pretending innocence.

"Your patients, your sick stones." He winked.

"Them? O they're fine now. Tobacco smoke was just the thing."

"I'm glad. At your service any time," he bowed.

To his eternal credit he never asked to see them.

The Devil
Behind the Cistern

Months went by; my brother was born; another year; and with one thing and another, I never got back up to the falls —not for years. My mother had always disapproved of these excursions, and now it took little to dissuade my father from taking me along. There was so much more work in the house. I might be of use, be helpful. The hold of other people upon my father was never very strong, and now, with a son in the house, he easily lost interest in me. Every so often he would casually pat me on the behind, call me, as before, his "little wife," but without conviction. I accepted, as one learns to accept what one cannot control. Tobacco smoke could not activate my father's affection!

Waka'tu and 'yaloko, at least, continued responsive to the only treatment I then knew; and for grown-up companionship and instruction, I turned, wholeheartedly whenever he was around, to the exuberant, and profound personality of Uncle Jochem. Puerto Rico, alas, was but one of his ports of call. I dreamed of him when he was off away elsewhere,

and often sent 'yaloko to whisper in his ear at night that his
Conchita was lonesome. I needed an ally. What I couldn't
bear was that my father no longer stood up for me; when
forced to intervene, he insisted mother knew best, it being
time—I suppose he thought, if he thought about it at all—
for me to start becoming a young lady. Which I had no intention of doing.

When my chores were done—coffee carefully roasted
over the grate, ground in the wooden mill, my brother's
linen scrubbed and stretched out over bushes in the yard,
plantain fried and mashed in the mortar—I used to dash
down the back stairs toward the mountain that had been
calling me all morning and gorge myself on mangoes with
the ragged squatters' kids who climbed those trees no faster
nor surer than I. Sometimes, while 'yaloko and waka'tu
stood guard, I went fishing with the boys on the flats by the
town dump or, if I felt like quiet, climbed partway up the
canyon formed by the right branch of Rio Grande to a
shaded pool discovered on my own. I took the stones along
and let them refresh themselves in a shallow place for a time
while I, stripped to my underclothes, taught myself to swim,
or simply lay on a flat rock gazing past blue, blue sky to the
band of white clouds forever forming and reforming on the
other side of the ridge that blocked all view of the farthest
mountains. Even during school term, there was time to play
after supper.

Infuriated by my unexplained absences, unable to prevent
what she could not predict, my mother concentrated on the
results—scolding me for the dirt on my legs, for the tears in
my clothes. And I, always able—while waka'tu and 'yaloko
kept her thoughts at bay—to slip off whenever I wanted,
learned to take unflinching all complaints and abuses.

I had, however, her unspoken permission to be outside
"until dark." By that time of day she was tired out and enjoyed sitting on the front balcony with my small brother on
her lap, watching people stroll by, occasionally exchanging

news or putting up with my grandmother's fixed opinions and indifferent silences. "Until dark," but if one second after, I risked a beating. Most often, this threat, together with my grandmother's vivid hints of what might be seen or even more nearly encountered if one lingered too late in the dusk, got me in promptly—the moment my father had finally decided to light the lamp hanging over the kitchen table, my grandmother to ask that the parlor shutters be closed, and Doña Lucinda next door to begin her nightly vigil. Occasionally, however, if playing hide-and-seek, we took our chances and stayed hid long enough to catch a forbidden glimpse of the night world. Then someone would chicken out, *all-y, all-y oxen all in free,* and we'd dash home to our separate beatings.

Crouched behind a bush, I remember, in full view of the cistern we had the nerve to use as base, watching out for José who had disappeared around the side of our house, trying to decide whether he'd gone far enough for me to make a break for it—I didn't want him to dash around and surprise me from behind . . . Where were the others? I could see Pepito's white shirt behind the chicken coop, but as for the rest, it was getting too thick to see. A firefly flicked past. Up in the acacia—was it waka'tu?—creaked. Somewhere a dog whined. Shivering with excitement, I strained to see the first of the dead souls float up out of the cistern.

Pins and needles, my left foot was asleep. Should I have taken that as a warning? Slowly I eased up until, were anyone behind, I could easily have been seen. Again that branch creaked. "Waka'tu? 'yaloko?" I called them silently. No answer. One of the kids must be hiding up there. Where *was* José? Had he played a trick on us and snuck home along the street? Was it the risen moon that made Pepito's shirt glow like a disembodied thing? Surely any minute now somebody would break it up, would scream *all-y, all-y oxen.* I, for one, could still get back in the house before my parents noticed.

The whine changed to a howl, infecting all dogs in the neighborhood. That did it. More fed up than frightened, I stepped free of my bush and began to slide along the dampening grass to the cistern. I would let myself in free according to the rules and go inside. To hell with the rest. Ghost lights would guide me. As I thought this, little flames began to sprout up behind the rim; but they didn't float off, as they usually did, to lose themselves among night twitterings. No, they continued to rise, now bound together in one continuous sheet, as if someone had covered the rainwater with kerosine and set a match to it. "José?" I feebly called. "Pepito? Maria?" My head began to pound. " 'Yaloko, waka'tu, where *are* you?" I thought in desperation. Again no answer. Only this incredible heat. Higher, the flames reached, as if drawing me in, for without intending I had moved perilously close. Sweating, I clenched my fists, forced my will full strength and succeeded in getting my right foot to move back one pace. "That did it!" said a low voice in my ear. The flames began to retreat. Then an uncontrollable chill seized me by the shoulders; and rising out of the dwindling flames I saw—the devil!

They say I screamed. I know I fainted. And even when I came to, I was in my right mind only on and off. As soon as I could speak at all, they questioned me. "The devil, I saw the devil!" Standing well back from my bed, clutching their crucifixes as if the danger were now in me and not out there in the cistern where I, for one, was sure I had left it, they would extract what information they could before I blacked out again. "Yes, he had wings, boned like a bat's, and three horns," I said, "not two, though the center one was thin as a knife blade. . . . Claws? Yes, laden with rings. And a white face, painted perhaps, for there were cracks in the skin . . . Eyes? Oh very black in that powdery face he wore, twisted with anger."

"Luzbel, I'm convinced of it," I heard my grandmother saying; but she went right ahead calling up all the devils she knew—from Beelzebub to Satan, commanding each unclean spirit, corrupter of youth, propagator of vice and disorder, in the name of God and merits of St. Michael to declare himself to the assembled company. Then she tried salt water. It being Holy Thursday, Padre Pepito could not possibly absent himself from the church, so my grandmother had to handle the emergency as best she could.

"But this is not," my mother kept insisting, "a case for the exorcist." And then, "Everything you're doing is highly unorthodox and," she stammered out in her impatience, "ridiculous." Which must have hurt grandmother's feelings a lot. "She's not possessed. She simply *saw* a devil. It was bound to happen sometime. All her life she's been a bad child, willful in everything. Besides, what she saw couldn't possibly have been the real devil. There's no such thing." At which my grandmother gasped. That my mother was a spiritist was no secret to the family. But she tried, I suppose, to keep two sets of opinions going: one for Padre Pepito and my grandmother (who themselves were usually at odds), and the other for Doña Montoya and her crowd of friends. Well, here the system broke down. Fed up with my grandmother, she persevered. "It could only have been a warning sent by the Good Lord himself . . ."

"The Good Lord," my grandmother solemnly reminded her, "has no time for such trivia. He's dying. Tomorrow will be dead. The entire world is susceptible to every kind of evil now, devils included; and only prayers of the right kind can help. Certainly not quarreling. And you, Dolores, will be getting boils on your tongue if you talk that way about poor Concha. You never should have allowed her outside today, certainly not tonight. When I was a girl, we used to keep the blinds closed Holy Thursday. You weren't keeping track of her at all. You were visiting with a neighbor."

Thus reproved, my mother slumped heavily down on the side of the bed. "You're right, I should not have spoken so harshly of Concha; nor should any of us have attacked her so with questions. For a while it was as though I could see him myself. Oh, I don't know what to think. Evil spirits of any sort are always so upsetting. I need a rogation." She got up and went to wash her face with cologne, as was her habit in times of distress. "The fault lies, I think," settling herself on the edge of the bed again, "with the child's guardian angel. Must be very weak. It has been on my mind to ask Doña Montoya to seek contact and try to work her up a bit."

"Her?" asked my grandmother, perking up.

"Yes, female. How else to account for such mismanagement, the lack of discipline she exerts on her charge? And, to judge by the living company Concha keeps," thinking I had fallen asleep, "she must belong to a most inferior stratum. Hardly evolved at all. In fact I wouldn't be surprised if . . ."

At this point my father burst out laughing. Until then he had been absolutely silent. "Shhhhh, you'll wake . . ." But he could not be contained in his guffawing.

"Perhaps you suspect, Dolores, Concha's guardian angel of being no better than she ought to have been in her former life. Poor fallen angel of my tomboy Concha's! Maybe she has bad hair as well. Maybe she's coal black, wouldn't that be shocking!" And he laughed till it seemed as if he would fall off his chair. It was hard not to smile myself. I had never heard him like that. But I preferred them to think me asleep; myself I wanted to be asleep. Instead I was burning, burning. Their conversation receded.

"I conjure you, ancient snake," my grandmother had gotten her second wind, resumed her ministrations. "And I conjure all unclean spirits of earth, air or water who may have insinuated themselves into this child, to be off. And when you shall have gone, may you extinguish this light!"

What light? I half-opened my eyes and saw that she had placed a long-burning candle on the little desk over by the closed doors to the balcony.

"We should all get some sleep now," my mother said. "Everyone's exhausted. Let us pray to the Blessed Mother of Sorrows for guidance."

"She's busy, too," said my grandmother in a husky voice, but my mother ignored her.

I *was* exhausted, but also, I knew by now, terribly ill and lacking the courage to say so. My cheek burned against the pillow. I tried the other side. Back and forth. Legs ached. And now I was again seized by that uncontrollable shaking, which I half-feared, half-hoped my grandmother would notice. But she was now totally preoccupied with undressing her skinny body.

Nightgown on, sparse hair brushed out, she slipped her hand under my neck and, lifting it slightly off the pillow, inserted a ribbon linking two rough pieces of cloth. The scapularies of Our Lady of Carmel! I had never known her, except when bathing, to take them off. How generous that was. "Thank you, Nana."

"Awake? You feel awfully hot, Concha."

"A touch of fever, I think, please don't call anyone."

"Fire cannot feel cold," she began, like old times.

"Water's never thirsty," I added.

"Breeze won't suffer heat, nor bread hunger," we completed the verse together.

"Now let's say a *Padre Nuestro* for *Santo Lázaro.*"

When we had finished, she put her hand on my forehead, the clever, twisted hand, and in a thin, cracked monotone began the old lullaby to which you can put any words you like so long as you begin, *And then turulete . . .*

> *Turulu, turula, turulete*
> *sing buttery rice,*
> *sing creamy,*
> *and he who hasn't got a cow*
> *won't drink milk at all.*

O turulu, turulete
and he who keeps one
drinks milk only.
Sing turulu, turulete . . .

As if caught in a web of her lace, I slept and dreamed all night of the waterfall. I was that thirsty.

The next day they wrapped me in wet sheets to bring the fever down. The sudden chill against my burning skin, the solemn efficiency with which this treatment was carried out, these frightened me more than the fever itself. It was a nightmarish day. No bells rang in Otoao. That night I heard muffled drums as the procession of the *Soledad* passed up our street and down to St. Michael's. Our Holy Mother searching for her son. In my mind's eye I could see her, swathed in black velvet, imploring hands, anguished face, pierced silver heart (worn outside her gown) exposed to the eery light of the mourners' candles.

Just before dawn I awoke, habit I suppose, tossed off my sweaty coverlet. If I didn't get a breath of air, I would suffocate, surely. My grandmother was breathing heavily in her sleep—her almost-snore. The coast was clear. I ran across the room, threw open the jalousies and there, on the balcony, was my guardian angel. I'd never seen her before, but knew her beautiful African face at once, name, everything: "Seraphina!" In her arms was a basket of leaves and flowers.

"Concha, I can't stay. Just popped in to have a look. Which is to say I wanted you awakened to see me. Every detail, clearly. Vanity, I suppose. Those insults from your family went a bit too far, don't you think? I've been to the plain (below the joining of the rivers, I could tell from the buttercups in her basket, the mint and sweet marjoram) and, it being Holy Saturday, I'm off to the mountain. I wish you could come." Narrowing her lively eyes the better to inspect my condition, she said, "But I'm afraid you'll have to wait until St. John's. That's a promise. Though the worst is past, you're still far from well and we've got to work the plants or you'll see the cemetery first." She laughed, becoming more informal with me.

"O Concha, you wouldn't believe my struggles. That *diabolito* had the nerve to attack me. But I fought and then bought him off with a whole barrel of white rum, one your small friends stole for me from Gonzales' tavern before *he* threw them back in their pond (don't worry, they'll come up), and a box of *his* favorite Havanas—I'm afraid those were your father's. Well, now we're quits. River spell has worn off, fire's died down, common sense reporting for duty."

"You can't imagine how glad I am to see you, Seraphina. I thought you were never coming, had begun to doubt . . ."

"No reproaches, Concha, never any reproaches. I came when I was really needed, didn't I? That's what counts. Now I really must be off while there's plenty of dew." She tapped one of the little bottle gourds nestled among the fresh things in her basket. "You must concentrate on getting well. Otherwise the things I give to the *curandera* won't be ef-fi-ca-cious." She pronounced the word just like that. "You've got a good strong will, but to get where you want, what you want, and to help others do the same, you must learn how to channel it into things; and never never turn it against yourself. Now, health, peace. Someday you'll learn how to say those things in African. Don't worry. Your St. Michael is a tricky one, but now at last the road is open." With that she stepped right into the room and pinched out the candle. Then she lifted her basket atop her head and vanished.

"Concha!" My grandmother sat up in alarm. "What are you doing out there? Get back into bed at once, foolish child."

"Grandmother, I couldn't help it. Thinking the cart had already rolled by, I rushed out to say a prayer to St. Michael; and suddenly the candle snuffed out. Look, it's still smoking. Now I know I have a good guardian angel."

"Well that's that," said my grandmother. "You'd better give me back my scapularies. So much," she winked, "for the devil!"

Secrets of
Mango Mountain

Later on in the morning the *curandera* came. Actually, at that time, there were two *curanderas* in Otoao: the respectable one who lived across the street from us in a neat yellow-painted house with ironwork balcony, and the other, who lived up the ravine, past the cemetery, in an old-fashioned hovel of lashed saplings. This Mama Titi had a reputation for putting the evil eye on children: cripplings and shrivelings, especially, were laid to her blame. For which reason I had never spoken to Mama Titi, though I'd seen her plenty of times, askance, on the way to my special bathing place. The respectable *curandera* had a Christian name, Paquita, to which everyone added the title Hermana (Sister). At work, either in the little kitchen she laughingly called her laboratory or by the bedside of her patients, Hermana Paquita wore a white, starched uniform with pearl buttons like that of a hospital nurse or beautician. Her graying hair was knotted smartly in a bun, and her dark eyes swam behind thick rimless glasses. Although she had a quick sense of humor, she was strict—without ever being unkind—that is to say, rigorous and thorough. While I was sick, and afterward, I learned a lot just watching her do things.

She began by giving me bark of mountain holly boiled with its own leaves to make me sweat and, for the same purpose, plastered my body with dampened tobacco leaves. Peeling these off, she rubbed me down with alcohol mixed with melagueta pepper seed powder, changed my gown and gave me bitterroot tea to drink, which she said never failed to finish off the stubbornest fevers. When, later in the afternoon, my fever went up again, Hermana Paquita did not despair but confidently gave me another dose of the same, wrapped me in a quilt, sat me in a chair and plunged my feet into a tub of water boiled with sweet-smelling sage, to which my grandmother for good luck insisted on adding basil, and for good measure three Our Fathers, three Credos and three Ave Marias. Before the *curandera* went home, she gave orders to let me sleep as long as I liked without interruption.

When I finally awoke, the room was filled with sunlight. *Bien-te-veo* birds were calling from the shrubs that lined our neighbor's balcony. Enameled plates and pans were banging away out in the kitchen (my little brother playing on the floor), and I felt serene, light-legged as I lay there between slightly scratchy linen sheets, and hungry! Easter was over. The sorrowing Mother had found her son on the steps of St. Michael's, where the separate processions of the *Soledad* and the Sacred Heart met and streamed down the aisle as one; while out in the square the boys of Otoao set fire to their scarecrow Judases. Without me watching. I'd slept through everything. Even Uncle Jochem's arrival and equally sudden departure. He'd stopped only one night and then gone on over to the southern part of the island. Back in a few days; meantime he'd left me a present and a hastily scrawled note: "Be a good girl. Stay quiet. Here's a nurse for all three of you. *Abracitos,* Uncle Jochem."

The brown paper parcel was wound and wound with string, so it took quite some doing to open. Ah, there she was—a black rag doll! Though not more than twelve inches high, she was complete: wore three full, flowered skirts, a lace blouse, lace-trimmed pantaloons, a woven shawl neatly folded across her right shoulder, gold earrings, red and brown seeds as necklace, beautiful red satin turban with a basket sewn on top of it. She even had fingernails—tiny pieces of wood inserted into her cotton fingers—and her features had been meticulously embroidered into just the right penetrating expression, with the slightest smile about to form on her correctly compressed lips. Seraphina on her good behavior. "How beautiful!" I exclaimed. How could Uncle Jochem possibly have known what she looked like?

Seraphina herself was delighted with the figure she cut. "Better than life," she said. "I always wanted plump arms. As soon as you get well, we'll fix her up so no one will ever be able to steal your shadow."

Now Seraphina began to keep me constant company. She found it relaxing to be able to slip inside the doll and talk to me from there. "Direct apparition is so tiring," she said. "Imagine the strain involved in making yourself visible all the time, like talking when you're more disposed to silence. It'll take a while for me to get used to. Guess I've grown lazy in my spirit life. Energetic I used to be—and how!— until my former destiny was accomplished. Then I had sense enough to throw it all up and run off with an Indian. Had I not done that, I'd be a sort of saint myself by now. But thank heavens I'm not. Proud, yes, but I've never been a snob. Which is why I get on so well with waka'tu and 'yaloko, I suppose—despite the opposition of their awful mother. Well, that's finished now. Out of the water and into the fire— what a roundabout way to the mountain! Lucky for you there's a stronger power than any of us fighting to fill your noggin. Now don't look so glum. I'm going to stick by you always; and no matter what's in store, we're going to have

ourselves a good time. Don't think you've got to dispense
with waka'tu and 'yaloko on my account. No, soon they'll
be working their way back to you. Everything adds up, not
down. So there'll come a time when you won't be the least
bit hurt to find out that I'm only a sort of substitute guardian
angel. Yes, when the real thing comes along, you'll be only
too pleased to call me something closer to what I really am,
or would be had I not left Africa. But," vigorously adjusting
her shawl, "we've got a long row to hoe. So concentrate on
getting well; before anything else happens we've got to get
you up to the mountain!"

She had promised to take me John the Baptist's Day in
the morning, when all living things are full of grace, all water sacred as the River Jordan, and young girls in my time
used to bathe at sunup in the Rio Grande—down by the
flats where it's wide and shallow.

St. John's Eve I told my grandmother that I planned to
sneak out and go bathing with some older girls from school.
She looked at me closely. "Why Concha, I didn't think you
gave a care to your appearance. Tell me," lowering her voice,
"not a word to your mother, that's understood, but have you
got a sweetheart?"

"No Nana, but I wouldn't mind, that is . . . I've got my
eye on someone."

"Mmmm," she nodded, "just as I thought. I, too, at your
age; but," she frowned, "that's no reason to risk drowning
in the river. All you have to do is fill a tub tonight, put red
roses, white chrysanthemums to float, wash tomorrow first
thing, and you'll come out beautiful as Candelaria. Besides,
having been ill, you might take cold."

"Please, Nana, it's important I go. Everyone these days
does. The river is much stronger than rainwater, you yourself would be the first to admit. I won't drown; I can swim.
Nor will I catch cold. My guardian angel will protect me.
In fact," confidentially, "it was her idea in the first place."

"Well, if that's the case, I suppose I mustn't try to stop you; but please be careful, Concha, and don't get back so late your mother finds out and comes down on us both." From her dressing table drawer she produced a little bottle. "Here," she said, in the excited whisper of the conspirator, "if you think of it, bring me some."

"Certainly, Nana."

Some of this was on the up-and-up. Following Seraphina's instructions, I would bathe before going to the mountain, but in a different place from the others. While it was still dark, she tapped me on the shoulder.

"Come on, Concha, let's get going." Under my pillow, wrapped in a handkerchief, I'd hidden my *toa-toa* stones, several grains of corn, my grandmother's flask, and a consecrated candle cut in three parts, one of which I now lit and set in the corner behind the door. Then I put on my old lace dress—the one grandmother had made for my first communion three years before. I took an ordinary pinafore out of the cupboard, a change of underwear, rolled these up into a ball containing the things from under my pillow, then tiptoed across the parlor to the kitchen. Taking a basket from the pile on the back porch, I put everything in that, then crept down the outside stairs, around the house and out onto the street.

Passing by St. Michael, I gave him a nod and would have gone right by had he not turned his head slightly and given me a malicious look. This was frightening, a bad beginning to our jaunt. "What does *he* want?" I whispered to Seraphina.

"His verse, naturally," she replied.

"But I don't *want* the sun to rise with its usual speed. Do we?"

"I'll say not! You'll have to change the wording."

"*Shadow of St. Michael,*" I began, "*evil darkness overcome . . .*" So far so good. "*Let St. John stay in bed awhile*

. . ." After that inspiration, I was stuck. Couldn't think of a rhyme. Never could. *"Until we get everything done,"* I concluded lamely. "O Seraphina, that's awful."

"Nonsense, don't be so vain. It says what we want accomplished, doesn't it? Now hurry up. And don't keep looking at him. Can't you see he's doing his wily best to detain you?"

Was he? I couldn't help it, looked again, and for a moment wondered if, overnight, St. Michael hadn't switched places with the dragon he was always stamping on. His stone wings seemed to be made of scales rather than feathers, and the little jacket of armor he wore over his gown looked pretty fishy, too. His face, his tongue . . . O this was horrible. I closed my eyes and hurried on into the whitish ground fog pouring down the ravine. It was all I could do, upon opening them again, to keep sight of Seraphina's turban.

On the way up the canyon we picked parsley, sage and goosefoot, which, as soon as we reached my special pool, we twined into a scrub brush. "Once you've been to the mountain properly," Seraphina said, "you'll be able to find any herb you want—even at night. They'll glow for you then. But mornings are best. Or so I've always found them."

On a flat stone slightly downstream from the pool, I lit the second piece of candle. Then holding one stone in each hand, hoping by this means to revive them, I stepped in, dress and all. "Tear it to shreds, tear it to shreds," came the awful voice of the Mother of the Waters.

"Put the stones down and do as she says," counseled Seraphina. "No danger now. This is our part of the bargain."

One by one those tattered strips of my grandmother's lace floated on the surface, hesitated at the lip of the pool, then allowed themselves to be sucked into the rushing water below. Past the candle they swirled. I watched until all were gone down where river and fog became indistinguishable. Then, joyously, I scrubbed myself with the scratchy herb brush, ducked under, came out and danced around on the flat rock until I heard Seraphina shouting through the mist, "That's enough, Concha, get dressed now, it's time to be getting to the mountain."

I'd been up and down countless times, of course, alone or with the squatters' kids who lived and played at the base of it; but this time was different from the very beginning, for we didn't go up the path you could see from our kitchen gallery, but roundabout, by way of a cutoff from the Adjuntas Road. About fifty yards or so up that path there was a termite mound where we stopped to light the third bit of candle and pay our "customs" as Seraphina called it. "At this stage a few grains of corn are enough," she said. "The Lame One knows that's all you can afford. But when you are older, you ought to bring rum, tobacco, a few coins as well."

As we walked the rest of the way she talked, her voice a clear singsong, the way you memorize a lesson: "Three tribes inhabit the mountain: trees, vines and grasses. Each of these has its own master, whom you must learn to call by name so each plant may be alerted to serve you—for good or evil. The paths are many, and games like these the mountain will teach you: tie-and-bind, sidle-and-dodge, hide-and-cover, strike-and-dwindle. Each leaf, bark, root is lively . . . Today you will meet the elders, those whose authority is greatest on the mountain."

A palm rose up out of the mist. "Greetings, Father. I should like your permission for my little friend Concha to listen." The crested crown remained motionless, but a lizard scurried down the bole, which Seraphina took to be affirmative, nodding. I moved closer, hung on and pressed my ear against stiff hairs of the unpeeled bark. "Hear anything?" The crackle and roar of flames, updraft, downdraft, like a living chimney. "That's enough!" Seraphina pried my hands off. Though there was no heat, no feel of burning, my fingertips were charred. And at my feet, horrors, a nest of vipers. I jumped back in alarm. "Don't be frightened. They won't hurt you. Look closer." In the center of this nest at the base of the palm was an iron casket full—for the lid was thrown back to display them—of gold coins. "Every St. John's Day what's hid discloses to those who can see. Uncle Jochem would love that, wouldn't he? You're going to be able to help him a lot."

Behind us, growing louder, was a steady humming. I turned and saw it wasn't bees, but rather a swarm of puff-balls, light as down, settling on the uppermost branches of a tree that bulked so large you could take the whole canopy in at once only by lying down. "What is it?" I whispered in awe.

"Grandfather of grandfathers," said Seraphina. "And I wouldn't be surprised . . ."

"From chips of that bark men were manufactured," interrupted 'yaloko, popping up by my side.

"Within was a flood destroyed the world," said waka'tu, sounding strangely pious.

"*And bones of the first man buried inside became sweet, sweet fishes,*" together they chanted.

"The dead come here," Seraphina persisted, ignoring both them and their remarks, "to catch up on the news and gossip. We have similar 'market trees' back home. This one's like a giant wisdom tooth aching along roots reaching all the way under the ocean to Africa."

"To me it's a cloud," I said, since likenesses seemed appropriate, "and I myself but one exploded drop of moisture like the rest of them." With that I felt suddenly dizzy and would have collapsed completely had not the three of them dragged me across the damp grass out of harm's way.

"You must first ask permission of its shadow," scolded Seraphina.

"I didn't see it. (True, the sun wasn't up.) I didn't know."

"You do now. There's no circle of ground on earth more dangerous, or for you, especially, more important. I think we've had enough exposure for today; but before we go, you're entitled to a gift from the mountain. Is there anything you'd like to accomplish? Someone you'd like to . . ."

"Help or harm?" suggested 'yaloko.

"Do in?" waka'tu with a leer.

"Cure?"

"As you like," Seraphina went on. "I was going to say 'do a favor for.' "

"Yes, actually, there are two."

"Greedy girl! Well, let's see how the Lame One responds to you. This is the formula . . ." as she told, I repeated after her:

> *Good morning, coolness of the mountain*
> *Good morning, green freshness,*
> *I have left my shelter,*
> *Silk Cotton give me shade;*
> *I have come to pluck,*
> *Royal Palm may there be no rain;*
> *I have come to gather,*
> *Please open the road for me,*
> *Earth's bitter joy,*
> *Hidden sweetness.*

No sooner had I finished than up spoke a smallish tree whose leaves are double colored: "*Star Apple has two faces; green without, red within; today yes, tomorrow no; Star Apple has two faces.*"

"Did you hear that?" cried Seraphina. "Just the thing to keep your uncle from falling into the hands of the authorities! I tell you Star Apple works wonders, with palm oil, brandy and the balsam at the foot of flamboyant. Pick it quickly, Concha, while the verse lingers."

Then, with the image of my grandmother before my eyes, and her full flask in my basket, I begged the mountain for one favor more. Again I was answered, this time by the feathery branches of the tamarind, "*Pin, rin, pillow within; sweet dreams to the fitful sleeper.*"

Such my introduction to the mountain. I was happy there, and so learned quickly. For the first time the things of this world began to make sense to me—everything jolted into order, even my grandmother's opinions. Early in the mornings before school (I said I was going ahead of time to help the teacher), Seraphina and I used to meet on the mountain. Sometimes I gathered herbs, for myself or "on commission" for Hermana Paquita, with whom to some extent I began sharing my secrets. At least she knew I knew where to find things, thought me clever, was willing to share what she knew with me; but there was a good deal I had to keep to myself: the meaning.

Like does right. That's how I can best express it. Take the song of bamboo clumps in soggy places. They creak, the inexperienced person might say. But if you concentrate you begin to hear those hollow pipes differently. In those days, I fancied I heard deep sounds like a roar of breakers on the southern shore where I went with Uncle Jochem, or a hubbub from an open-air market like the one set up in front of St. Michael's. So when Hermana Paquita showed me how boiled roots of bamboo could be used to cure asthma, I *knew* that remedy would work because the sounds I'd heard were the opposite of suffocation. And if I thought of these as I applied the juice, I knew it would work even quicker.

There remains one missing link. My grandmother insisted that if asthma, or even bronchitis, was what you had, no concoction could be of the least use without calling first on the merits of St. Lazarus. Well that in a sense was just what Seraphina meant by summoning first the master. In fact, she called the owner of all giant grasses by that very name, St. Lazarus, partly because she was, admittedly, afraid of his African one, but also because she said the African powers had instructed her to teach me first in Catholic rather than in some foreign language I would find confusing.

For a long time I thought all African languages must be

the same, nor was Seraphina the one to set me straight on that. I'm not even sure she's Yoruba for she prefers to keep her past life somewhat vague. "Why shouldn't I," she says, "when there was so much suffering?" Bitter I imagine her memories as the aloe Hermana Paquita used to purify the blood and clean out the kidneys. A plant so strong, 'yaloko and waka'tu told me, that should it ever fall into the river all fishes, frogs and turtles within a certain distance would die immediately. Aloe belongs by rights to the Mother of the Waters. We call her one thing, the Indians—what's left of them—another. So even the dwarfs had plenty to teach me.

But too heavy a burden of golden fruit on the mango tree portends misfortune. This I didn't learn right away, but thought the opposite—good eating! All summer long, flies buzzed about the base of those trees the squatters' kids and I used to climb. An empty sack, the Puerto Rican people say, won't stay as is; but a full sack better. I'd absorbed just about all I then could when Uncle Jochem took me to the Cave of the Dead. That made the bag of my happiness burst, my mind turn, again, despairing.

Secrets
of the Cemetery

When we got home from the cave, I sat politely in the parlor for a while; then, feeling fidgety, slipped out into the backyard thinking to bury my new treasure beneath the acacia tree, so the dwarfs could watch it.

"O no you don't," said 'yaloko. "Not him. Either you take that fellow elsewhere or I for one am leaving."

"Blackwood on the mountain," said waka'tu (maliciously, I should have suspected), "soil at the base of that tree stops footsteps stalking."

"What are you talking about?"

"Toe bones, Scare feet. Wherever you've a mind creep. Bury it—anywhere except under our acacia."

"Rum and tobacco?" I asked. They shrugged their shoulders.

"Shall I light a candle?" This, back in my room, to Seraphina, who had curled up inside her image and gone off to sleep. Lips sewn tight together as a lizard's, eyes fixed into a stare that frightened me: it was a bad sign she wouldn't answer. So, planning to take it to the mountain next day, I put the bone in my bureau drawer and joined my family in the parlor. My uncle had bought a bottle of Holland's gin to celebrate, as he said with a wink, our new "alliance." My mother, not knowing what to make of this, said "Jochem, I wish once in a while you'd take us seriously," and sent me into the kitchen for a tray of glasses.

It fell from my hand and smashed on the tile floor of the hallway. Stupid, clumsy Concha.

All night long the jalousie banged. "Lock it, Concha."

"But Nana, I did, I think it's unhinged."

From then on that banging followed me. Into the kitchen next morning to grind coffee: "What's got into you, Concha? Can't you do anything without making a racket?" It wasn't me. It was the cast iron kettle bouncing on the grate when she wasn't looking. That day I was sent home from school for tapping on the desk, so the teacher said, continuously.

"But it's not me; the pencil, yes; but there's a difference."

"Impertinent!"

"Where's Uncle Jochem?"

"Off to Arecibo, on horseback," said my mother with set lips. "He's cross with you also. The Ford wouldn't start, and opening the hood, he found certain innards missing."

"But he knows I wouldn't do such a thing!"

"What else is he to think? 'She's the only one around here who'd dare touch it.' And with that he stomped off to Don Montoya's stable."

It was true, the neighborhood kids stood in awe of Uncle Jochem and his car—the only one most of them had ever seen, let alone ridden in. Señor Montoya kept his locked up in the blacksmith's extra shed and took it out only for occasional business trips to San Juan. Whereas Uncle Jochem didn't mind taking a whole gang for short spins, which didn't mean anyone was ever fresh with him. On the contrary. Only Concha.

Well, all this, bad enough, was just the beginning. The following morning I awoke to find my sheets tied in knots and my hair so matted with something like pitch that no one could comb it out. Eventually my father had to cut it off short as a boy's.

Still the knocking and banging continued at night, driving my grandmother into a sleepless frenzy. Tamarind branch under her pillow did not one whit of good, nor teas, nor prayers to St. Lucy. And I hardly dared move for fear of wrecking something. Everything I picked up seemed to want to fall down. Chairs slid, as it were, into snares for tripping. My grandmother, naturally suspecting the devil again, in every corner placed candles, which, no sooner lit, went out. So she put on her storm slippers and went scuffing all over the house sprinkling salt water left to right, up and down, calling upon Saints Blas and Michael.

How did I feel? Empty, deserted—as if the river of my strength had run off, and with it 'yaloko and waka'tu, who wouldn't be smoked out for anything. Nor would Seraphina appear. The doll on the bureau continued to mock me with its grim look; and, strangely, the little wooden fingernails were splintered and stained.

("Did you try to fight him off by clawing and scratching?"

"As if that would do any good! No, I had sweet marjoram, pith of custard apple, and was trying, before the wind blew out of me, to tear the heart from a swallow.")

This is where my mother comes into the story. She was, as I may have said, a spiritist. Every Saturday evening she and our neighbor, Señora Hernandez, dressed themselves in white instead of their usual black and, wrapped in shawls, strode across town to the blacksmith's house, while he, "Clavito" Gomez, walked in the other direction, toward our house to play poker on the kitchen porch with my father. Mother considered "working the spirits" more interesting, as my grandmother justly suspected, than anything Padre Pepito had to offer, which was why he was cagey enough to ignore what went on at the Gomez "residence."

This is the way they talked when they were together. For not only did such work bring about elevation of the spirit, but by putting "gifted" ladies like my mother and her friends in contact with Doña Montoya, spiritism brought them all up a social notch as well. No one invited Mama Titi, though no one conversed with spirits half so intimately as she, for you had to be respectable first, then gifted. Doña Montoya, a languid woman with dark circles under her eyes and pale, heavy arms, was their medium. She had been told by her spirits to keep active or perish, and in exchange they would do their best to upgrade the auras of those who sat round table with her. Doña Montoya's principal control was a turbaned Indian named Krishna P. Divanda, Doctor of Occult Philosophy.

The "devil" all over again, my mother figured out, and so ceased to hold me responsible for all the pranks and terrors. Me, she now considered the victim of "fascination" by some mean and inferior spirit who, having once seen fit to appear as an hallucination, had now switched to material means of accomplishing evil designs, from which Doctor Divanda ought to be called upon to dissuade him. Afterward, Seraphina would have to be summoned to account and by prayer strengthened.

About this last step I was skeptical. I doubted she'd even appear to defend herself before such a crowd of goody-goody spirits. Besides, how could anyone at the séance make contact with her when I couldn't? And, further, how could I tell them on her behalf that Seraphina had no desire to "evolve," that she was perfectly happy the way she was?

After all, she could have had, she emphasized, the very morning that we went off on that ill-fated adventure with Uncle Jochem, regular sacrifices in her honor, beautiful dances, her praises sounded by drums the likes of which I'd never heard; but Seraphina thought that kind of power would be exhausting to keep up and so had chosen to remain, as she put it, "vanished queen, half-forgotten founder, the stone in the jar from which no one removes the lid, a mere communal memory, summoned once a year as part of a whole crowd of receding ancestors. . . . And do I care? Mind-reading herbalist is good enough for me—chatty, relaxed, lots of fresh air, intuitive, and," she added, with a witty-wise look at me, "temporary teacher, substitute guardian angel. Nothing permanent." Which also suited her just fine, a well-defined—and limited!—responsibility. But that did not mean, she hastened to reassure me, that we would not always be the closest of friends. Loyalty was part of her skin.

But not at the moment. So when my mother insisted I attend the next séance, I offered not the slightest resistance. Indeed, I had always been curious, had sometimes begged my mother to take me along just to see what would happen, if by any chance I too mightn't be "gifted." But there always had been some excuse. Underneath perhaps, apart from my disheveled lack of respectability, was a fear on my mother's part of competition. That I had to get out of this mess, overrode all previous objections. Agreed. My mother had her own theories, as I've stated. For my part I was terribly afraid, with Seraphina missing, of coming down with the fever again; also that my poor grandmother would break under the strain of so little sleeping; afraid Uncle Jochem would be found out and I forbidden to go on any more expeditions with him.

In my dazed and anxious state, I was quite aware that he never should have taken me into the cave, nor gone himself in the first place. That was trespassing. The cave belonged to Carabalí and his men, who had somehow made their peace with the ancient spirits clustered like bats upon the ceiling.

Why it never occurred to me that perhaps Uncle Jochem had made some kind of pact with Carabalí in order to hide the treasure there, I just don't know. Maybe because, in his own adventurous way, Uncle Jochem seemed so innocent. It actually occurred to me that because of Uncle Jochem's natural imperviousness to harm, Carabalí might be wreaking his vengeance on him through me, ready victim of anyone's anger. Maybe there was a curse on the treasure, too; but that I hadn't touched at that time, so its malevolence seemed less likely. The bone buried beneath the blackwood, could it have been made to speak out, would surely have explained everything. But how? I dared not go near the place without someone to help me. Were Uncle Jochem to come back, next week, next month, I doubted even he would be adequate to that task. Only Seraphina . . . but indefinitely is too long to wait for either the dead or the living. As to which of all my jealously guarded "secrets" would come out at the séance—well, I simply had to take my chances.

We left our shoes in the parlor and with courteous whispers were ushered into the bedroom—got up as if for a wake. The scent of carnations was overpowering. I half expected to see a young child's corpse laid out on the table. Instead there was only a white damask cloth upon which various objects had been neatly arranged: pitcher of water, several glasses, cigar box, a tapping bell, two bottles of scent and one of hand lotion, and every place "set" with a tablet of letter paper and pencil. The blinds were firmly shut. Upon the chiffonier glowed candles in iron sconces. The bed, I noticed, had been pushed way back in the corner. At every place was a straight chair, upon two of which my mother and I were beckoned to sit down. A few others joined us. The rest piled onto the bed. Everyone sat eyes cast down while Señora Gomez, our hostess, got us in the correct mood with prayer.

After a few minutes, there was a stir in the adjoining parlor. Doña Montoya had arrived. As she entered, everyone sat erect. Soon it would begin. You could feel the tension in those straight backs. But first she went about greeting everyone, which in her fashion meant embracing each participant, whispering a series of what seemed like condolences but were probably mere inquiries as to health and family.

When she came to me, guest of honor, Doña Montoya bent down, kissed me on both cheeks and said, with a sort of threatening sweetness—loud enough so all could hear—that she hoped everything would progress for the good of all present; for in the evolution of a single soul, all were involved; from one soul's distress, all hoped to learn something. "Amen," said Señora Hernandez, crossing herself, and the others followed. Upon which, with no warning at all, Doña Montoya passed her hand over my forehead. She was not a fake. That hand was cool, electric. My arms were gooseflesh.

Doña Montoya seated herself at the head of the table. Taking up the scented lotion, she rubbed her hands and face with it and then, to my astonishment, opened a cigar box, took out a fine Havana (were imported cigars more elevating?), bit, spit, lit up, took a few puffs and passed it round. I drew and puffed a couple of times, careful not to get the end wet. I thought of 'yaloko and waka'tu, of Seraphina.

"Right here," a faint voice said, seemingly from the middle of the biggest bunch of carnations. "It's easy to get through such atmosphere. You thought I wouldn't show up? Wouldn't miss this show for anything. Shhhhh." The voice was certainly Seraphina's, albeit subdued. So was her appearance most indistinct, a sort of pastel haze. And what on earth had happened to her turban? Why pink? Faded? Or was she specially got up for the occasion? I smiled affectionately in the direction of the carnations and gave a little signifying nod, which Doña Montoya caught, and under heavy eyelids darted a quick glance there. Did she see Seraphina, too?

". . . I pray God Omnipotent," she went on, "to permit my guide to communicate with me, and I pray that all guardians in this room will give their assistance in keeping away all evil spirits, with the exception, of course, of the misguided soul we shall attempt to reach this evening . . ."

At the opposite end of the table, frail little Señora Gomez began to buck like a horse. Doña Montoya dinged her bell. The spasms ceased. Hunching over her place, pencil in hand, Señora Gomez began to scribble. When she had filled three or four sheets with ripples (rather than words), she jutted out her chin, shuddered her thin shoulders and sank back into a sort of stupor. Somebody handed Doña Montoya what Señora Gomez had written. "Mmmmmm, in-ter-est-ingggggg" she said, running down, as if the scribbles were putting her to sleep. "Eh?" she gave a start. Her voice had changed. "What did you say your cognomen was?" a curious nasal drawl, clearly a foreign accent.

"That's Doctor Divanda speaking," whispered my mother.

"Dolores, concentrate," Doctor Divanda reproved, then repeated the question three times with the tired patience of the educated.

"MIERDA" a bass voice unmistakably said. Everyone looked at Señora Gomez, who looked nowhere, eyes rolled up into their lids, oblivious of what was coming from her lips.

"Again? Either I did not hear correctly or you are behaving in a most inappropriate manner," said Doctor Divanda. "Name please?"

"MIERDA (shit)," the voice boomed again. " 'Name please?' Nonsense. Got no name of my own, no family. To them I weren't no person at all, only a place. Call me Carabalí, and you call my country. No one's apt to forget where

I come from, at least. Nor where I now live. Call me Mierda then. All adds up to the same thing, don't it? Nothing definite, and very dirty. Out of the hole into the sink. No footprints. Well I guess it's only natural to ask a man his name, though in my case you got to dig for it. Shouldn't ask me to write anything, however. Don't you prissy sisters know I'm il-lit-er-it as shit? So are you, Doctor Lavender water. So's everyone here except the kid, and she's so smart I'm going to teach her the spiritual alphabet, first six letters of which are . . ."

"M-I-E-R-D-A." I came up from somewhere screaming it, or rather throwing it up. Much to my mother's horror and everyone's consternation, I was being sick all over that clean white damask. My head split. I was being struck—by a whip? Deep inside was a sobbing I couldn't get at. Outside a quiet commotion, hands busy changing the tablecloth, folding it half over, the way you change a bedsheet when there's a sick person lying on it. The room began to reek of scent. Florida water. I crumpled into the darkness behind my eyelids, lay like a piece of meat about which flies buzzed, vultures circled. I could feel the heavy beat of their wings. Smoke—smell. Awful heat. Too tight the collar of my dress. Indians were being burned in their villages. I could hear their shrieks. "By Saint James!" the Spaniards shouted through silver mouthpieces of their helmets. Banners flapped in the sea breeze, triumphant. Trumpets. Then silence. *Twang, thungk*—a broken guitar string. And I could feel the strain at the leash, collar burning into muscular flesh about the neck. Bare feet were pounding along the packed path between cane stalks. A volley of shots, echoing across the valley. Rumble of thunder. Cane stalks, hide me. Lightning. I received it. Carabalí, Carabalí!

Why was everything so quiet? I opened my eyes and looked tentatively around the table. All eyes politely cast down, Doña Montoya was saying "Our Father . . ." The séance was over.

"Well at least he's put his cards on the table," said Señora Hernandez to my mother as we shuffled home through the night. "Now all we have to do is work him out of this sphere into another," she answered.

". . . Hewers of wood and drawers of water, sent to perform the same work, on the spirit level, that our servants perform in everyday life," Doña Montoya informed us. "All they need is direction. They too can learn to behave responsibly."

But not Carabalí and Seraphina, who it would seem had become so intimately linked that you could simply not get rid of the one and call up the other. She refused to be contacted by Doctor Divanda or any of the spirits at the table. "Question of principle," she told me fleetingly. "In my last life I loved a revolutionary." And Carabalí vowed he would keep Seraphina hostage and continue his destructive course with me until I agreed to devote my life to avenging his wrongs. I suited him perfectly.

Indeed the strength he was able to borrow from me astonished everyone. All I had to do was place my hands on the table, and together we could make it mount to the ceiling. For a while feats like these excited everyone, but after a few weeks the ladies became bored with the sessions and refused to attend them. So long as Carabalí was present, no other spirit—save only the persistent Doctor Divanda—dared appear. No dead parents, no relatives absent in America could be called up, no instructive work done nor moral progress made. When, finally, even Doctor Divanda refused to have anything more to do with us, Doña Montoya politely informed my mother that enough was enough, and I would have to stop attending séances in Otoao.

There had begun to be serious consequences in the larger community. Without advice from the dead, how could the living avoid accidents? A rotten porch step having gone spiritually undetected, Señora Gomez's mother-in-law fell and broke her hip. Who knew which grandchild next might fall from what second floor balcony?

So that was it. I'd have to take steps to get rid of Carabalí myself. And this seemed well nigh impossible. I seriously thought, despite the dread that place now held for me, of going back into the *Cueva de los Muertos* and throwing that bone down where it came from. But would that do any good? I doubted it. For his contact with me no longer depended on anything like a talisman.

Not that I didn't stand in awe of Carabalí. There was even a sense in which I was proud he had chosen me as his vehicle. But at the same time I felt he had misread my character. Mischievous, yes. There was a side of me that enjoyed kicking over the traces, even smashing things now and again, but not at the expense of those I wished well. Nor did I see what possible good to him could come of all this. We had become a public nuisance. He was tearing me to bits. At this rate I'd go out of my head before I was old enough to relieve anyone else's torments, tend to the injustices of this world. To that extent I suppose his maniacal insistence had prevailed. For all the crippled lives led I now felt myself—in a strange, remote way—responsible. Somehow, if I lived, I would try to make Carabalí's outrage felt. Which was enough of a promise, apparently, to suit Seraphina.

We were sitting, dismally, in the shade of the silk cotton tree when, after weeks of evasiveness, she suddenly said, "Neither I nor anyone on the mountain can possibly speak to you in your present condition. And there is only one person in Otoao who can help you get rid . . ." It was Mama Titi.

New moon I greet thee,
New moon, give me health, tranquility,
*   peace to the world,*

No more war, no sickness,
May I never lack, nor my friends, nor my enemies
Bread to eat.
New Moon I greet thee.

So saying, Mama Titi, leading a black dog on a leash, opened the iron gate and motioned me to follow. In front of the largest cedar tree, to which she tied the dog, Mama Titi stooped down and arranged the things she'd brought tied up in her apron. The required number of corn kernels were placed in the form of a cross, and tobacco smoke blown toward each of the four directions. So far so good.

"That's just like Seraphina and I do when we go to the mountain."

"Of course." She clucked her tongue against her wide-spaced teeth. "Mountain and cemetery are the same, only the reverse; so you must never confuse them, no more than waxing and waning." She set nine *pesados* face down in a circle about the kernels, then sprayed rum from her mouth and lit a candle in the center, saying:

Water from the heavens,
Water from the sea,
Holy water of St. John,
Dewpoints—and the white flame.

From four little gourd flasks she poured these various waters into the iron pot I'd been carrying.

Earth from the crossroads,
Earth from the grave,
Earth from the marketplace,
Sweepings—and the black sting.

In went the four soils and the scorpion. Then she sacrificed the dog. It was the first time I'd ever seen that done. Surely, whatever the outcome, my life could never again be the same.

"The warm blood."

I poured it in.

"The cold bone."

I handed it over, at last! The proper place!

"Red pepper. Root fibers."

I produced them.

"Feathers, for speed." I had none and for a moment she couldn't remember what she'd done with them. "Eh! Here they are." Stuck up under the rags she bound her head with.

"Now, Carabalí–Matebo!" she cried, "Come live here!" The ground within the circle of *pesados* trembled. Just to make sure, she set her knife on top of the pot containing the ingredients. "Carabalí–Matebo, come live here!" she repeated. The knife swung around as if magnetized until it pointed due west. Or so she said. "Ha! *Non hay mal que por bien no venga!* Congratulations, Conchita, you got yourself a very strong pledge." With nine more of Uncle Jochem's coins I paid her. "Now, don't forget what I told you. You must take it to the mountain and bury it under silk cotton. Leave it there three Fridays, then come back to me and I'll show you how to feed it, how to get it going. Maybe you like to keep it at my place all the time for security?" No, I didn't want to do that.

"Don't worry, Mama Titi, I'll find a safe place."

"Now run along, child, I want to catch her when she dips. Eyes white as milk set out in cat's dish can blind the beginner. But sometime you'll be up to it, eh? If we take good care of your servant. I think we going to be fast friends now, Concha."

"Yes, Mama Titi. I'll come by and see you whenever I can, and in three weeks certainly. Thank you for everything."

"Don't mention it." She grinned.

Once out of the gate: there was Seraphina. I knew she'd be.

"You were perfectly right to keep a little distance from Mama Titi. Learn from her what you like, but remember Carabalí is *your* pledge, not hers. Those who work with the dead can never be entirely trusted."

"I guess that includes me now, Seraphina, meaning you'll continue to keep your distance?" I teased her.

"Silly, of course not. Only, when you go in there, I'll wait outside. Well, that's over," wiping her brow with the end of her shawl. "And I know it's for the best. Fated, naturally. There must be order . . ."

Suddenly I understood. "Seraphina! You gave him up for me!"

"Forget it. I will eventually. It becomes easier when you have to do it over and over. Besides, he got what he wanted, didn't he?"

"Who knows? I imagine he'd have liked Seraphina and me more political. Well, we were for a time—over there, where it would do some good. But not after we came to America."

I had never been to the mountain at night before. By the time we got there, the new moon had vanished, her seven sisters bent low in the sky. I picked a few leaves of sage from my favorite bush, and they glowed in my hand like furry minnows. 'Yaloko suddenly appeared, looking more rabbit-like than ever before, his eyes misty with tenderness. He bounded onto my shoulder, pressed his clammy nose to my neck and whispered, "Did you see her when she came down?" I shook my head, wondering. A strange rumbling, a slight heaving of the ground beneath my feet:

"What's going on?"

"Shhh, look there," Seraphina pointed. "It's the silk cotton returning home."

"What? From where? Can it really? . . ."

"Visiting the others hereabouts. Had a good time, too, see—it's dancing."

And so it was, ponderous, gracefully rocking from side to side, pulling itself along by its buttress roots as if they were crutches. The most extraordinary sight in the world. Few are fortunate enough to be allowed to see it. We waited until the silk cotton settled down, fifty paces from the royal palm to which it bowed, and was in turn acknowledged. High up, loose twig ends, still swaying, playfully brushed away the swarm of glowing souls at their alighting.

"Let us roost where we can. Dawn will find us all far away from Africa," sighed Seraphina. "Now, Concha, ask permission to bury your dead and let's be getting you on home before the shadow of St. Michael . . ."

RAYMOND

Directions

I

Though my city is inner, I'm hardly disadvantaged. On the contrary. I was born on a pirate ship: repeat, holding your tongue and you'll get my meaning. That's Manhattan Island —other side of the tropics. No church bells. No rickety cart. No *bien te veos.* Starlings, though, and sea gulls mewing in the night.

My birthday began with the reservoir in Central Park, concluded with stickball on asphalt. You think I feel sorry for myself? Well you're wrong. The first sound I awake to every morning is the honey wagon going down Madison Avenue grinding everything as it goes along, except maybe a teddy bear salvaged from the wreck of somebody else's childhood. Pale blue, life-sized (maybe some grown-up won it at an office party), strapped to the biting backside of the Department of Sanitation truck—reborn as a mascot. Good luck! We need it; we're running down. Without that Sanitation truck, the packages put around everything would pile up, nudge us out. Instead, all that cardboard, Styrofoam and so on, destined for fill, gets chewed up in vast charnel houses strategically located along the edges of the city. The one I know best is on the East River near the fireboat station, south of the footbridge to Ward's Island.

Those that can't make it mentally on the mainland are shunted off here to take the sun, when it shines, on concrete benches behind barbed wire. Island-within-an-island, further insulated by a park where our lower school takes its June outings in the disdainful shadow of the Tri-Borough Bridge, remotely bypassing Ward's Island on its way from 125th Street to Flushing.

Cut off? Follow the refuse. ──⟶ This way lies salvation. ⌐↘ Imagine such signs installed at key points about the city. Your choice—gone for the most part undetected—where every traffic light blinks odd, blinks even.

Once it has chosen you, Santería reveals a living patron for everything, even sewers, certainly barges. Okada is the divinity of garbage. Climb up on a mound sometime and have a look at the plume on his headdress: doesn't bloom so much as ooze a mealy growth smelling like low tide on the Sound: All-Good, vulgarly known as "Stinking Goosefoot." Combined with honey, vinegar and salt, it makes a fine poultice—I bet Melissa would know for what kind of swelling. If you want to keep a tattletale from talking, just wrap the roots with lizard's tongue in a strip of white cotton. In that half-kidding, half-sinister way of his, Ferryman has threatened to use this jinx on me if I don't well disguise the truth of what I'm writing. No problem. Either both or neither of us be unscrupulous betrayers. So long as you keep the lid on, nothing wrong in showing the pot, says Ferryman. I say, my story's a ball of yarn the unraveling of which will get you only to the end of it. Not until you roll it back up in your own mind does it need fastening. How else can I explain? Reality, right on the surface, camouflages itself.

Hence the mystery of the chameleon. Or, until you've begun to follow, you won't even notice the signs.

Here's how I got started.

We were sitting at the kitchen table when all of a sudden an escaped parrakeet—the green and yellow kind—flew in through the broken pane the super has never gotten around to fixing. Hopping along the counter to the sink, it abruptly changed its mind, took off and flung at the window. Bonk, back again on the counter. Can't he see the grease on the pane? No, only the light he's after, taking his chances on an opening. Over and over, blunders; shorter thrusts, frantic feather fusses, blunted. "Not there, over to the right!" I shout. Startled, he swerves, flutters high onto the curtain rod. While he's doing this I jump to open the window.

Neither of us till then had moved or spoken. That thing had us hypnotized. I propped the frame with the plunger (sash being the old chain kind, and broken), then tiptoed back to my place at the table. "Now the coast is clear! hit a homer!" The bird had been cautiously clawing his way down the curtain. Startled, he dove out into the room, veered round and headed straight for the open window. Meeting no resistance, showing no surprise, he sailed right over the airshaft, swerved to miss the adjoining building and continued through the gap toward all we could see of our reservoir in the distance.

I got up to close the window, wondering why on earth neither of us had thought of trying to keep him. We could have closed the curtains, caught him under the colander, found a secondhand cage for him on Third Avenue . . .

"A typical case of hysterical behavior," my sister was saying. She was, then, a psychology major, with a strong minor in the classics. "If you hadn't opened the window, he'd still be at it—to the death, unless by accident . . ."

Sometimes I found Miss Hunter College irritating. "So you think you've got all the answers! How about the fact it flew in at all? Well, I'm going out. Lucky I know where the door is. . . . Say, when's lunch?" I called from the corridor.

"Not till one. Charlie's coming over to study. I've got errands. Raymond," she added, "don't be mad." And then, not in tune at all, "I just hope that bird finds its way back to where it came from. Obviously he's a pet. Some old lady, some kid, will be just as frantically searching . . ."

"Better find him," I called briskly. "Starlings in the park will tear him to bits; if he doesn't die of cold first." I zipped up my jacket.

Heading off around the reservoir, I thought I'd check out the museum. I was still early enough to be there when it opened. Saturday mornings are okay—until the crowds come. I kept thinking I might catch a glimpse of the parrakeet. Just a few shreds of plastic in the trees. Leaves' fall discloses everything. Lost kites, birds' nests. No parrakeet. Out on the ridge that divides the reservoir in two (you can actually see it in summer when the water ebbs), the usual line of gulls stood awaiting orders. White against gray water. When the cinder path began to curve north, I jumped over the wire.

Where to go? After a quick run through Birds of the World, I elevatored up to the Hall of Man in Africa.

To spend an hour or so in there can be a very strange experience. Not so much because it's spooky, though it is that. Mr. Thornskyl—he's the Curator of African ethnology— set it up as a sort of darkroom where indirectly lit "symbols of power" are slowly being developed. How? Take the masks, for example. Strung on invisible wires they appear to float—white moon with horns, hollow-eyed crocodile with a twisted jaw—like ghosts of what they really are, which is what you can't tell yet, and maybe never will know. And all the time there's this African music being piped softly through the room: sweet xylophones, distant stampede of drums.

A well-lit anteroom leads into the dark. Here the visitor

is supposed to stop and shed false ideas, learn what the African continent is really all about. Tarzan–anti-Tarzan. On the walls are blowups of the way it really looks, people, children in ordinary schoolrooms, young man in a welder's helmet, woman walking to market with a stack of enamel basins on her head, old men in loose robes talking. Some of these photographs were taken by my parents, the Hunts—maybe you've heard of them. On one of their trips they got mixed up in a revolution. Their Land Rover crossed the border with guns, meant for the guerrillas, hidden under their photographic equipment, and for this they were shot up by mercenaries. Or so the story goes. I was only nine at the time and, as you might imagine, all shook up. The leader of the Freedom party, a professor, friend of my father's, wrote a personal letter to me and my sister at the time, saying one day he'd take us where it happened and explain what had been going on. Meanwhile, our great loss was shared by all who believed in human dignity, and we should consider him an adopted uncle, ready to help us out whenever we needed . . . My sister answered; but by then he'd sort of gone into hiding, I guess, and we didn't hear anything after that. Two years ago a bomb went off in his briefcase. Although there's no plaque, which my parents certainly would not have wanted, the blowups remain as a kind of public memorial, so Mr. Thornskyl explained over the public address system when we came down from Middlefield for the opening.

Middlefield, that's in the Berkshires where we were sent to live with our real aunt and uncle. They are both writers who left New York about ten years ago, bought an old wreck of a farmhouse that they've gradually been fixing up themselves, plank by plank—even the plumbing—which is where they were at when we came into their lives. No furnace yet. We spent the whole first winter around a wood stove in the kitchen—my aunt, my sister and I. My uncle had his typewriter next to an electric heater in their bedroom. We all got on each others' nerves somewhat, but we made do, and

by spring, despite the mud, which drove my aunt crazy, I
was loving it. My uncle helped me build a lookout in the
apple tree, and I helped him dam the stream so we could
have a pond by summer. But my sister was bored, down in
the dumps. My aunt is pretty enough, even now, to be a
model, likes to dress up in old fashioned clothes to go with
the house, refinish antique furniture. She writes pretty good
poetry, though of course I'm no judge, but on the whole *is*
rather childish—my sister's verdict, she herself being ma-
ture from the word go. I mean, unlike my aunt, Marty's
never been one to avoid responsibilities. By the time she was
in second grade, Marty could cook almost as well as my
mother and better than the various baby-sitters they got to
stay with us when they went off to Africa.

There was nobody, she said, for her to talk to in Middlefield, nobody her type, nobody even interested except the
biology teacher, a ridiculous man who got a crush on her.
We called him Mr. Peepers. The first winter Marty skipped
a grade, started to study Greek and Latin on her own because that's what she wanted. I didn't care. I don't depend on
school—and it certainly can't depend on me. I like to read,
and there were plenty of old books at the fussy little library
open two days a week and paperbacks to be pried out of my
aunt and uncle's still unpacked cartons. But Marty couldn't
stand it, and after two years, when she was fifteen, she began making my aunt and uncle think about letting us move
back to New York so she could finish high school at Walton.
Marty's persistence always pays off. They had to admit she
was perfectly competent to take care of me, and finally let us
do it.

We wanted to find an apartment near the school. With my
uncle's help we found one right on Madison, just two blocks
south of where we used to live—three rooms in the back,
sixth floor.

In the beginning my uncle came down from Middlefield
every once in a while to see how we were getting on. The

first year we went up for Thanksgiving, the second only for Christmas and spring vacation. This year we stayed right where we were. I thought Christmas on our own would be kind of lonely, but it was actually more fun.

Marty can do what she likes, but I think I'll always keep going back to Middlefield summers. After all I've been through, I appreciate that country—how shall I say? for its calmness, long views of the hills from the back meadow, light-flecked woods, and the vegetable garden—cleared, plowed and planted. If local divinities there are, they're sleeping. Sometimes a strong wind tries to shake old secrets out of the trees. They submit their branches to the storm, but remain silent. The noon sun softens the haunches of granite slabs through which the Mad River once cut its way into the next valley. These days the river, now only a stream, seems misnamed, placid rather, the color of amber, here and there carnelian deep. After a swim you, too, can fall asleep contoured in smooth depressions of those comforting old rocks. This summer I'd thought of setting up a little shrine or two, but so far it has seemed inappropriate. Maybe a good thing too. Might bring strife and disaster down upon Middlefield. It would seem the roving gods of the world are attracted to places where the action is—like New York City.

That day, as I started into the Hall of Man in Africa, I saw something I'd never noticed before. To the right of the entrance to the photographic exhibit, cut into the wall was a cube-shaped niche sealed over with glass. Not even indirect lighting, so you were forced to peer inside. There was a strange lump, a sort of head with cowrie shell eyes and spurs for ears, sitting in the kind of raised rimmed clay plate you put under a flowerpot. On the floor of the cubicle, below the shelf that held this creature, stood a three-legged cast-iron pot containing a collection of miniature tools. A rusty horseshoe sat astride the edge—one leg out, one leg in the pot. A

printed card stuck up against the inside of the glass gave the
following explanation:

SHRINE OF ESHU-LAROYE
with *Guehierro*
presented by one of the many
Afro-Americans
who have preserved the
African tradition
in this country

You don't say! I stepped back a couple of paces to try to
figure out what was going on. Shrine? How would I know
what a real one was supposed to look like? And who was this
Eshu-Laroye glinting at me as if I ought to have known him
but didn't? *Guehierro*. Clearly that was Spanish, a mixture,
it would seem, of iron and warrior, or perhaps a new word
we hadn't come to yet in our *Essentials of Spanish* vocabulary. The horseshoe—for good luck. That much was clear.
Tools? They work. I get it—*Guehierro* means what he says.
If you're on his side, you'll have good luck. He'll work it out
for you. Like deciphering a rebus. But Eshu-Laroye himself
said nothing.

Preserved tradition? No blacks I knew had anything like
Eshu-Laroye shrines in their apartments. Only blink boxes.
Same size, though. For all I knew, at midnight these kids and
their families gathered in front of the screen—a closed circuit Afro-American program came on—to worship Eshu-
Laroye. Glinting eyes in a puff of smoke. Right on, Eshu,
you tell us what's what. How the Spanish caldron can brew
hard and fast good luck. Nonsense—that card was a put-on.
But "one of the many" was enough for my 'satiable curiosity to go on.

Luckily, although it was Saturday, Mr. Thornskyl was in
his office. He'd been on a field trip, just got back and had, as
I could see, a lot to catch up on. True, I hadn't seen him for

a long while, but then I hadn't tried. He was really my parents' friend, not mine. He looked thinner than I'd remembered him, a bit lined, his blue eyes surprises in his tanned face. Otherwise, same beard, same pipe, same cable-knit sweater. Around his bony wrist was wrapped a chain, a sort of bracelet—not silver, iron. When he caught me staring, he casually pulled the cuff of his sweater down, smiling,

"Well, Raymond, what can I do for you?"

"I came to find out something, sir. That shrine to Eshu-Laroye outside the Hall—new, isn't it?"

"Yes, a fairly recent acquisition."

"You must know all about it. Of course, to you it's nothing new, but I really had no idea such things had been preserved since slave times. And there's nothing as real as that in the rest of the exhibit; I mean nothing as close to home. Do you know the person who presented it? I mean do you know him personally?"

"O Ferryman," he laughed. "He's quite a character. Knows far more about the religion than the average Yoruba."

I knew the name. Quite a few of the "symbols of power" on exhibit were marked "Yoruba."

"Are all the African traditions preserved, like the sign says, in this country Yoruba? Only Yoruba?"

"So far as I know, maybe there are others."

"And this guy, Ferryman, how come he knows so much? I suppose he's traveled a lot; and his ancestors—maybe they were Yoruba?"

Thornskyl laughed. "Ferryman's never been farther across the Atlantic than Cuba. And he's sophisticated enough not to give a damn about who his ancestors really were. All he cares about is that he's got it now."

"Got what?"

"The power," said Thornskyl, leaning forward, an intense look in those light eyes. "*Ashe* is the Yoruba word for it."

"Well I can see that's what Eshu-Laroye has got, same

with the Spanish caldron—in a more, how can I put it? obvious, nitty-gritty manner. Eshu-Laroye seems much more mysterious."

"Spanish caldron?"

"The *Guehierro,* that's what it says. Spanish caldron is just what I call it."

"Call it rather Ogun; that warrior is Ogun, Yoruba god of iron. Of course there are others."

"*Ogun*—" as his voice hit bottom and came up dragging the deep tone, I fell in love with the sound. "*Ogun*," I repeated it. Which amused him.

"Look Raymond, I have a hunch. I'm very busy." He gestured at the clutter before him. "If you're really interested, why don't you go see Ferryman yourself? I'll give you his phone number, and a warning. He's harmless, but you must never go there without calling him first . . ."

"Where does he live? What part of Harlem?"

"Not in Harlem at all, not far from you as a matter of fact, on 91st Street, over by the river. Now, one more thing, you mustn't tell him who sent you. Don't let on that you know me, even mention my name. I'd rather not."

"What if he asks? He'll think it odd if I call up just like that, won't he?"

"Tell him a friend told you about him . . . anything. I leave it up to your imagination. Only, I repeat, don't bring me into it." He looked very stern now.

"I won't. Thanks a lot, Mr. Thornskyl."

"Not at all; let me know how it works out. What a joke on good old Ferryman!" This rather hurt my feelings. But I wouldn't have put him wise to that for the world. There was, beneath all the man-to-man cordiality, something cold about Thornskyl, something that pretended to be close but was really remote. Was it arrogance? He, too, knew a lot, a lot he wasn't telling, would never tell *me*. He too was a *guehierro*.

II

Well I was in for it now. I'd gotten Ferryman on the pay phone, and he'd said, "Okay. How far away did you say you were? (I hadn't.) Across the park? Well then, you can start on over. By the time you get here I'll be *all* finished." (With what?)

I tried to keep my nervousness down when I talked to my sister. "I'm calling from the museum. Might be a little late for lunch. Don't worry." I'd been tempted to add, "If I don't show up at all, start looking for me at 444 East . . . but I hadn't, and here I was—what on earth for? On my way down that steep hill, looking on the right side for the correct number. In front of a row of red-brick houses was double-parked a beautiful white delivery truck—MAR-VEL MILK. It was the only live car on the block. The rest were drab sheep nuzzled up against the curb, slowly—here and there a hub-cap already stolen—decomposing into the glass-strewn asphalt. As I tentatively started up the steps of 444, a burly figure in starched white coveralls, shirt and cap came bounding out of the door. Took the steps two at a time, swung himself into the cab of the truck, slouched for a moment—time out to mop his brow with a red bandanna. Though it was far from summer, that man was hot. Hotter still, he lit a cigar and started her up. I stood right where I was, all admiration, wondering what private joke it was made him slap his stocky thigh, bend forward in soundless laughter.

"Hey baby," he called, noticing, leaning across the cab to get a better look at me. "Where you going?"

"Dunno," I said with great embarrassment; ran on up those steps, and four flights more.

"It's Raymond, Raymond Hunt who spoke to you just now on the phone." The battered old door swung open at my touch, pitching me forward into the bare room.

"Hello kid, give that door a shove, will you," said Ferryman, sitting propped up against the opposite wall. "Shall I get you a chair? There's one in the other room."

"O no, this'll do fine," I said, sinking down to the floor as unobtrusively as I could, beside a low table, which looked to be the only real piece of furniture in the room.

Next to the open window some plants—various herbs and tropicals crowded into pots of different sizes, all small—caught the bright morning sun, which came right on in, dancing with dust motes to further yellow the pages of old newspapers and dog-eared *Police Gazettes* stacked up at that end of the room. The plants stood on a shelf formed by a continuous row of crates housing black loose-leaved notebooks. In the corner an overloaded metal wastebasket disgorged a tuna fish can, angrily crumpled papers, cork-tipped cigarette butts. The old stove in the corner was heaped with pots, the nearby washstand with plates. And here and there scattered about the floor was a paper cup turned on its side —wooden stirring stick drooling a few last drops of "take-out" coffee—two jelly glasses—an inch or so of wine slowly evaporating into a brownish red scum—mason jar lids overflowing with butts that had given up hope of ever finding a place in the crowded wastebasket. This room, in short, despite Ferryman's considerable presence, looked almost moved-out-of. Clearly, behind the curtain in the next one was where the action, if any, was. The mere fact of a chair's being in there implied, contrasted with this bareness, much. Over by the door I noticed, out of the corner of my eye, a flowerpot lid containing Eshu-Laroye. I rotated around slightly.

"That's not necessary. You can keep your back to him. No need to be afraid of that fellow; he's fond of children. Who'd you say sent you?"

"I didn't, and would rather not if you don't mind too much."

Ferryman looked thoughtful, almost worried. "Whyever

didn't whats-his-name come along with you? Sending a kid to see someone as frightening as me alone—what sort of a friend is that?"

"A busy one," I said, and we both laughed. Now for the first time I dared look at him directly. He didn't seem too old, maybe forty. Nor did he look too well. Apart from his still being in his pajamas, his face was yellowish, a bit saggy. Eyes—cloudy, and he often squinted, as though they bothered him. No, I didn't want a reading. (Cards? Was he a kind of fortune-teller?) Well, what then?

"My friend, the one who sent me, said you knew more than anyone else about African traditions." Ferryman's scanty eyebrows went up, making his forehead wrinkle. "About Eshu-Laroye, Ogun—and stuff like that."

"Hmmm, did he now? Then perhaps he's more my friend than yours." He paused to let that sink in. "True, of course," he went on modestly, "though why this should be any business of yours I can't imagine."

Because it's Saturday and I haven't any other business, I thought of saying—much too flip. Because a parrakeet flew in our window—too nonsensical. "Because, although we're not blacks, my mother and father knew Africa quite well, spent a lot of time, got killed over there in fact—not by Africans, though, by whites—mercenaries—helping to put down the revolution my parents were involved in, rather by accident I believe, but nonetheless . . ."

"I understand. And I'm sorry kid. Bad destiny. I guess that does give you a right to ask a few questions." Again he paused, seemingly distracted. "You know we've got a revolution going on right here in this city. There's enough power in the next room to blow the whole frigging island to pieces. I could call up the mayor this minute and force him to do anything I ask."

"Wow!"

"But we're laying low for a time," he continued, "till we've got all our demands together. Then either Whitey gives in, or we give it to him. Most people out there on the sidewalks have no idea they're walking through fire—flames shooting up like devil's weed through cracks in the pavement. That's what the old volcano is saying—small talk from the core of the earth. Like this." He lit a cigarette. "Listen, once fire alone was creator—long before water. Get it? There's a lot of stuff in the newspapers about violence. The crime rate in New York, they say, is a hundred times greater than in London. A kid your age can get knifed in a scuffle over a Coke bottle. Put it out? Nonsense. Someone ought to get wise, hook up to it, tap that fire in its pure state, bottle it—what a hustle! Ah, but it's not too easy to play with fire. You go through changes when you tap that violence . . ."

"When you're little they say you mustn't, never turn on the gas, never play with matches," I contributed, feeling safely in the drift of the conversation.

"That's right, kid, and when you're big they say, 'That guy must be crazy, man; it's a wonder they don't lock him up in the slammers.' Listen, you're all right. For $4,000 I could do the whole thing, set your head right forever. You say you can't cross over? I'll carry you on my back. You say them ravens' beaks is empty? I'll see they bring you meat. When old Ferryman does the job, I mean it sits. I wonder who has put in a bid for you. Ogun? He's tough, but even so, 4,000 would cover it."

What was he talking about? "I hate to tell you, Mr. Ferryman, but I don't have a cent. No more than carfare. How could someone like me possibly raise $4,000?"

"Gee kid, I forget." He looked disappointed. "Well, you'll know where to find me should anything come up. If the Big Lottery really wants you to win, he (pointing to Eshu-Laroye) will find you the bread to put on your ticket, spread it right out there on the street for you to sweep up. I mean I've actually known it to happen."

"Even without the money, couldn't I just come by again sometime and talk?"

"Sure, talk is cheap, if that's all you want, and you can follow what I'm saying, don't ask for too many explanations —sure, that would be fine. But like most kids, I bet you'd rather be where you can get with it. Now I haven't had anything going for a long time," he gestured around the room apologetically. "Time was when I used to throw *bembes* right and left—that's what we call drumming up the power and the glory. But unless I've got a saint to make, I don't go in for the fun and games anymore. Not worth the preparation. I've got more serious homework to do. Sometime, when you're more familiar, I'll let you in on a few minor things. A little jinx never hurt anyone, and in this town, if you can't go the whole way, it's a good idea to know how to protect yourself in small ones." He stopped, evidently coming to some sort of decision. "Obalete now," he went on, "you might be interested to go see what he's got on the fire. Lots of action there. Funky Obalete with his chorus of reborn babes. These days he really whips it up. From all I hear. You might drop in some Sunday afternoon at the Yoruba Temple—117th Street, corner of Lenox. Just stroll by and see if those humpty-dumpty drumskins have anything to say to your head. All the king's horses with their bad behinds trying to get it together again. Obalete's something else, I tell you. And if you decide to go on in, introduce yourself, say old Ferryman sent you. Any friend of mine has got to be a friend of his. . . ."

He looked depressed, tired, but was too polite to get rid of me. Up to me to take the hint. "Well, so long, Mr. Ferryman, thanks a lot."

"That's all right, kid. What did you say your name was?"

"Raymond. You wrote it down, if I'm not mistaken, when I came in."

"Did I? O yes, little black book. Better give me your tele-

phone number while you're at it. Come back and see me
sometime, no matter what. Do you want to learn how to say
hello and good-bye to our friend over there? Just give three
taps on the floor and say 'with your kind permission, Eshu-
Laroye.' Got any small coins? Even a penny or two? That's
it, just put them in the collection plate, and I guarantee they
won't be embezzled by the preacher."

"Take care," I called, pulling the door softly toward me
until it clicked.

Going down those rickety, stinkity stairs, I had an image
of Thornskyl at his desk and thought how strange it was that
alliances could so easily shift. I might not know anything
more about the preservation of African traditions, but as of
now I was definitely on Ferryman's side of things and
wouldn't dream of reporting back to Thornskyl.

"Well, what have you been up to?" asked my sister, looking at me over her horn-rims with stern amusement. "What's
going on at the museum?" They were taking time out to
listen to some drawn-out medieval music in the living room
—sitting on the rollaway (my) bed, his head in her lap.

"Looks like the Dark Ages itself in here," I said. "Marty,
if you don't wash the windows, I'm going to have to. You
guys ought to go out for a walk while it's still nice."

"We've been," said my sister. "I picked up your good
shoes at the repairman's."

"Thanks."

"Listen, Charlie's got the car tomorrow. He said he'd
drive us up to Bear Mountain. We can go skating. Anyone
you'd like to ask?"

"Thanks, but no thanks for that unless we can get home
by lunchtime. In the afternoon I'm busy."

"O are you? What's on the fire?"

"Everything!" I laughed. "The entire city. But don't tell

anyone so I can find a private way to cash in. Now, if you guys will excuse me, I'm going to take a nap, in your room, Marty—okay?—I'm pooped."

"No lunch?"

"Well, a bite I guess."

"I wonder what's got into him?" said my sister. I could hear her easily from the kitchen.

"Raymond's all right. Let him alone," said Charlie. "If he wants to tell you what's on his mind, he will."

"Right on, Charlie." I walked back through, my mouth full of peanut butter. "You'd flip, wouldn't you cats, if I told you that only five blocks from here lives a genuine African witch doctor in yellow flannel pajamas. A living tradition, maybe not too well preserved—all bottled up, though, in intelligence."

III

I'd never walked into Harlem before. Taken the bus, yes —up to Edgecombe Avenue where a friend from school lives; and I remember going to the Schomburg library with my mother now and again when I was very little. I used to take copies of *Hue, Sepia* and *Ebony* off the magazine racks and look at them while she took notes from the books piled before her, intent, as she was fond of saying, on separating myth from fact about Africa. Nor did the facts of Harlem escape her notice, and she took pains to point them out to me as we rode by. But she never got out and took photographs. That, she said, was the business of black photographers like DeCarava.

Would she have understood what I was doing now— starting up Lenox Avenue on a sunny Sunday (two bright days in a row, cold spring in the middle of January) with my hands clutched for courage in my jacket pockets (I had my good clothes on underneath) and only my eyes for camera? I'd told my sister I was going uptown to a birthday party, by which she probably thought I meant Morningside Heights, so we left it with no further questions asked— thanks to Charlie's respect for my independence.

I was struck, as I suppose all white visitors of any age are, by the number of churches and funeral parlors. Whatever else these people hadn't—no service from the Sanitation Department, that was for sure—death and religion they did have; and as they came by in snappy pantsuits, men in chesterfield coats, kids in herringbone caps, little girls with white fluffy skirts sticking out beneath their heavy toppers, I thought of the Mahalia Jackson record we had: *"They gon' walk! Rise up and walk! . . . kick a holy step across heaven."* And smiling shyly as I passed, hoping they wouldn't stare back (which nobody did, though one little girl stuck out her tongue), I strode on up to 117th Street.

That I'd come to the right place was obvious. The storefront windows had been painted out with thick colors. You could even see the strokes of the brush that had formed the blue ☥ (ankh—ancient Egyptian "sign of life"; I knew that from the museum) against a green background, red ⋈ ("double-ax," said Marty when I drew it to ask her) against black. On the whitewashed wall itself, black, green and red letters formed the following advertisement:

AFRICAN GODS
Revived
YORUBA TEMPLE
of Obatala

In front of this sign a little boy in short pants and Eton jacket stood crying—completely, sobbing out loud as the tears flowed down his plump cheeks. Other people began to gather along the sidewalk. The place was also, I realized, a bus stop. A green dragon lumbered up to the curb; the other people got on; the green dragon farted off leaving the little black prince alone on the sidewalk. Well, there'd be another one. I felt around in my pants pocket for bus fare. He stopped crying long enough to take a good look at the coins, then shook his head manfully and went on crying. So, thinking of Eshu-Laroye and his being kind to children, I set the fare down on the sidewalk in his name and swung around to the entrance, a beaded curtain at this hour, a steel door by night.

That I had arrived too early was also obvious. Rather than hang around outside, I went in. The room was long, narrow and empty of people, though rows of folding chairs anticipated quite a crowd. On the street end, where the afternoon sun through the painted windows cast colored lights on the white linoleum floor, a straw mat had been placed to accommodate Eshu-Laroye in his dish and, I was pleased to see, the cast-iron caldron of tools beside. "Ogun," I said to myself. "*Guehierro.*" Both objects were stuck all over with feathers and surrounded by tidbits of food set out in small sauce dishes. After tapping on the floor three times, "with your kind permission," as Ferryman taught me, I stood up and cautiously walked the length of the room to the far end, where a set of congas caught my eye. They were really beautiful drums, newly painted with black and white diamonds, and stood slightly to the left of a tall cabinet with closed doors, before which a straw mat had been laid out lengthwise. To the right was a white canvas curtain, with voices coming from behind. In back of the drums was an open alcove where, in the half-light, a small gnarled man in a navy watch cap sat bent over some task. Well here was someone. I drew closer. By his feet was a ball of cord, in his teeth a pearl-handled knife. He was repairing the beaded net stretched around a calabash shaker. I just stood there waiting for him to look up, which he did in his own time.

"*Alafia?*" giving me a sly glance. "*Shay Alafia ni?*"

If this was a test, I'd have to flunk it. But I tried repeating the word, "*Alafia.*"

He nodded.

"Sorry, I don't speak Yoruba—yet," I put in for good measure.

"Mmmmm." He squinted at me for a closer look. "You come to see Baba?"

"That's right." My own boldness surprised me.

"He's in there—" pointing to the curtain.

"Well, maybe I'll come back some other time."

"O? Don't you want to wait till he comes out? Want me to let him know you're here?"

"Is that what one does? Trouble is, he won't know me from Adam."

"Are you sure about that? Adam was a black man!" He gave an explosive laugh. "What's your name, kid?"

"Hunt, Raymond Hunt," feeling terribly out of place.

With that he put the calabash down, lurched forward, pulled over one of the drums and began to smack out a pattern, repeated it three times. I wished the floor would swallow me up. "That's okay, kid, relax; Baba doesn't really understand drum language anyhow, not this kind." With which, horrors, he went on to call out, "Hey, Baba, there's this little white dude of a Hunter-man to see you."

"O please . . ." I was perspiring.

"I'll be right with you." A most carefully groomed and pitched voice. Without looking back at the man in the watch cap, I moved over to stand directly in front of the curtain. "My dear," the voice, slightly disdainful now, "you can 'think it over' all you like, but I tell you, your physical health will begin to suffer."

"It's only the money that's keeping me back, Baba, honestly," rejoined a woman. Then he said something I couldn't catch, and she began to back out through the curtain. I stepped aside.

"Next please." Long beringed fingers held the canvas back so I could slip in easily.

"Most of them," immediately taking me into his confidence, "don't seem to realize what's wrong with them."

I nodded sympathetically. "Too bad, though, isn't it, in her case; she's awfully pretty."

"Seems." His elegant hands gestured helplessly. "In reality all that black beauty wasted, wasting away. Inside," he bent forward to let me in on the secret, "rotten. Rotting," he corrected himself. "Now, young fellow, what can I do for you?"

How to answer? I should have thought things out better in advance. But how could I? . . . Ought to be able to think now, but . . . it was difficult to do anything but look at that incredible person. Under the white peaked cap, Obalete's face was lean and handsome, nose long and slightly arched along the bridge, eyes clear, terribly intense and at the same time genial. He wore a voluminous white African robe of some very heavy material embroidered in a slightly contrasting cream color, and about his neck, stretching down as far as his waist, hung about five pounds of necklaces and talismans. We were in a tiny cubicle, room for only two chairs with an ice-cream-parlor type table between. Nothing on the walls. No place to look except right at him. Surely he was getting impatient. I had to say something. "Ferryman sent me."

"O?" Intimacy, to both our reliefs, restored. "How's he doing these days? Getting it together bit by bit? We used to be good friends, then he began to drop out. Jealousy perhaps. What do you think?"

"I don't know him well enough to judge. Sure, he's a little odd, I guess, but he seems like an intelligent person to me."

"Very."

"Well, it's like you say, he, being kind of out of things, thought I might like to come up here and check out the Yoruba Temple." Did that sound too cheeky? Outside, the room was filling up. Above the heavy impulse of talk came the sound of drums tuning. "I suppose you wonder why? . . ." How could I explain it? That ever since yesterday I'd had the feeling of a magnet pulling me like a stray paper clip, a pinch of iron filings, I couldn't say against my will, but definitely outside it, and a thousand times more powerful, so that resistance would have been comical. Or sometimes, whatever it was spun me round and round and then withdrew, as in a game of blind man's buff, leaving me like a little boy compass needle with lost bearings. O dear, he must wonder why I don't say anything, think me odder than . . .

"My dear boy," Obalete was saying, "ten years ago I would have been glad to accommodate you—toddler as you would have been then!" He smiled benignly. "But the situation has changed. I can't imagine why Ferryman wouldn't have clued you in. He's not that out of touch. Nowadays it is very important for the Yoruba Temple to be at the forefront, if not at the center," he sighed, "of the Nationalist Movement. Otherwise, a black life-style can only be a white capitalist game—a chance for middlemen to grow fat on mahogany picks sold in incense-burning boutiques, soul food, soul drink—the same old soda pop that ruins our people's teeth. Without religion at the base, all this return-to-Africa is a mockery. What's the point of sprouting an Afro if the head beneath is nothing but confusion? Better shave it off, as we do, completely. There's a lot of jive talk about vibrations—but how are these communicated except through the sacred medium of language? And I don't mean slang; I mean the mother tongue behind the fashionable black English. Which is where we begin here at the Temple, with the Yoruba alphabet. The loaded word, the correct intonation, that's the only way the brothers will ever be able to change things. Call it educated conjuring. Not just *Latin 'n' soul* on the congas, but genuine Yoruba patterns, which 2,000 years ago were discovered to release the power of the great divinities."

He paused on the last phrase, giving me a chance to speak, and what popped into my head was, "And the Black Muslims? How do they fit in?"

Which triggered him off again: "A foreign creed, with all apologies to the regretted Malcolm, imposed on us—no different in that regard from Christianity—whatever their myths say. No slave name, agreed, but why call yourself X when you can answer to a name that means something in your own tradition? A name recalling the aspect of divinity that rules your head, lifts you up, gives you an identity beside which all other forms of 'blackness' are but skin deep. Why a dark suit? Why all the discipline, not to say mortification of the flesh? I'm Obatala, I can't drink; but how ridiculous to keep Shango away from liquor! Islam, I say, is foreign to our temperament. We, too, are clean. We, too, have dietary rules, but they depend on who you are, what jibes with your personality, your power, the direction your fate takes, not on a single prophet's prohibitions. For, our prophets, like our divinities, are many."

He searched in the folds of his gown, drew out a silver watch on a fob and said, "Long past three, I'm afraid I must dismiss you and get on with my other duties. By now it must be clear I would personally very much enjoy working with a young person of your obvious gifts (How would he know? I hadn't said anything.) but my people would never understand. Were your hair just a little bit crinkled, your nose slightly spread—anything to suggest you had at least one black grandparent. But as it is . . ." He threw up his hands. "Well, you get the drift. My first wife, however, was, is a white woman. I'm going to send you to her *madrina*—that means godmother—the one who initiated her. This woman is a Puerto Rican, takes in all kinds, mostly Spanish, but likes to listen to anyone's troubles, except," he laughed, "those of whom she up and decides to disapprove. Then she can be really fierce. Don't worry. She'll like you all right. Here's her phone number. Bronx—she'll tell you how to get there. Tell her Obalete said to get in touch. Later on, when you've got your beads, as an authorized visitor from another house you can drop in on us to see what's going on—no questions asked, so long as you don't come too often. She's Obatala, too," he added. "But a different road. Call hers Calvary and mine the Wilderness of Judea—if you want Christian comparisons." For the first time there was the curl of envy, of bitterness about his aristocratic mouth, a pinch to the flesh beside his nostrils.

"I really don't." I tried to joke. "But I'll ask someone. You see, I don't know very much about the Christian religion either."

"Well then," he relaxed a bit, "you've got a fresh start. No hang-ups, as you young people put it. Let me warn you, though, a little religion can be a dangerous thing, especially this one. The risk of offending our divinities is as great as the benefits we hope to get from them."

"I can imagine! Well, thanks a lot, Mr. Obalete. You've been awfully generous with your time. (You could feel the crowd outside was becoming impatient.) I'm sorry things are as they are, but I guess that's history, or fate, or whatever . . ."

"Like everything that comes out of the sixteen doors, my boy, if you only knew how . . . inevitable. You can stay for the beginning if you wish, the sending away of Eshu . . . And please give my regards to Concha—that's what everyone calls her."

"I will, and thanks again. *Alafia?*" I said, tentatively.

"*Alafia modupe,*" said Obalete, giving me a special double handshake.

Well, it wasn't easy to walk down the center of that hall with everybody staring at shamefaced little whitey, responsible for their waiting so long. The floor was strewn with "no comment." A small crowd in ordinary clothes stood gathered just inside the beaded curtain, where I kept my eyes fixed. But I observed the chairs filled with youngish people wearing white African-style clothes. Interspersed were others in bright African fabrics, dark glasses.

Suddenly an old woman in flowered print and turban came rushing out from the alcove where the drummers sat.

It was Mama Télé-Télé, I later learned, Concha's sworn enemy and most important rival. She was hauling a heavy bucket, whose sloshing contents could barely be contained until she reached the entrance. Crossly warning us bystanders out of the way, she heaved the bulk of the water through the curtain onto the sidewalk. A cowbell back in the alcove struck up a regular beat, accompanied by a piercing tenor:

Yyyyyyyyyy-bara-go, O
Mo Yuba

a phrase repeated as everyone cut right in behind him,

O
Mo Yuba

Led by the man in the watch cap, the drummers attacked, and when they'd established a wild lilt, a tall fellow took up the mended shaker and backed up the cowbell's crazy off-beat phrasing, *Mo Yuba* on and on until . . . O Wow! Obalete splendidly emerged from behind his white curtain, arms stretched up and out in an ecstatic posture of blessing. He did a half pirouette this way, that, flourishing an enormous key with which, back toward us now, he unlocked the cabinet and dramatically flung open the doors for all to see gleaming pots, festooned with heavy ropes of beads, that contained—the mystery. A young woman rushed to fling herself face down upon the mat. As the others rose from the chairs and crowded forward, presumably with the same intention, I knew it was time for me to split.

IV

Change at 161st and River Avenue for the D train. Get off at 175th Street and walk east. Precise directions; but it's confusing down here. Concrete space, held up by squared metal pillars, wants to press in. Tiled tunnels overhung with signs that mean nothing to me slink off obliquely. Out of one of these I finally emerge into the sooty gray light of next Saturday afternoon, turn left (east?) and start up a street that steepens into a ramp leading me high along the edge of the Cross Bronx Expressway. One bridge I count, then another, a third, after which the ramp sheds its streetness, narrows into a railed sidewalk and slants on down to the dead end of a street that turns out to be . . .

Anthony Avenue. Here I am. Now which? . . . The easternmost row of houses tar-papered, abuts on a cliff. To the west, the last stretch of ramp walk has, I observe, been skirting an upheaved ridge, the top of which, tumultuous with boulders and trash, backs up against the sullen side wall of a six-floor tenement. On the fourth floor—southeast corner—Concha lives.

Ever since, but once, I've continued to take that ramp along the Expressway, even if it is somewhat quicker to go out another tunnel and walk across 175th, and I always look up. Open window airing mop and rags—that's the kitchen. Closed window stuffed with plants—that's the bathroom where she speaks to the dead, bathes the heads of the living, and keeps goats if she can't get the man on the ground floor across the street to take them in. Double windows with fancy plastic curtains—that's the formal sitting room; and the last two, set at right angles—bedroom combined with bustling inner sanctum.

Now it's hard to imagine that the first time I didn't look up, but of course I had no idea which windows were hers or even which building would wear the number given.

That's it, that tall brick one next to the high lot. Up the steps I walk, across the courtyard and into the south entry. Past a row of bashed-in mailboxes, a stone staircase leads from one neglected landing to another—steel doors all painted with a brownish red paint guaranteed to last forever. And these closed doors really mean it. There's a dog, to judge from the barks, behind every one of them. Sometimes a bit of excited advertising from the Spanish radio station makes its way through the heavy insulation, an occasional outraged voice—one-half of a quarrel—penetrates to linger unanswered. Otherwise, only dampness and cockroach spray cling to those no man's landings. I step back against the wall to let someone with an innerspring mattress on his back go down like a weird tortoise. Moving out? Where? Where else is there?

4D. Finally. Just like all the others. No giveaway, and no bell. My knuckles dent the outer layer of tin, upon which the dog behind, hoarse with barking, throws himself against the inside layer. Finally the chain slides back and I am let in. By whom?

It is a weary man in a brown gabardine suit and nylon sport shirt, who, without even looking at me, slouches back into the only visible room, and wedges himself into place on the nearest couch between a well-dressed middle-aged woman, smoking, and, huddled in a black coat, the similar shape and features of her mother, whose ankles swell beneath elastic stockings. I nod and make my way to an empty straight chair over by the window. To my left there's another couch, also covered with plastic, upon which a young couple, in the white African-style outfits of the Yoruba Temple, sit impassively. If there were any magazines to thumb through, would they?

Propped up in a puffy chair next to them, there's a black doll fancily dressed in the old-fashioned way—skirt-upon-skirt upon petticoats, ruffled. On her head a red turban, around her neck bright beads. This—although of course I don't know it yet—is Seraphina. I look around the room again, more carefully. No Eshu to be seen. A framed certificate over the nearer couch says that Concepción Montaña y Rios, having passed all examinations, is entitled, by the Holy Apostles Eastern Orthodox Christian Church, to practice as a medium. I have only a very vague idea of what this means. ("To impress the police," says Concha.) At the far corner of the room, behind the doll, a large umbrella stand sprouts peacock feathers. On top of the nondescript cabinet next to the wide door stand a pair of plastic babies with nodding heads, incidentally dressed in Indian costumes. They look won at some carnival. Shango is also represented here in Concha's waiting room, though of course no more than I recognize the others do I see him beneath the too-smooth tourist-trade ebony skin of a chieftain wearing, somewhat incongruously, a red-and-white necklace. At this point I have no idea who Shango is.

A bowl of white carnations on the coffee table, a whirligig stuck into the radiator next to the window where I sit, a roly-poly brass Buddha, a child's bow and arrow nailed above the door, a spear—these, indeed all the decorations in the room turn out to be tokens of divinity more serious aspects of which are hidden away in Concha's bedroom, which can't be seen because the door is closed for privacy of consultation.

An hour passes. The older Spanish woman has gone in and come out again, then the daughter, finally the husband, who at last escorts all three to the front door. The dog barks. From another region of the apartment a bulky woman in white uniform emerges to let the newcomers in. The young couple have their turn together. Me next. As they leave, I step up to the half-open door.

"Uhhuh, come on in." I duck under a dangling bunch of blackened bananas and pull the door shut behind them.

She is standing in the center of the room and comes forward with friendly curiosity to greet me. A stout, comfortable woman in baggy wash dress and carpet slippers, she is slightly shorter than I, has gently rounded features, slightly flustered hair, wears modest gold earrings, one strand of white beads—everything about her muted, homey, that is to say, nothing formidable except her eyes, which, despite their humorous reserve, cut right through me. No nonsense. And no fake formalities. Her presence insists I make the first move, declare myself at once to be . . .

"Raymond Hunt. Mr. Obalete sent me." I remind her of what I said on the phone, but this is superfluous. Her expression indicates she knows perfectly well. "He wishes you'd drop into the Temple sometime," I conclude lamely.

"Is that so?" she twinkles. "I don't have to go downtown to know what that guy is up to. Tell me, you look like a smart boy, is it true that over in Africa priests are allowed to have a lot of wives? Many as a dozen? I've seen some on television. Once in a while one of my godsons brings an African student by for a reading. Of course most of those aren't even married. And they're all so quiet, gentlemanly, I find it hard to believe. Obalete thinks he knows everything, but after all, the nearest he's ever got to Africa is the farthest any of us have ever been . . ."

"Cuba?" She nods, not at all surprised. I say I have no idea how many wives Africans have these days. Priests of the old religions, not having been forced by missionaries to give them up, might still have several. "I know someone at the museum who visits Africa a lot. I could ask him."

"Sometime—when you think of it," she says lightly. "Now, come over here and sit down. Let's look it over."

By "looking it over" she means your situation, your life as it can for a moment or two be spread out upon the white cloth nailed to a breadboard, which she balances on both our knees and then proceeds to throw the cowries. The shells fall in a pattern incomprehensible to me—some showing broken backsides, others smiling crookedly. But she confidently writes the score down in a little black book. All the while, between throws, I'm to do my part by moving two stones back and forth from closed fist to closed fist and showing, when she asks, which the right hand holds, or the left, depending.

Now as she begins to tell the upshot of these maneuvers, this no-nonsense lady sometimes glances at the book, sometimes at a spot above my head, mostly looks directly at me to see how I'm taking what she says. She knows about that pull-of-a-hidden-magnet feeling, of the special attraction Ogun has for me, knows family things as well, about my mother and father, the sort of person my sister is. Most important of all—for that's the way this intelligence makes me feel—is her recognition of me the moment I entered the room, a recognition by gooseflesh. I get it, too. Recognized what? Something I carry inside me, something I've been cut out for, something I've been playing down without realizing and this has been making me moody, confused, short-tempered sometimes. No? Yes. The cowrie shells say I must begin by learning to speak to the dead. How? A glass of water by my bedside always, and then concentrating at the source, where the running water is, for . . .

Up the drain, up the peeling lead pipes we had bandaged with rags so they'd leak less, from subterranean springs beneath our industrial-gray painted basement, the dead would come—were I to call them correctly—into the sink, or the bathtub, or even into the antiquated wooden tank above the toilet. Sounds odd? So to me at first, as I, with a certain hilarity, imagined the process; but then, I never could shake my childish belief that our drinking water actually came from the reservoir I could see.

There is a certain urgency in what she now says about my sacrificing a rooster to Ogun, which means she will have to do it on my behalf and this, since I ask, will cost five dollars; but if I don't have the money never mind, I can pay later. And she must wash my head. For that I will have to come up early some Saturday and stay all morning. Why? What's going on? She volunteers very little beyond the measures of avoidance to be taken and, strange to say, I don't ask, afraid I guess; so it is not until later when Ferryman tells me a story about Ogun's wife being stolen from him by Shango that I am able to fit the facts together. Desperate to get his river-goddess back, Ogun occasionally enlists human beings like myself to help him. But all I know from this first meeting with Concha is that Ogun for some reason or other is after me, and in addition to the foregoing acts I must be careful to avoid switchblades, sharp tools of any kind. For seven days I must stay out of cellars and caves, avoid all machinery, stick close to my neighborhood—no trips. How about the subway? How can I get home? Never mind one ride; what can't be avoided must be sidled past. She will give me insurance against incidental hazards.

She puts the shells away in a little bag, takes the consulting board off our knees and leads me over to the cabinet in the corner. There on the floor is the *Guehierro* caldron. "Ogun," I say, in solemn recognition. Eshu, too. I hesitate, then tap the floor three times, "with your kind permission."

"Who taught you that?"

"Ferryman. Is that right? Do you know him?"

"Of course I do. He's tried to kill me plenty of times, but I'm not afraid of his jinx; anyhow I'm always warned. But you got to be careful of him, Reymundo. He's evil."

"Not just crazy?"

"No, evil—and crazy, too, if you like. And bright as the devil. Off-by-himself, that he gets from *Agaju-Sola*. The rest is his own character, or lack of it."

I say no more. From the caldron she pulls out an iron bracelet—solid, hoop-shaped—says some Yoruba words over it, then drops it on the mat for me to pick up. "So you can recognize enemies," and with a stern look that contains some playfulness, "I think you have trouble separating sheep from wolves. But you must do it. You fight a lot, which is okay, but go easy. Remember: melted iron passes through cold water."

Putting on the bracelet, I feel better already. So how bad had I felt before? Maybe worse than I thought. "Mrs. Montoya . . ."

"Concha, everybody calls me that."

"Well, Concha then. Do you have drumming here sometimes? *Bembe* is what I think you call it."

"You'd like to come? Sure, I'll let you know."

"Thanks. And I'll call you when the seven days are up—before that, may I? if there's trouble."

"Don't go looking for it, and there won't be any. But call whenever you like. Don't worry. I'll take care of everything."

I knew she would. I trusted her. Whatever I was in for, she was at the center and would hold fast. "And if in any way I could ever help *you* out? . . ." Brash kid, I suppose, but my impulse was to make it even. All I really had to offer thus on the threshold of a new existence was unqualified loyalty. She saw this, laughed affectionately at my chivalric stance, and with all the wealth of her intuitive generosity took me up on it:

"Maybe someday. You got a lot of good things coming to you, and how!"

On my way down the stairs, I met the fellow I'd seen coming out of Ferryman's place a week before, the burly driver of the milk truck. But this time he is leading a goat. Hauling that stubborn animal up the stairs takes some doing. Nodding politely, I start to ease by.

"Why, hello baby." He recognizes me. "You sure get around, don't you."

"Guess so," I mutter.

Water drips through the steel beams overhead onto the ties between the tracks. I wait. No one in sight. Finally, down the dark tunnel a light blinks green. With a rush of wind the big red square with a white D emblazoned on it charges, steel stallion at the lists. No uptown bound opponent on the adjoining track. The challenger stops forlornly to pick up such an inconsequential passenger, then roars away again, flinging me down on the slippery Fiberglas seat. *Guehierro 71* with a black spray can it is writ. And, just below, slightly askew: *Ogun lives!*

Bembe

That whole week I lay low, as Concha said I should, coming right home after school—the model pupil, for once, catching up on all my assignments.

I spent a good half hour in the bathroom every evening —tap running slightly in both washbasin and tub—trying to get in touch with the ghosts of my father and mother. No luck. So, sitting there on the tattletale gray chenille toilet seat cover, I tried thinking back to my less immediate ancestors. Maybe one of *them*. Surely the drains were clogged with cockroach messengers. No news for me? Alas, too vague. My parents had never talked much about their families.

I knew my mother to be distantly Dutch. There were a couple of maiden ladies, second cousins of a different generation, whom we had visited once in upstate New York, Glens Falls I think. But of grandparents I could recall none. My father was, as they say in history books, of English "stock." I remember his telling me that though white might not be beautiful, industriousness and fair play *were* traditions to be proud of. He grew up in Manhattan in a town house somewhere in the 70s, long since sold and renovated into apartments. I think his parents were separated, which is why, my sister says, he became an artist; at any rate he never mentioned them. Nor his Uncle James. No wonder, after years of neglect, dead forebears should resist my summoning.

I also took Concha's advice about caves and caverns. Although my sister was somewhat mystified when I told her that for seven days I'd rather not take the garbage to the basement, nor the clothes to the washer-dryer down there, she agreed to change jobs with me temporarily. I'd clean up the apartment, scrub the bathroom (which suited me fine) and the kitchen..The rest of the work would go on as before. Her boyfriend Charlie had been gradually doing more and more of the cooking, while we shared table setting and dishwashing. "Just so long as you're not getting phobic about basements," staring at me over the rims of her glasses in that humorous way of hers.

"Marty," I countered, "you ought to go down to Orchard Street and get contacts."

"Speaking of which, I've been meaning to ask you where you picked up that far-out teething ring," pointing to my bracelet.

"Just you try to sink your teeth in it, and you'll find out what it's made of. Concha gave it to me."

"Who's Concha?"

"Wouldn't you like to know? If you're a good sister, I might take you to meet her some time."

"That's okay, Raymond," a little wistfully. "I was just curious."

I waited until about nine on Sunday morning to call her up, figuring any earlier wouldn't be polite; but she had already gone out, a voice on the end of the wire informed me.

"When do you expect her back? . . . Not till midnight? O . . ."

"Whassah maddah, you sick awsumpum?"

"No, it's just that I'm stuck. My seven days are up and I don't know what to do, where to go from here? Can't explain. Well, tell her Raymond called . . ."

"You cuwed cawl her yahself. Where she's at." There was a pause. "Heresah phonumbah."

"Gee, that's nice of you. Thanks a lot."

A confusion of voices in the background: someone shouted, "Concha . . ." and she came to the phone. "Unnn-huh?"

"It's me, Raymond. . . . I'm fine. It's just that my seven days are up and I . . . O Gee, can I? That would be great . . . Yeah, I've got it. Thanks ever so much, Concha. So long."

It turned out she was at a certain Manuela's house on Hoe Street, helping get things set up for a *bembe* to be held there in the afternoon. I was to take the number 5 train, get off at 174th and Southern Boulevard, walk east, then south. I could hardly contain my excitement. Charlie and Marty were going to a concert. That I had "other plans" didn't bother my sister at all. She looked pleased. "Raymond's got a girl friend," she announced, "a Spanish señorita, if I'm not mistaken. See how he's got himself up—white shirt, still yet. He even borrowed my shoe polish, used up the rest of the can oxblooding his good shoes."

"Cut it out, Marty. Someone might think you were jealous or something."

"Nonsense. Break it up, kids," said Charlie.

After 149th Street the subway turns elevated. Despite my being all dressed up, I couldn't resist stepping out between cars, hanging on to the handles out there and letting the wind fill me out like a kite, as we tore by lofts and living rooms, cutting straight through brick walls to zoom in on those old stilted stations. People waiting under the shed draw up at our approach. Bleary-eyed shutter slides back. Time. Step in like clockwork. Slides shut, and off we go again. Side streets provide discreet depth of focus: fire escapes crisscrossed with laundry: work pants, undershirts, diapers. Hey, Sweetie, where-dja hang my death? Dunno, why? Private lives inscribed on public conveyances. Colorfast mottled luck serpentines us by.

Manuela's house is in the middle of a block of two- or three-flight walk-ups. There's a Spanish–American grocery store on the corner that sells everything from plantains to blue jeans, and pop-tops in all weather. Insulated wires zigzag across the street, tapping energy and shooting it from one building to another. And from these dangle gym shoes, same as above Anthony Avenue, high-topped Keds tied in pairs and loop-the-looped footloose like prayer flags. Where-dja say you hung my death? On a telephone pole with sixteen branches; on a power line with sixteen connections. Cinders, ticker-tape confetti from the sky.

I rang the bell, and a woman dressed in white let me in. "Concha, there's an American kid . . ."

At the end of the dark corridor, in the kitchen, cooking up a stiff kettle of rice, "So far so good." She turned off the gas, put on the lid and wiped her face with the corner of her apron. "How you feeling?"

Taking my arm, she went round introducing me. "This is my new godson, Raymond." There must have been fifteen people crowded into that little kitchen. At a table in the corner two young women in white blouses and turbans were carefully cutting the centers out of a heap of black-eyed peas. Some men in loose-fitting white suits were gathered about the icebox drinking beer. Out on the glassed-in back porch, an immense and very black woman with red headcloth and suggestion of goatee was vigorously leading a team of chicken pluckers. This was Manuela, owner of the house, hostess of the feast. We shook hands.

"*Cumpleaño de Chango*—Shango's birthday party. Me three years," she explained. "He gonna be pleased and happy. Nothing too good for Shango. Come see."

"You can speak to him in Spanish, if you speak slowly," Concha said. "He studies it in school."

"That so? I got a nephew in high school. He does very good. Someday I send for him," said Manuela, leading us into the living room where her saints were displayed in all their glory.

It's hard to explain if you've never seen it—all those covered casseroles festooned with heavy necklaces, each raised on a pedestal covered with bright satin cloth. Like islands in a sea of fruits, for there were dozens and dozens of oranges, arranged in circular patterns, incorporating grapefruits, golden delicious apples, mangoes, melons and pomegranates. All out of season. Manuela had spent, so Concha whispered to me, $125 on fruit alone, not counting animals slaughtered, drinks and so on. Here and there had been set down sauce dishes containing such ritual foods as cornmeal mush and stewed okra. Front and center, a basket of dollar bills. But the crowning glory was the cake toward which all the fruit patterns pointed: two-and-a-half feet in diameter, ringed with red sugar roses, a vast tablet of white frosting upon which was written:

Feliz Año
Kawo Kabie Sile
CHANGO

As we stood on the brink of the feast admiring, others began to drift in, and soon Manuela and Concha were busy responding to salutations of guests prostrating themselves, first before the splendid company of saints, and then before each other, the *santeros*. In front of Shango, the pile of dollar bills grew bounteous. I dug into my pocket for an embarrassingly modest contribution. As the room filled, it became a forest of risings and fallings governed, as Concha ex-

plained in a free moment, by the principle of seniority. All
were obliged to prostrate before those longer in the priest-
hood than they. Chronological age had nothing to do with it.
A young girl no older than I arrived with her mother and
immediately queues formed to salute both of them.

"Obalete's first wife and daughter," Concha whispered.
"The girl is a Shango priestess, initiated ten years ago—after
the accident."

"What accident?"

"You see her older brother belonged to the spirit world.
We call them *abiku*. Kept trying to go back and, one day,
when the woman supposed to be minding him wasn't looking, the poor kid fell out of the window. Nothing anyone
could do."

"How awful!" I glanced at the blond mother's face. It was
gaunt and kind, with an intense animation in the hazel eyes
that reminded me of my mother's. "Is that kind of thing
common?" I whispered to Concha, who shook her head,
meaning can't talk now.

As senior priestess in the room, she had much, too much
to do to explain things to a newcomer, so I shut up and
stood by, feeling somewhat lost, dutifully smiling whenever
introduced—fortunately not often.

Meanwhile, a critical situation had been developing in
the saints' part of the room. A diviner had arrived and begun
to throw pieces of coconut down to see whether Shango was
indeed satisfied (as Manuela so confidently hoped) with the
feast spread out before him. Much to the bystanders' surprise and Manuela's horror, by means of these counters,
Shango declared he was not. Eventually the salutations
ceased and everyone pressed forward to watch the divina-
tion.

To each offer of something additional—money, another
goat and so on—all four pieces of coconut, face down,
angrily gave the same negative answer. You could have cut
the tension with a sacrificial knife. Finally Concha, the di-

viner and Manuela left the room to confer on the back porch. This the resulting proposal:

Would Shango be satisfied with a new initiate? The diviner dramatically asked the question three times, in Spanish, English, Yoruba; and the coconut pieces replied, all face up, three times in a row, meaning the road was clear, the *bembe* could go on. However, somebody there tonight would be called upon to "make it."

At the time I understood little beyond the feelings of the crowd, which now began, with relief, to applaud. The diviner shook a pair of red maracas, Concha her silver bell and Manuela, her face again alight, rushed off to change her clothes.

But there was plenty of time. The drummers, it turned out, were already two hours late. Having played a nightclub engagement in Philly, they were on their way up the Turnpike, when a rear wheel of the car they were riding in came all the way off. Luckily no one was even hurt; but by the time they got to Manuela's the men's nerves were so unstrung they asked for a couple of beers each before tuning up.

"Hey baby," said the lead drummer. I gave a start. He had his arm around Concha's waist and was treating her like his best girl friend.

Concha, surprised, "You know each other?"

"Only by sight," he said. "Better make it official. My name's Jamón."

"Pleased to meet you," I bowed, catching his sense of fun, "mine's Raymond."

"Reymundo, king of the world, so that's where you're at," said the irrepressible fellow I'd first seen in front of Ferryman's. "No wonder you get around. Shall we fight it out on some mountain? Transport's my line. Mother's milk direct to your door. Just ask for Jamón and you'll get peppered. What's that sitting on your head?"

Baffled, I put my hand up and he burst out laughing.

"Never mind, you'll find out sooner or later, my boy. Tools of the trade. Guess you have to be credited with their invention; but now the shackle's on the other foot and you're all screwed up, understand?"

I said I didn't exactly. How hostile was he, really? How much just playacting?

"Well you know how to balance on the head of a pin. I'll hand you that. Cool's where the o-ri-sha (he hyphenated them out) are really at, right, Godmother?"

"Don't be fresh, Jamón; Raymond doesn't understand that sort of language."

Jamón disagreed by slapping me on the back. "God-mother doesn't approve, like she doesn't really understand; but you and me, we're the younger generation, and that's how we rap, right?"

"Right . . . right on," I faltered.

This broke him up. "You're fore and aft, Reymundo; if you keep on swinging we might even get to be friends."

I said I'd like that, and meant it.

The kitchen clock said almost six. I thought I'd better find a phone and call my sister. Maybe there'd be a booth on the corner by the Spanish–American grocery. I didn't want to call her amid all the hubbub at Manuela's.

By the time I got back, the drummers were striking the pegs of their handmade congas. Everybody was gathered about the perimeter of the front room. Concha had already performed the opening ceremony with water. A very black, very energetic man with a cowbell began calling the chants. Drums and maracas moved in, and two or three people, led by Manuela, began to dance. She was wearing an old-fashioned red-and-white checked dress trimmed with eyelet ruffles and looked really nice.

Iba ara ago o, moyuba
Ee Elegua Eshu lona . . .

Everybody took up the chorus. The dancers faced the drums and moved in a little two-step, swaying slightly back and forth while their arms and hands worked a pulling motion, as if hauling something into themselves, into all of us. That something is *ashe,* force.

When the tune shifted to *Ogun de!* (Here comes Ogun!) Concha winked and went out on the floor to show me how his step was done. She's a wonderful dancer, light on her feet, emphatic on the accents as she shuffles right, touches down, shuffles left, touches down, pushing out, pressing in. Despite her age, her weight, her swollen ankles and twisted toes that I know pain her a lot, when she does dance, Concha is eloquent, as she never can be in talk.

Now, Ogun cuts a wide swath with his machete, and when you dance him, as your right arm moves back, your torso must tilt with it. Flinging your left arm and leg out for balance, you crouch lower and lower, right knee taking all the strain. If you get tired doing this, you can simply fall back into the simple two-step again; but that day at Manuela's, Concha kept on calling the god of iron for me, until Jamón mercifully changed the rhythm. When it was over, I wanted to rush over, embrace her, wipe the sweat from her face, bring her something cool to drink, but I was far too shy that day to do anything of the kind. I simply caught her eye and she looked back with amused affection, as though to say, "Not bad for an old lady, eh, Raymond? You take it from here."

The drums swept on to songs for the other saints; more and more people crowded into the cleared space, forcing those on the periphery to keep swaying or be crushed, so that after a time there wasn't much distinction between those who were dancing and those who were merely moving, watching and singing. There was plenty of *ashe,* but no possessions until Shango's *kan kan* rhythm began. Then the thin wall that holds the invisible back burst through the most susceptible place, and we were in for it.

Manuela did a few steps by herself, before others joined in. After a few turns, Manuela began to snort, to stagger; fell back against another woman who shoved her onto her feet again; after which Manuela began to spin—arms outstretched—driving her fellow dancers back as close to the wall as they could get. And then, eyes closed, upper lip and jaw thrust up, sweating profusely, the great shelf of her buttocks jutting out almost perpendicular to her legs, Manuela, egged on by Jamón, who slapped the dotted accents down with a vengeance, began to bombard the room with imaginary thunderbolts.

More commotion by the door. Another orisha had come down over there. As we all craned to see who had been affected, Jamón slowed the drums to a different tune—stranding Manuela. She gave a terrible lurch and fell into the waiting arms of Concha. A couple of young men rushed up to help ease her away into a small bedroom off the kitchen.

KE KE KE la la la la LALA

went the chorus of the new song, whose saucy, sentimental lilt Jamón emphasized to the verge of mockery. Soon the floor was crowded with women, moving in formation for the first time, counterclockwise around the room. Hands daintily picking up their skirts, they swished them back and forth in coquettish wavelike motions. In the center of this whirlpool the possessed man danced alone, trousers rolled up, shirt open to the navel, a bit of blue satin hastily wound about his head. Over his heavy shoulders someone had thrown an elegant fringed shawl, the corners of which he grasped outstretched, this way as from tiptoe he dipped flatfoot and flowed, now that, while the circling dancers either encouraged or taunted him—I couldn't tell which—their high nasalized voices all but screaming the chorus: *KE KE KE la la la la LALA*.

His sagging face was not at all in keeping with the romantic dance he did. On the contrary. Heavy eyebrows were contracted into a permanent angry frown, a lolling tongue lapped away at his lower lip. All of a sudden he made a dash for the corner where the feast for the gods was set out. Seizing the platter that held the cake, he lifted it high above his head and began to spin round and round until it seemed he must surely lose his balance; but no, catching himself just in time, with the flourish of a proud chef he set his precarious offering down before the drums. Then, by a disdainful flick of his wrist, he invited Jamón and the others to join him as, kneeling down, he dug right in, himself—with both hands. (Gasps from the crowd.) Continuing to stuff his own mouth, with the other hand he threatened to smear Jamón's drumhead with squishy frosting unless the drummer took a bite, which Jamón now laughingly, did. After which, this spaced-out Yemaja, mother of us all, got off his knees and gestured to the rest of the crowd to come and get it.

And we were hungry, we discovered. Here it was almost eight o'clock. Some had been milling around for hours with nothing to eat. Three or four little kids who had been pressed against bystanders in the back, delighted with the turn events had taken, now rushed forward. What parent dared stop them? Me, too. We all surged toward the forbidden feast. Some of us were fed by Yemaja's own hands, others groveled and grabbed. A neat lady named Inez produced a stack of paper plates (intended for the rice, stew and beans); somebody else handed around plastic spoons. Jamón whipped out his pocketknife and began to cut slices for the more fastidious.

Eventually the drummers went out to the kitchen for beer, while the rest of us were served soda, as we sat around on the floor gorging ourselves, until there was nothing left but a film of frosting all over the place. Whereupon Inez and some other ladies brought wet dish towels for our faces and fingers, sponges, a mop for the floor; and within half an hour everything was pretty much back to normal—except for the two guests from heaven, Shango (whose cake it was, after all) and generous Yemaja.

When Manuela, come to herself again in the bedroom, found out what had happened, her rage knew no bounds. Red turban askew, she came rushing into the tail end of the cleaning-up. Spotting the culprit, Manuela discharged a volley of Spanish cuss words, then charged him head on, like a ram, possessed as he was. "*Sacrilegio!*" shouted the crowd. Only Shango himself could have prevented her from killing "Yemaja," and down like a shot Shango came. Manuela staggered, spun, put her hand to her forehead and, disoriented, forgot her vengeance and burst out sobbing. While Concha comforted her, Jamón and some other men eased Yemaja out of the room, out of the house altogether. A couple of young priests drove Jean-Claude, for that was his name, home.

"Don't worry, baby," said Jamón, noticing me at the door. "They'll wrap him up good in the car and stay right by his side until he comes out of it."

Although I gathered that eventually the *bembe* would pick up where it had left off and that after all the gods had been sung for, there'd be—Inez warmly assured us—paper plates or not, plenty of good food. Still, all things considered, I thought I ought to be getting on home myself. When I went to pull my coat off the pile in the bedroom, I found Concha dressing Manuela in a red satin suit.

"Excuse me, I should have knocked."

"That's okay Raymond. She's decent. Goodness, I'd all but forgotten you were here . . . Were you to wait a while, I'm sure someone would give you a ride . . . All the same, you shouldn't go to the subway alone after dark. Find Jamón, I'll ask him to walk you over."

I didn't object to that. I wanted to hear what he would say about the cake eating.

As we were going out, a woman I recognized was coming

up the stairs with a couple of fellows. All three had Yoruba Temple costumes on under their overcoats. She smiled. Ah, she was the one who had been talking to Obalete. "Slumming," said Jamón contemptuously. I grinned back over my shoulder. "Hey baby," Jamón poked me in the ribs. "There must be something about you, half-pint, that doesn't show on the surface. One of these days maybe we gwine to have to laaaak horns."

I said I sure hoped not, and he, mercifully, decided to change the subject. "Well, how'd you like your first *bembe*? Pretty strong stuff, eh? Too bad you have to leave so early. That was just the warm-up. Main feature ain't even started yet. Something tells me that sassy little broad from downtown's going to cook up a real storm. Wanna bet?"

"Not against you, Jamón, not against your drumming."

He laughed, delighted with himself and me. I asked him if he had any idea of what Manuela had done to make Shango so angry and was it to punish Shango for his sulkiness that Yemaja had made a mess of his cake? Or did that fellow Jean-Claude personally have it in for Manuela? In short, I found the whole business awfully confusing.

"Baby, no wonder. You don't even know where the o-risha's at, let alone the human component. Well, to begin at the bottom of the heap: Manuela's born for trouble. Nothing she can do about that. Shango hasn't much to say there except to give her a hard time. And Jean-Claude, well you saw him, starved for affection, like most of us, his kind especially. So let them eat cake! That's the French rev-o-lushun. His real mother, they say, is a baaad woman from Martinique. Now as for Shango, despite the cake-bit, he had to duck in at the last moment to keep *his* mother from being insulted. Not that she didn't ask for it. Trouble is what the big mother wanted. Ya see, Yemaja, she likes love—all sweetness beginning with the mouth. And when she sees too much tough swaggering around, she's got to put the kibosh on her own son. Time was, in the old country, when Yemaja was bigger than anyone—except Obatala, and he's kind of special. Everyone scared stiff of woman power. All the men's jiving to Yemaja. But over here and now, Shango's really got it made, most of all in this town. Which is fine by me." He clowned a cool swagger. "Nor, on the other hand, do I mind, once in a while, a little put-down. You saw how I joined in. Shango's not the only one in charge. Yemaja's my mother, understand? Like you got Oya."

"What?"

"Never mind. Just a guess. You'll find out all about that soon enough. Anyhow, since I know where my double ax is coming from, I'm careful to tote both barrels at all times, get it? Well, here we are, everything straight now? All those extra wrinkles ironed out?"

"Well, anyhow, thanks a lot, Jamón. I think I understand a little better. Can't expect to take in everything all at once."

"Don't mention it, baby. And don't attempt the impossible. Even Ogun doesn't go running around half-cocked. Remember what I told you, control—that's where the religion's really at. *Bembes* are special. Anything goes. For when the orisha hit the deck, there's no controlling *them.* But the rest of the time, easy does it. That's why I go for godmother. She's got a built-in cool, no speedups, no breakdowns, level to the hilt, if you know where I'm coming from."

I wasn't sure, but I was charmed by his talk, which even in the act of making fun of itself kept a bead on the target. "I'll do my best to find out! Thanks again. See you around, Jamón."

When I got home, Charlie was still there, working on his architectural project that involved, it turned out, developing a lot of pictures. My sister and he had decided that very evening to convert our bath into a darkroom.

"Hope you don't mind, Raymond, I had to move the plants out so's we can keep the shade down all the time. Charlie has to . . ."

"Fine by me, so long as you move them back afterward."
I had to laugh. Suppose some of the dead came up and got
themselves into the negatives—little unaccountable blobs of
light, an eerie hand, a misty bit of cloth that never would
come sharply into focus.

"What's so funny?" asked my sister sharply. "And look
here, Raymond, you'd better be more explicit as to your
whereabouts. How far away does this girl friend of yours
live?"

"In the Bronx." My sister didn't know any more about
that part of the world than I did.

"Way up there?"

"Which section? that makes all the difference," said Charlie sensibly.

"Where the Grand Concourse crosses the Expressway,
that's Concha's pad. But the party was over on Hoe Street."

"Hoe Street? You'd better be careful up there, Raymond,"
said Charlie. "That's gangsville—Ghetto Brothers, Bachelors, Black Spades . . ."

"Oh? Funny, I didn't notice that type of thing at all. In
fact, the streets seemed peaceful by comparison . . ." They
looked puzzled, but didn't say anything. "Anyhow," I went
on, holding out my bracelet, "Concha's already shot me up
against all the worst hazards of the city—if you know where
I'm coming from."

"Raymond," said my sister, "what are you talking about?
And whom," suspiciously, "are you imitating?"

"Concha's big brother?" suggested Charlie.

"Best friend, rather, cause he's really a lot younger. Well,
if you two'll excuse me, I'm going to sack out."

"O Charlie, what'll I do?" My sister's voice floated down
the hall. "I'm afraid he's getting mixed up in a life he can't
possibly cope with."

"I know it's tough, but after a point you've got to rely on
his judgment. He's almost fifteen. When I was that age, I'd

have given my right arm for the kind of freedom he's got. Why I used to think it a big thing to go out to Astoria to play soccer on the Greek team—don't ask me why I wanted to do that—buy baklava on the way home. My mother had no idea what a tough neighborhood that was or she'd never . . ."

"Yes, but you're different, and you don't really know Raymond," answered Marty. "He seems able to get on in any situation, that's his peculiar charm. But he really lives in a world of his own construction, which is why, for all his independence, he's just the kind to get into trouble without knowing it."

"But the fact he's got a girl friend is a good sign, Marty, any friend for that matter. The trouble with Raymond is his having been terribly lonely."

Ebo

I

When I got home from school the next day I called Concha.

"So far so good."

"Anything special happen after I left?"

"Mmmmm . . ." She didn't know what I meant by "special."

Could I come up and see her Saturday?

Yes, but it would have to be early.

Like what time?

Soon as I could make it . . . No, 7:30 would be just fine.

I heard the dog barking in the background. That meant somebody was at the door. "Okay, Concha, see you then." I hung up feeling let down or, I suppose, as Charlie said, lonely . . .

I walked in to find everything changed around. The bedroom had been cleaned up so Concha could share it with someone else. Stretched out on a mat, with pillow and quilt to make her more comfortable, my friend from the Yoruba Temple! "What's she doing here?" I asked Concha.

"Shhhh, let her sleep a while longer. She's got a big day and a long night ahead of her."

We went into the kitchen. "Do you like these hard rolls? (Concha's favorites) Okay, you can butter them." While I did so, Concha made coffee in a flannel bag, heated up milk to the boiling point. While we ate, she told me what had happened.

After the drumming started up again, more and more people got possessed, all *santeros*. Then Shango suddenly came down bang on an outsider—Doreen, the girl in the bedroom—and it was all Concha could do to bring her out of it. A consultation with the diviner confirmed what everybody already knew. That girl was the one he had chosen. Her life was in danger. A heavy protection of beads was put right on. Nor could she go home, but had to go straight away into seclusion and be initiated as soon as possible.

"What a mess!" continued Concha. "I'd never laid eyes on her before, but she clung to me, sobbing, insisting I be the one to make her saint. I called Obalete right up. Who am I to go around stealing his chickens? But to save face that conceited fellow passed the buck. 'Go ahead, my dear Concha,' he says, 'you are welcome to her. I've been telling that little baggage to get herself together for weeks now, and so she goes and gets herself possessed someplace else. Serves her right. Good riddance.' And with that he hangs up. So here am I stuck. She can't pay a cent, or so she says. I've got to do the whole business on credit. Seraphina says . . . you don't know her, but anyhow, she says it's a question of chickens coming home to the right place to roost, it having been my bright idea to pacify Shango with a new initiate. But I tell Seraphina that Manuela was making the offerings in the first place and so Doreen ought to be her responsibility. The trouble is Manuela herself. She's broke, you have no idea how in the hole. All that money she'd collected, birthday money for Shango that would have helped her pay back some of what she already owed, well, after everyone went home, she hid it in his own mortar and next morning when she got up to look for it—gone."

"But who could have stolen it?"

"Anyone. You saw how crowded the place was."

"You think it was an inside job? That it wouldn't be difficult to guess where she'd put the cash? But how could anyone dare steal sacred money? Surely no one who believed in the religion would."

"Well, it might be those tenants of hers upstairs. That's what Manuela thinks, but there's no proof. As soon as she found the money missing, she went charging on up and ransacked the filthy place. Nothing. I've told her time and again that guy is a crook. Doesn't even live there, in and out, and the woman in bed all the time, who knows what she's got. But Manuela refuses to kick them out because of the children. Well, who can blame her for that. It's just her bad luck she was born with. She's offered to come over here and take charge of the cooking. That's nice of her; and anything more would risk bad luck for Doreen. I've asked Inez to be Doreen's Yabona—that's like sponsor at a baptism, maid of honor at a wedding. You met Inez the other night. Remember the good-looking Oshun priestess I introduced you to?"

"You mean the one who passed out the paper plates? Yes, she was nice." Wondering why in the world she was telling me all this news and gossip. Obalete, too, though the content was different. Neither of them wanted my opinion, really. Queer, as if they were talking through me to someone else growing out of my shoes. Sounding board, old friend . . .

"That is, when she shows up," Concha pursued. "As Yabona, she's supposed to have been helping me run around getting everything collected (seven white towels, seven com-

plete changes of underwear, all white, and so on, for each
saint, an appropriate container). The girl can't leave the
house, and since she won't let anyone know where she lives
—her boyfriends skipped out right away—I've even had to
buy her a toothbrush. I've been calling Inez all week, but
she keeps saying her husband's just about to go to the hospital to be operated on for an ulcer. She promised, though,
to get here ahead of time this morning. I'll believe it when
I . . ."

The dog barked.

"Ah, there she is now."

At a nod from Concha, I jumped up to let Inez in. She
sure looked elegant that day: white nylon pantsuit, yellow
chiffon scarf, and a yellow pile coat, which she said she'd
rather keep on awhile till she warmed up. "What weather!"
she said, taking off her white kid gloves and stuffing them
in her pocket. "The poor girl will freeze tonight in the
river. What's your name again, dear? I know I met you the
other night, but there was so much confusion."

"Raymond."

"You must be just about my Benny's age. He's the young-
est. The others are all girls. (I marveled; she didn't look all
that much older than Marty.) Concha's told me all about
you, how you've come up from Manhattan on your own. I
think it's wonderful. Few kids nowadays are interested in
anything but groups and clothes. I was born in Cuba, but
my kids are just as American as you are—three of them
priests, though they don't do much with it. Too bad, it's
such a beautiful religion. My husband's Jewish, but he respects the saints. We've got a nice place out on Long Island.
You'll have to come and see us someday. Summer is
best. We've got a swimming pool right in the backyard.
Thanks, now I can take it off, I guess. My heels, too." From
her purse she produced a pair of slippers and an apron.
"Ready to get to work! O Concha," (coming out of the

kitchen, shopping bag in hand) "how are you, darling?
Where do you want me to start?"

Concha, decidedly cool: "The *ebos* are all ready, but we
got to cleanse her first. When I go out—the boy's going
along to help me carry the pigeons—you can fix her coffee,
and maybe a little lunch for the girls coming in to do the
room. Manuela's taking care of the rest of the food. You'll
find everything you need in the icebox. Now, let's see, I've
got her morning dress all pinned, but haven't got round to
hemming yet. If you have a chance, you might whip it up,
thread's in the drawer of the sewing machine. And . . . Oh,
Jamón might call from the corner. You got to make sure the
coast is clear so he can bring the animals up. Don't want no
complaints. He'll see to the stairs, after. Which reminds me,"
taking an envelope out of her pocket, "slip this under the
super's door, please Raymond. You might as well get your
coat and go on out. I'll be down in five minutes."

A half an hour later Concha appeared with the shopping
bag, which she insisted on carrying herself. "I just want you
to take my arm," she said, companionably, "in case I should
start to slip on the ice. There isn't much, but with my feet it
takes only a little." We walked along the ramp until we came
to the first bridge. Here on the corner there's a little vacant
lot, mostly dry grass and rubbish, with a cluster of boulders
in the center. I helped Concha up onto the bottommost of
these, then stood respectfully back while she took a little
plastic sack of what looked like cornmeal mush out of the
big shopping bag, said some Yoruba words, then slipped it
into a crevice. "This," she explained, "is for the Guardian of
the Mountain." *Ebo*-littering I call it.

We crossed the bridge and sat for a while on a bench in
the midst of a traffic island that doubles as a park. Two
sweeper trucks were converging upon the narrow roundabout at the same moment, and a small crowd had gathered

to see which would give way. Meanwhile, the mailman, parking his truck well above the intersection so he could back out, began to weave through the traffic to our little refuge. Unlocking the blue and red mailbox, he pulled open his canvas bag and began stuffing in letters. At which point Concha got up and strolled around close to the curb, casually leaving a small deposit in four widely separated places: points of the compass, as I know now. Nobody saw her do it; and even if they had, I suppose they would have thought she was only one more crazy old woman feeding pigeons.

Then, leaving the traffic in a snarl, we went on down one of the narrow side streets to where there's a footbridge over the railway tracks. Leaning on the balustrade, we stood for a time looking over a tangle of grape and briar bush to dark creosoted ties on the gravel bed below. The tracks themselves were not rusted over, but shone like beams from some steel eye at the vanishing point. *"Mo fe re fun Ogun,"* as she threw a Baggie of baked beans down. Aha, he *is* watching me, I thought, getting frightened.

Back across the Expressway we went, up Anthony to Tremont, took a number 36 bus to Southern Boulevard, got off and walked the rest of the way to a little cemetery screened from the public eye by skeletal oaks and beeches. Domino soldiers guarded by their rusty cannons.

"No matter if we can't get in," said Concha, as I helped her up the eroded bank on the high side where the fence was lowest. "Oya guards the edge of the graveyard only. It is Oba who lives inside."

Something like a cat began to snuggle against my ankle. Even through my boot I could feel the touch of warm fur. I glanced down. Nothing. A cold wind brushed past my cheek to rattle dry twigs against the wire fence. I remembered what Jamón had said. How informed was his guess? "Concha," I refrained from asking, "is it true Oya is my mother?"

Across the street there's a power station, concrete platforms bristling with transformers. NO TRESPASSING. "Convenient, isn't it," chuckled Concha. "Well here's one thing they can't KEEP OUT." With girlish mischief in her eyes, she planted her suede hush-puppies squarely on the sidewalk and popped Shango's packet neatly over the fence. "*Kawo Kabiesi!*" she exclaimed; then together we exclaimed, in triumph.

We walked on down 180th Street hill toward the Boston Road and there at last . . .

You'll say I'm crazy, or that I'm putting you on; you'll say no person ever falls in love, especially at first sight, with a river. And in such an unprepossessing place, you might add when you see it. Well, blame it on my bad destiny, if you want, but there I stood astonished, all my wildest fantasies caught by the vivacious, defiant nakedness of that moment as she plunged, and continues to plunge, come what may, over the weir, joyously into a welter of junk.

Does the sight continually shock her, as it shocked me the first time? Or, as I was inclined to think even then, does each successive ream of her know full well what lies below the brink: Landslides of automobile tires; whole chassis; broken baby carriages; market carts; battered fridges; rotten two-by-fours porcupined with nails; busted barrels with rusted staves; bashed-in crates; kerosine cans; and more pop-tops than could ever be counted. These must have eased down the east bank of her bed night after night, year after year, sunk in, piled up, formed promontories, detached into islets. To continue to rush with such pure energy through such stinking turmoil was another marvel. To seek such shores, and after such a reception to continue to be a river at all—that took courage no mortal could ever equal. She had me then—hook, line and the proverbial sinker.

I walked to the other side of the bridge. Beyond the falls —the place where she generates all this glorious, ironic energy—inside the park, she rested then, as now, calm as a lake, content to absorb the reflection of accumulated clouds, snarls of leafless twigs. I ran to the downstream side again. A hundred yards beyond the avalanche of metallic misery, a trestled railway curved a protective arm high across the stream—dark reassurance of iron as it ought to be. Not even gods remain the same. So who am I at this the beginning of her leap thus to cry, silently, "Forgive me. . . ."

I shook myself as if I'd been asleep and saw Concha looking at me curiously. "You would have liked," she said, "the Salto de Merovis. Well, here goes!" and she hurled the last Baggie (frozen shrimps) down into the eddy.

We watched that *ebo* bob along until, halfway to the trestle, it snagged, together with the old rags and other pieces of plastic, midstream upon a clump of barbed wire that projects from a feckless fence post—itself once caught up in its careening course by the submerged carcass of some obsolete machine. Far below, in the shadow cast by the bent arm of the railroad trellis, a bloated cab top surfaced like a hippopotamus. "Accepted," laconically said Concha.

We took the elevated five stops south, then walked up Westchester Avenue to the place where once the fashionable Harlem branch of the New York, New Haven and Hartford crossed the Bronx River. Nothing's left of those excursions now save a ramshackle Victorian station, embellished with greenish iron worked into vines still visible beneath real brambles and summertime morning glories mounting up from the corrugated tin roof of the shed over the sidetracks, where dead boxcars await the long haul. The new NY, NH and H crosses farther up, and the old bridge has been converted to a thoroughfare for cars. Safe on the pedestrian boardwalk (rattling transit to Pelham Bay above), we crossed, continuing along Westchester until we came to an inconspicuous turnoff marked Elder Avene. Here the diviner they call Pedro Cartero lives; Peter-the-mailman who delivers the big news from heaven.

He came to the door himself. Although by this time it was almost twelve noon, he was still in his pajamas, like Ferryman. But Pedro's jowlish face hung low, almost to his chest. She had come, Concha briskly announced, to negotiate prices. The diviner's soft, brown eyes narrowed defensively as he straightened up, yet he continued his friendly line of Spanish apologies as he showed us down to the basement. A little office had been partitioned off from the rest—an indeterminate cement area, into which, closing the door behind them, he purposefully led Concha.

I sat alone in that cell-like consulting room of his, which boasted but one decoration—a color print of St. Francis, in brown robe, holding out his hand to a sparrow, one window —barred, high up at street level—two chairs and a table. A pine staircase, newly constructed, led into the place where I presumed he lived, and down this his wife eventually descended, scuffs ca-clunking. She was still in her dressing gown, yellow tulle, her hair militantly controlled by curlers. She was smooth-complexioned, on the plump side, definitely a pouter. "Where are they?" she asked in Spanish. I said, "In there," and pointed.

A while later all three emerged, apparently on the best of terms, Concha and the wife talking animatedly. "Concha told me about you," Pedro Cartero said, coming over to shake my hand. His English was perfect. "It's very unusual, an American boy . . . more power to you. Concha won't wait for coffee, says today is too hectic; but I've made her promise to bring you by again so we can get acquainted. You look very intelligent. Maybe you'd like to study to be a *babalao*. Next time we'll look it over. I was the first . . ." he shrugged his substantial sliding shoulders ". . . to bring the religion over from Cuba. That was twenty-five years ago. At first no one would listen. I lived like a beggar. Now I look around at what's happening and feel pretty smug. But I don't want any publicity. Not like some. And as for rich clients, you wouldn't catch me moving out to the Island. No, I'm staying right where I am. Got more work here than I can possibly handle."

I thanked him for his kind interest, and praised him for his pioneering. While Concha and his wife embraced, we shook hands a second time, and he showed us out with cheerful gallantry.

"Whew," said Concha. "Good thing she didn't get down those stairs any sooner. And I couldn't wait to get out for fear she'd make him change his mind. Half his age, married only six months, and already she runs him."

"But you seemed such friends."

"I knew her before; she's an Oshun priestess—diviner's wives always are. That rule goes way back. His first died ten years ago. A real friend of mine, of everyone's, she was a wonderful person. Too bad about this one, but he was lonely."

"And Pedro himself? Is he really wise? He's kind as well as crafty—you can see both in his eyes. He talked to me about himself with such dignity; why then does he seem, and from what he says he needn't be, so awfully run-down, so shabby?"

Concha laughed. "Pedro's okay so far as diviners go. Besides, who else is there? The others? Ugh, you can have them. My godmother's husband? But that's a long story. I wish I had *the knife*. Then I could sacrifice animals on my own and wouldn't have to depend so much on Pedro Cartero. Somebody told me Ogun does allow certain women to have it over in Africa. No one would dream of such a thing here. The diviners have that business all sewed up. Nor would they in Cuba. I know; I tried. No, for the knife I'd have to go all the way to Africa."

At the corner of Westchester and Elder, we went into a dingy little shop to pick up a cardboard carton of pigeons with Concha's name chalk-marked upon it. Holes punched in the sides allowed the birds to breathe and there was a handle folded up so I could carry it easily.

"This business is really a sideline of Pedro Cartero's," Concha explained outside. "That fellow at the counter is his first wife's brother. Raises them in Jersey for practically nothing and sells them to *santeros* at wholesale prices. Now we got to go to the pet shop and buy a turtle for Shango; then we're all set."

By now, clearly, Concha was tired. "Are you sure you don't want coffee? I noticed a doughnut place this side of the bridge. Come on, I'll treat you. I've got money."

"Sure, that sounds very nice."

After coffee (she insisted on paying for the doughnuts) we walked back across the way we had come. Locked into a pond between a low-slung railroad bridge and the one we were on, a subdued river mirrored only metal—the tapering necks of derricks poised along the farthest edge, the heavy zigzags of the distant trestle.

II

I went back to Concha's next afternoon for the *bembe*. Though I came an hour later than she said, the drummers were still "on their way over," but the place was jammed with the most distinguished *santeros* in town. As Inez said when she greeted me at the door, "When Concha makes saint, that saint is really made. Come and see the throne."

In twenty-four hours Concha's goddaughters had converted her bedroom into a palace. One corner was all you could see of it, quite enough to suggest an infinity of antechambers, warriors, women and priests. Beneath a crimson canopy sat Doreen in a red satin suit trimmed with gold braid, her throne an authentic mortar stool imported, Inez told me, from Africa. Even the wedge-shaped recess behind her had been covered with red satin industriously appliquéd with thunderbolts and double axes.

She wore a soft velvet crown, fitted to her forehead and puffed over onto one side. About her shoulders hung a short military cape. Her costume, though not exactly African, certainly did convey an impression of royalty. Her face, incapable it would seem of fierceness, was, rather saintly in its pallor—indifferent alike to roaring of lions, of fire. I hesitated to greet her in such state, but Inez said I must. And when I got up off the mat, she smiled kindly, though without recognition.

I slipped into the living room. Couches, easy chairs, even the borrowed collapsibles were taken. I felt shy about standing with no one to talk to, so I perched tentatively on the arm of the nearest sofa. A sullen-looking girl in dark glasses —probably about my sister's age—was saying, "Sometime I'm going to stop talking. I'm not going to rap no more. I just don't see the sense in it. If I really need to know something, then I'll ask a question, but no talk for talk's sake merely. Like you said . . ." I craned to see the person she was talking to. It was Obalete! "Only a blind man sees everything. Well, I ain't ever going to hear anything till I stop using words." What he replied I didn't catch, but I can imagine.

In the center of the room, a stocky bearded man in a three-piece pinstripe (complete with gold watch chain and Phi Beta Kappa key) was addressing an Afro-headed Nationalist bedizened with mean-looking amulets. "It's not a case of 'Blacks go back to Africa,' an atavistic retreat. Our ancestors, through us, have something to offer to *humanity*."

"Right on, Professor," said the Nationalist, laughing.

There was a commotion at the front door: Jamón and the band, at last! I saw Concha rush over to scold him, saw him jokingly fend her off; then, seeing her weaken, put his arm around her waist and promenade into the throne room.

I got up and followed them as far as the door, uncertain

as to whether or not at this moment I should enter. *"Santeros* only," said Obalete sweeping past me, his handsome face set in that ecstatic smile that seemed to throw wide the world to him. A few others followed, including, to my surprise, the professor. Me, I clung to the doorjamb, determined not to be dislodged by the crowd filing in behind me. Kitty-corner from the palace, Concha, Jamón and some of the others—backs turned to all observers in the corridor— were busy doing something to the drums. Waiting for them to finish, I noticed something very odd. The fresh bunch of bananas suspended from the lintel had, from heat generated by the crowd perhaps, already begun to go bad, attracting, in the process, a swarm of insects so small no one else seemed to notice them. Then, before my astonished eyes, these bananas began to glow like a chandelier in the oncoming darkness of the winter afternoon. Someone, as if reading my mind, flipped the switch in the hall. "That's better," murmured voices.

All chatter in the hall outside subsided. Inside, the litany of the Saints had begun: Jamón, alone at the lead drum, going through his repertoire of rhythms.

Suddenly there was a terrific rumble, then a crash as the wind tore through one of the cracked panes in the bedroom. As glass tinkled on the floor, the *santeros* turned to each other with knowing looks, and Jamón, half in fun to judge by his expression, began to imitate the sound of thunder on his drum. *Crash! HarrroooomBRRROOOOM!* Real thunder responded. *"Kabiesi, Shango!"* shouted Obalete, constantly alive, to his very fingertips, with a fine sense of the dramatic. Still another roll, and a terrific gust that swung the bananas back and forth. *"Kabiesi,"* shouted everyone this time, *"Kabiesi, Shango!"* Concha, from the pocket of her beautiful white lace dress, took out a crook-shaped silver bell, shook it high, shook it low, shook it all around the room to discharge the tension.

"Look!" screamed Inez. Doreen had risen to her feet and,

without going beyond the edge of the mat, began to dance gracefully. Jamón burst forth with Shango's most important rhythm, thus forcing her off into the center of the room. The *santeros* cleared a space for her. The other drummers rushed to their instruments. Faster, faster, the drums told Doreen to kick out her left foot and hop around on her right, then the reverse. Round and round she spun until she was but a flaming whirl of red satin.

"Sock it to 'em, Shango!" shouted the Nationalist.

When I left, it was still snowing outside, a wet snow blossoming from the tops of overstuffed garbage cans lined up along Anthony Avenue, clinging to the bare limbs of telephone poles, turning the sidewalk into a soundless coverlet, thus bestowing purity upon ugliness, forgetfulness upon yesterday, compassion upon tomorrow.

III

The morning after, a holiday, it was still snowing. I decided to go back and see if I could help clean up or something.

A young man in white robe and peaked cap let me in. The borrowed plates and glasses were stacked in cardboard cartons in the entrance hall; the floor was immaculate; plastic covers had been put back on the living room furniture; in short, everything, to my surprise was already restored to normalcy. Concha? She'd gone out to find a deli open somewhere. Inez? Gone home to her husband and five children. "I'm baby-sitting," the young man said pleasantly. "I guess you'll want to visit Kanyola (Doreen's new name). I'll be in the kitchen. Just let me know if you, or she, want anything."

Paying calls on the newly initiated is common. That wasn't exactly why I'd come, but I went in anyway.

I found her, in an ordinary white dress, stretched out on a mat beneath the fancy canopy. "How are you feeling?"

"Just fine. Kind of tired, though"; and, obviously, delighted to have someone to talk to. "I'm sure not looking forward to this week. It's nice to relax, have everything done for you; but I've already had several days like this and it can be dull. My thoughts go round and round. And when people come, they just sit down and start talking Spanish among themselves. Pay no attention to me at all."

She was worried about having to find another apartment. "I can't possibly go back to that place I had before. The walls was beginning to cave in on me. All sorts of bad vibes, as if it be haunted. I want to start all over in decent surroundings . . ."

I reminded her of our first meeting. "Obalete was part of my problem. He told me I was Oshun, and he was dead wrong. Godmother says it's because he uses the (diviner's) chain, when he's got no authority. He ain't no *babalao*. Ought to throw the shells like an ordinary priest, but he got to be special. Well, Shango has me right where he wants me now, so I guess my worries are over." She yawned.

I said I sure hoped so.

"You know why I quit dancing with Ogundoti's company?"

I said sorry, I didn't know who Ogundoti was, or even that she—though I might have guessed from the good shape she was in—danced professionally.

"Oh? I thought you knew everything that was going on. You mean to say you don't know Ogundoti, lead drummer at the Yoruba Temple? I thought you'd been talking, before . . ."

"O that guy, with the watch cap, sure, I just didn't know his name, that's all."

"Well, anyhow, he's got what he calls the African Performance Group, plays engagements all around; he's really booked up tight, or was till I got off the floor. Three weeks ago now. Ogundoti thinks Obalete got me to stop working for him; but that's not the case at all. I just quit cause I couldn't stand being driven so. The dancing, the teaching, I could have taken those in my stride. But I had to handle his correspondence, pay his bills—or fend off the creditors—answer the phone to boot. It got so's I couldn't sleep nights I was so wore out. And when the numbers said someone was tying me down, that cinched it.

"My ex-boyfriend's agent is trying to get me a new job. He says there's a Voodoo picture coming up and maybe I could get the part of a priestess-like. It'll probably fall through, but I sure hope it don't. I'm not afraid of getting possessed anymore. Godmother's promised to tell me how to control it—that's the whole thing with orisha, you know."

"Yes, that's what Jamón told me. Too bad he doesn't have a band. You could dance for him. I bet he'd treat you fairly. Say, how about coffee?"

"Sure, thanks, wouldn't mind at all. But godmother's gone out shopping. Funny she isn't back by now. Must have stopped in someplace. You think you can make it? That dude in there doesn't look as if he knew how to face the stove. And I don't dare leave this mat—except to pee and sneak a smoke in the bathroom."

I said I'd try. I'd watched Concha. "My sister and I use Chemex," I added, "but the bag thing's something else!"

The "baby-sitter" was sitting at the kitchen table studying a Yoruba grammar. "Want some coffee? I'm going to make some for Doreen, er, Kanyola, and myself."

"No thanks," he said cheerfully, "not allowed by my *ita;* but go right ahead. Hope you can find everything. I don't see how Godmother can stand to live in all this confusion. You should see our place: neat as a pin. We take turns with the cooking; that is, the Sisters do. The Brothers tackle everything that requires know-how—wiring, plumbing, plaster."

If she heard that, Marty would flip. "You part of a commune?"

"Hmmm, might call it that. We call ourselves the *Egbe.* That means 'society' in Yoruba. *Egbe ile Bukuli;* the closest we can get to Brooklyn by way of Yoruba pronunciation. Say, when my year is up, I'm going to throw a big *bembe*. Then you can come and have a look around, meet the Brothers. Godmother will let you know when, and what train to take."

"Gee, that's nice of you." I put the milk on to boil, fixed the coffee in the bag and set it in the enamel pot. Then I ran water in, just high enough. "How did you hear about Concha?" I asked, feeling more at ease with him now.

"A Brother. A friend and I used to go see him. This cat did a lot of things around the house. We thought he was crazy. Then he took us to see Godmother. She read me, told me things nobody knew about before. That was it, man. I don't have nothing on my mind no more but the religion."

"Same with me, but it's great how thorough you are, I mean your getting into the language and all. Are you taking courses someplace?"

"No. Just study on my own. But the spirit helps me a lot. Sometimes I take my drum down to the East River and songs come to me, in Yoruba:

> *ye ye a l'odo*
> *ago mo juba*
> *ye ye*
> *bobo iku ago mo juba, ye ye*

"Say, that's nice. Don't know what it means, of course."

"That one is for my mother. My father is Obatala, but not the same as Godmother's. They say mine's pretty hot. You know," he went on, "they used to carry candles down to the East River for Yemaja. But not anymore. Too many people jumping right on in. Now me, I go down and sit at the very edge of the water; but I'm not frightened. I figure if she wants me, she'll get me no matter what. And you know, if something like that should ever happen to me, I'd consider it an honor. For it would mean I was called upon to do something on a higher plane of existence."

I took off the milk, turned the coffee way down, pushed the rags on the curtain rod aside and looked out of the window. Traffic was moving very slowly along the Expressway, on account of the snow. Right below us I saw no crevices in the rock I knew to be mined with rubbish. A light gray haze enveloped the acreage of tenements usually visible from Concha's hilltop windows. Harsh flat roofs became vague farm plots. A man with an eight-foot davenport strapped to his back walked cautiously down the path from the basement door to the gate marked DELIVERIES ONLY. Super moving out? Or was it the man I'd seen on the stairs the day of my first visit? You couldn't tell from above. Well, someday they would all move out, one by one, carrying everything portable, leaving the rest to the junkies, then to the rats. Gangs of boys, Black Spades and Bachelors emblazoned on their jackets, would descend to hurl chrome javelins at the retreating figures. Then they, too, would move on, driven away by packs of wild dogs, roving those desolate streets: Ogun's hunters, he himself behind them with a bulldozer. Then it would snow again, and this time the snow would cover everything, once and for all.

"Existence?" I said. "Sorry. I fogged out. What you said just now was really beautiful; started me thinking off in nowheresville. You know, I didn't get your name. Mine's Raymond, Raymond Hunt."

"Pleased to meet you, Brother. I'm Ebo, Ebo Jones. My name means offering, sacrifice,—or purification," he added.

Footpaths
I Wanted to Follow

Saturday, February 27. Took the first of my walks along the river.

This was meant to be the beginning of a journal; but though I took the walks, I never kept a record. I might have, had I begun them now; but then I was much too disorganized. Besides, the first turned out to be the most important, and of it I can remember almost every detail. After that, one set of impressions gets overlaid upon another, isolating only the most unusual. Although at any time, around any bend, the unexpected may always be met with—a new adventure, or a drab bush I'd never noticed before may suddenly flower —still, the first time maps the contours of all subsequent discoveries.

"Why do you climb a mountain?" someone asked a mountaineer. "Because it's there," he replied. Same with me, and why along the river? Just as Ebo Jones sits himself resignedly down and sings what he hears—if he hasn't fallen in yet, haven't seen him since Concha left. Except mine is a different river—not salty, for one thing—and my mode of creativity is also different. Has to do with physical exertion, encounters, a more staccato way of perceiving.

Since I seemed to be the only one to find that curious affinity for the desolate banks of the River Bronx, I more than ever wanted to follow them, see where that affinity, those banks, would lead me. Into—I presumed, though not in any conscious way I could have laid on the line—the World of Santería, which from the outside had been so generously presented to me by Concha. Out of the partials into the tone. For that world has many accesses, entrances, doorways, portals. Sixteen is only the square root of how many there are, says Ferryman. Well, I had to beat my own way through the bush.

What sort of a strange bird was I to have found myself at those *bembes* instead of, like everyone else in my grade, at the movies? What were the implications of Concha's reading? What, unawares, had I already got myself in for? Who was Concha to me, really? Or I to Ogun? Not to mention those veiled and somewhat sinister references to Oya. And why did I feel that curious way about the river? I needed time and space and privacy to absorb everything that had been happening to me pell-mell since my parrakeet flew in the window. And maybe this longing wasn't all that odd, maybe Santería wasn't such an exotic compulsion. Did not the alongness of the river call me, I realized late one night, as one by one it had called my battered childhood companions off the shelf: Moley, Paddle-to-the-sea and Tarka? But then again, what a different river, what a different me!

Ferryman, to whom, despite Concha's warnings, I'd turned that snowy Monday after, said as Ogun's child it was not surprising for me to be attracted to a river goddess. "But remember," he cautioned, "there are three—all Bitches-Brew—don't be deceived; and Shango has the stronger medicine for attracting women." Ogun—lonely hunter, grimy smith, bloody warrior. But abandoned mill wheels could turn, escaped quarry be hunted down again, wrongs forgiven, fair captives wrested from the enemy. "Perhaps that's the ante you're in for," he suggested. More than these elusive bits and snatches he refused to tell me. "Find out for yourself, kid; otherwise there'd be no truth in the old tales; now would there?" And when I told him about the strange vision I'd had looking out of the absent Concha's kitchen window, he said it was merely a sequel to the one he dreamed every time he checked out his explosives. "Obatala is the beginning—of the end," said he. "Generation and dissolution are the same. And there's nothing new under the sun except Eshu."

So, armed with these mysterious resonances, I began at 180th Street, just below the falls, and walked that first Saturday all the way down to the end.

Footpaths I wanted to follow, ancient ones—this phrase came to me the moment I set foot on them. Well worn, yet hidden from the vulgar eye, they led me down and back I can't say how many times that spring. And still, when a certain mood takes hold, I follow them. They are like the little highways and byways my toy cars used to make under ivy tendrils, between roots of locust trees, where the hidden blackberry bush fruited (before pollution got it) in that place along the reservoir where I used to play by the hour while my mother stretched out in the high grass, reading.

And as I went along, everything I noticed had meaning, or at least I took it in meaningfully. Like those "signs and portents" of which they speak in *Caesar*. Do you know what I mean? Soothsayers of old used to "read" innards of animals, they say, like flights of birds, comets. Well, some days the very litter on the ground makes sense to me, and the most casual happenings resound with a strange importance. Maybe those old derelict women with bound feet one sees examining trash cans early in the morning are really augurers by appointment to his majesty the mayor of New York City.

Ferryman would like that. Must remember to tell him next time, if ever again, I go by his place. For me, simply to walk those paths along the water's edge is to invite experiences that cause gooseflesh, reverberate, continue long afterward to shine with the yellow urgency of forsythia.

For example, scrambling down the gravel to the riverside that first day, I saw at the foot of the junk slide on the opposite bank three burned-out overstuffed chairs. Spectators of the bathing. I see them still. And as I write I'm reminded of a little verse Concha recited one day when I was asking her about Christmas in Otoao. Here it is, freely, from the Spanish:

> *Came the Three Kings*
> *Barren fields flowered—*
> *daffodils, wild strawberries*
> *Nobody welcomed them*
> *Vanished the Three Kings*
> *Desolation followed.*

That last line, may tradition pardon me, is my own invention.

Caught in the branches of a leafless tree that twisted up to meet the underside of the bridge was someone's cast-off *Santería* necklace, all colors, and that gave me confidence.

Picking my way through rubble to the cement wall that keeps the river from undermining the trestle supporting the elevated, there at the loop I found the path. And the river, her mood now serene after all that impetuosity at the junk slide, flows beneath the curved span half-asleep . . . until she bumps smack into a wrecked car, a two-door sedan that has somehow managed to hold most of itself together, keep its tin topside above water anyway, bent on becoming a permanent obstruction.

A tree trunk connects wreck to shore. Surveying the situation from atop the cab, here's how I reenacted it for the imaginary benefit of the *New York Times:*

A DETERMINED HUNK OF DETERIORATION
taking advantage of having landed nuzzle-thrust
against a sizable rock (which protected his body from
the down-drag), the battered veteran of turnpikes at
once slyly began to pile up pieces of driftwood in his
smashed hood's cavity. Some roots, branches, even logs
gradually pushed their way through the broken wind-
shield into the front seat. What could river force do then
but sidle around the exposed flank, eddy on up the protected side, lap against the outflung door (still miracu-
lously intact) and, having succeeded only in further
consolidating his attachment to the rock, retreat with a
mere lick of rusted paint for her pains and the hope of
someday managing to pry a sodden tire from the mud
into which it had fallen free when the car rolled (or was
pushed?)
>   down
>   the
>   bank . . .

I imagine that even before the car began to create a sort
of pond, the shore was always pleasant in that place. Soggy,
perhaps. Still there was grass beneath the beer cans, rusted
washers and other discards from the factory to which I now
climbed to have a look. Operations had long ceased; but
part of the ground floor had been converted into a garage.
A lonely mechanic offered me a beer.

"No thanks, but if you've got soda, I'll take one," digging
into my jacket pocket for a quarter. He cancelled out this
gesture with a generous indication of his own.

"This one's on me. What are you up to, sonny?"

"Nothing really, just taking a stroll along the river."

"Ah," he said, a new look coming into his eyes, "it was
really beautiful along here no more than fifteen years ago,
the best fishing. You could catch a cod a foot long. I grew
up over there," pointing across the river. "Cedars of Leb-

anon Street, beautiful. Now it's mostly parking lot. The city no longer keeps it paved. In those days the old men and women who didn't work anymore used to come and drop a line in. Now they're pushing drugs along the river, getting rid of stolen cars—look."

I said I'd seen.

"I don't feel so bad for you and me," he went on, "but for those old people. They're the ones who suffer. Suppose the city should stop dumping here and fix the place up so's they who can hardly walk could come out here and relax, like the old days. Catch a fish, enjoy a bit of sun, or shade, depending . . ."

"I feel the way you do." What more was there to say? "Well, I've got to be going now. Thanks for the talk, for the soda."

"So long, son, stop by again some time."

"I will." He opened another can of beer. He too refused to go down, though his breath, poor fellow, stank of what was sinking him.

Forced to flow under the Expressway, the river turns sullen with exhaustion, pouts through the viaduct. Loves trains, hates cars. I went right along with her, jogging the steep paved bank, afraid of slipping, of being mugged in the dark, and came out—to my great relief—upon a lake of junk. Some neighborhood kids were living it up in a yellow rubber boat. I waved.

"Want a ride?"

"No thanks, not today, another time." Younger than me, or at least smaller, they were all bundled up in plastic leather coats with their caps pulled down over their ears. Two paddled with thin pieces of crate, while the others fended off with lengths of tubing. The river, exasperated with the size of the obstacles thrown in her way, twisted this way and that, threatening to collide the kids against a bathtub, toilet bowl

or old-fashioned icebox. But they weren't afraid, mainly because they knew her temper was not really directed against
them. Three months later I saw that same bunch swimming
amid the same junk, with the same trust.

At home their human, harassed housecoated mothers
waited.

Another bridge, still in process of construction, and then
the rubble along both shores vanishes into park: green
fields stretching wide as a couple of city blocks. Gently
nudged into a nobler density, between handsome stone dikes
the river, winding as through some half-forgotten old-world
countryside, is redolent of once-upon-a-time grapes, huckle-
berries, strawberries so plentiful that in June the fields were
dyed red and you could get high on the smell of peaches.
Three hundred years ago, say my guides, the grass was as
tall as a man's knees in summer. "Still is, can't you see it?"
I reply. In patches along the west bank between the viaduct
and the turning basin, tall enough to hide the footpath from
all but accustomed feet, initiated eyes.

I run as I write, reliving the springing pace of time. In
February, my sneakers slipped on the mud as I, sidling along
dried hawthorn bushes meshed in crinkly grapevine, grabbed
at willow branches to keep from sliding down the embank-
ment. But by March, the clay underfoot had begun to dry,
the brambles to inch back with the approach of my stride;
and by late April, I was running on packed ground, clearing
roots with a practiced leap, plunging blind through green
thicket (the solemn, wind-flecked river always at my side),
surprised as I flung myself into the sunlight, onto the mown
grass of the open promontory, to find my arms covered with
scratches.

Here, that first Saturday I saw a young man in an old
man's overcoat twice his size sitting on a gunnysack, warm-
ing his hands over a little rag fire. He had everything for his

fix spread out neatly before him on a white handkerchief; but he turned his head to let me pass by without seeing him, as a hiding child covers his eyes.

A month or so later, in exactly the same place, I saw a crazy old woman flying a kite. Good at it, too. Flicking the nylon cord held in her right hand (gloved, to avoid cutting), she jerked the line taut at just the right time, then payed it out clean with the updraft. When the kite was no more than a dust mote in the sky and the plastic detergent bottle she held in her left hand had but one knotted turn of line around it, she began hauling in—stalking about the field like a crane, me following. The cloth wings—rainbow striped— beat back, fighting to stay aloft; but the old gal hung on, gradually easing in until the pressure slackened. Then she reached up and caught it, fluttering, by the ring attached to the traverse guy.

"See, it comes to hand like a falcon," she said delightedly. "Want to try?"

"No, not today, another time."

"Never then," she replied, catching my conscience with her bright, slightly squinted eyes. "There being only two alternatives."

If you start down one of the trails on the left side of the aquaduct, fine, you're on the east bank from the start and it's a quick run to the promontory opposite the place where the strange lady flies her kite. And this point is even more beautiful because here the field slopes up to form a knoll overlooking the long, low dam at the start of the turning basin. But if you've started down on the right, as I did the first time, to arrive at the knoll you have to go down to the railroad bridge, which is rather dangerous to get up on be- cause of all the exposed high tension wires. From the ties (having kept a wary eye out for a sign of trains coming), you drop down onto a concrete wall. From thence a narrow metal ladder leads you further down to a hidden wharf, which runs back under the girders of the bridge itself.

Here, I say, the God of Iron claims his river bride, clamps her to him with riveted elbow joints and solid angular knees. And the sleek oil upon her face reflects him back—Ogun above, Ogun beneath. And yet, despite the intensity of concentration, imperceptibly below the slick, do not her thoughts (deep down, where barnacles cling to the creosoted piles) elude him still, inevitably glide by?

Back up the ladder then, Raymond, along the retaining wall and through a miniature grove of poplars to the eastern promontory. Here, a pickup band comes out Saturday afternoons to practice: guitar, cowbell, congas, and sometimes a steel drum, recalling the beauties of Luiza Aldea, the prowess of some soccer player from Ponce, and—worse luck—Shango's fire.

Flowing sedately under Westchester Bridge, as daughters in time resemble their mothers, the river develops the voluptuous curves and, ultimately, the girth of an almost estuary. Broader, but also deeper, wiser, she patiently begins to tolerate burdens—first commercial fishing boats, then barges.

Below the Victorian railway station, a ratty structure consisting of piles, gangplanks and moorings juts out midstream like a harness. Hand-painted signs advertise the 7:00 A.M. departure of *Bronx Queen* and her sisters, *Sea Witch* and *Claire*, for herring and mackerel banks off Long Island. On my way up the ramp to Bruckner Boulevard I saw the first of these returning with a haul of hatted, muffled men crammed onto the foredeck. Spirits high, they cheered, as I waved, pointing with their upraised beer cans toward the fish flag flying above the conning tower: red on white.

Heavy-bellied barges, pride of the New York Trap Rock Company, dock downstream beside lime troughs. As I cautiously pad by giant funnels overflowing with aggregate, idle cement mixers, pent-roofed silos seven stories high, a pack of barking dogs suddenly surrounds me. I put my hands in my pockets, clench them tight, and, whistling casually, heart pounding with fear, saunter on past the shingled, and seemingly deserted, guardhouse. Safely arrived at a sort of high-and-dry jetty, I pick up my pace and begin to leap from slab to slab of quarried granite, across crevices filled with rusted cable, crowbars and contorted bits of siding.

Safely arrived on Edgewater Avenue, my ordinary route lies straight on. That stiff wire fence about the dockyards no longer puts me off. I simply crawl around it and jump down to a little beach you can follow all the way round to the breakwater. But that first day, once I got past those dogs, my purpose had begun to peter out. I felt cold, tired, very much alone and I wondered if anywhere along that cracked and weedy sidewalk was a place you could get a really good cup of coffee, not unlike Concha's.

A block ahead I saw a forlorn herd of white delivery trucks huddled in front of a long, low building. My hopes rose. I thought of Jamón. But when I got there, I found I was wrong. Not MAR-VEL, but DELICIOSO. Nobody about. The swinging door pushed easily in. Nobody in the cashier's box either. But the display case confirmed right away the sort of place it was: three-tiered wedding cakes, sugared birdcages filled with candied swans, *Buen Viaje* cakes, toy ocean liners plunging through billows of butter cream icing, moon-faced birthday cakes with sweet names like Rosalita, Margarita and Nuestra Señora de las Mercedes. *Feliz Cumpleaño*. Remembering Shango's birthday cake, I was emboldened to push on through to the pantry.

Young women in white kerchiefs were leisurely putting the last squirts upon row-after-row of monuments to buried cravings and beloved hungers. "Is there any place nearby where you can get a cup of coffee?" I asked, in my careful textbook Spanish, staring incredulously at the giant Mixmaster, its super paddles frozen to a stop.

"Try the Cosy Corner—up the hill, on your left. Care for a lick, honey?"

From the outside, the little diner looks bleak; but once inside you can see it's well kept up. No other customers at that hour: behold the black Formica counter spotless, each salt and pepper shaker in its proper slot, each bottle of catsup, each easi-pour sugar spout. A smooth-haired dark lady wearing a starched white uniform rises as I enter. "Good afternoon, young fellow. You look as though you could use a cup of something hot. How about chocolate?"

"Good afternoon. If you don't mind, I'd rather have coffee—heavy on the milk. Have any doughnuts?"

"Sorry, all out. How about homemade cornbread? Bran muffin? buttered English?"

"They all sound good."

"Then try a little of each." She really has a beautiful face, I thought, doesn't look old at all. The flesh was still firm, almost plump, across her prominent cheekbones. Her manner was deliberate, quiet. "I'll bet you're hungry."

"Sure am. Didn't have any lunch. Mostly cold though. Say, Ma'm, would you happen to have a bathroom in the back where I could wash up?"

"First door on the left."

It is immaculate, even dainty. There is a fresh folded towel on the rack, a new bar of Palmolive on the rubber trivet . . .

"Here's your coffee."

"Thanks." I measure out two large teaspoon flows of sugar. It is thick, really hot, every bit as good as Concha's. Toasted English looks good, too, soaked in butter. Cornbread moist. I decide to save the bran muffin for later.

She leans her elbows confidentially on the counter.

"Well, how did you get so far out of your neighborhood?"

"How did you know?"

"That's easy. I've never seen you around before. So either you've just moved in, which isn't likely—most of them are moving out, or you're from? . . ."

"Manhattan," I manage, with my mouth full. My, it's warm in here. I should have taken off my jacket first. Too much trouble now. Steam had fogged over the window, blotting out the street, or maybe it was frosting over on the outside.

"I'm from the South." She smiles, lighting a cigarette. "And I'm in no hurry to get anywhere else. For me, right here is the end of the line. Where did you say you was going?"

"I didn't, though I will if you like. . . ." I have to stop and think. "No place special. Just along the river."

"Sightseeing?" She chuckles.

"I guess you might call it that."

"Most American kids your age don't drink coffee," changing the subject.

"I didn't either—all that much—until recently. Could I please have another? I mean, if it's all made up. A Spanish friend got me hooked on it."

"Where are *your* folks from?" This with her back turned, filling my cup.

"Funny you should ask. I've been thinking a lot about that. Don't know, exactly; but I mean to find out. I've . . . been trying to get in touch with my ancestors—if that doesn't sound too odd."

"Not at all." She smiles pleasantly as ever. "If I was you," she goes on in that marvelous unhurried way of hers, "I'd check out the graveyards first off. You say you're following the river? Well, you're not far from the mouth, less than a mile. Hunt's Point—where the market is. Closed now though. Halfway down along Hunt's Point Avenue," she points behind her, "you'll come to a little cemetery on the right, set in a park. There's a fence around, but you can look in, at least, and get some idea. It's very old. No more than twenty tombstones or so. Names kind of wore off, but maybe your eyes is better than mine. Pleasant atmosphere. Sometimes on my way home from work I go by and sit down on a bench in the park for a while . . ."

Mmm, I wonder . . . "You haven't ever heard of *Santería,* by any chance, have you?"

"*San-te-rí-a?* Can't say as I have. Would that be some kind of wine?"

"No." I laugh. "Well, maybe. Also, it's a religion."

"You don't say! Well, I'm a Baptist myself. Took the plunge at thirteen."

I glance at the clock. Her calm is making me strangely restless. Or is it the coffee? 2:15. "Gee, I'd better be getting on. Nice talking to you."

"The pleasure was mutual, young fellow; come back again real soon."

"O dear, I nearly forgot. How much do I owe you?"

"Twenty-five cents for the hot-buttered, twenty-five for the cornbread. You didn't touch the bran muffin; I can put it back."

"And the coffee?"

"That's on me, this time." She smiles. "Next time you come in you can bring me a souvenir. One customer brought me an ashtray from Niagara Falls." She points to the large arm of the chair she'd been smoking in when I came. "Someone else, a handsome gentleman from Barbados, brought me a piece of gen-u-ine coral." There, on top of the cash register; funny I hadn't noticed. "No obligation, though," she says pleasantly. "Coffee's always on the house for strangers."

"Thanks." By now it's become so hot inside the place I feel dizzy. "Thanks again, I really enjoyed everything."

"Don't mention it. And on your way down to the Point don't forget to stop in at the cemetery. You never can tell. Take care . . ."

"I will." (If I ever get out of here.) "I will."

The little cemetery cannot be seen from the street on account of the semitrailers lined up front-to-end around the circular park. And the lady at the Cosy Corner was right, even against the fence it's hard to see much—so close together are the wrought-iron bars, so indistinct the weathered writing.

But I kept at it, walking all the way round, peering through at intervals, and sure enough, on four of the pinkish brown stones, set all in a clump, I finally made out the name Hunt. Think of it—two Hannahs, an Elizabeth and one Thomas!

Prongs, too, difficult to climb, but luckily, on the side farthest from the Avenue, there's a tree with branches—two of them—extending over the fence so that it's possible to shinny the trunk, walk out on one branch while grasping the other for balance, then jump—right in the midst of all the Hunts. For there were others, names worn off, whose position convinced me that they—even as I, in the exhilaration of my discovery—belonged to the family.

Imposingly fenced off from the rest lay, I assumed, our patriarch, old Noah, perhaps Jacob Hunt, or whoever it was brought us over to America; but no, an intruder— hence probably the partition:

Joseph Rodman Drake
1795–1818

Green be the turf above thee,
Friend of my better days!
None knew thee but to love thee,
Nor named thee but to praise.
        —FITZ-GREENE HALLECK

Well, who was Drake? And what was he doing here any-how? Staring at the inscription, I eventually became aware of a boy's voice, high in the tree I had climbed in by, ex-claiming, "Go, go preach the gospel to the Indians, Josiah." A pause, then repeat, "Go . . . Josiah," and finally, a burst of laughter. "There, that'll fix him. You'll see. He'll ask my father leave to depart on a heaven-sent mission, and I'll have no more beastly lessons!"

I rubbed my eyes. That last remark must have been meant for me. There *was* a boy up there, about my own age, Colo-nial in brown velvet britches. He winked, jumped down from the tree exactly as I had, and stood, hands behind his back, which—maddeningly—was turned toward me. A shadowy crowd began to fill in behind him, gathering about a new-dug grave; and as I watched, the boy seemed to grow taller, broader in the shoulders. A nasal voice began to speak, or rather read to the assembled company, ". . . Whereas I for-merly intended to have made my nephew, son of my de-ceased brother, my sole executor, his many and great mis-carriages and disobediences, his causeless absenting of him-self from my house, I do as a consequence . . ." The voice trailed off.

"Well then," said the solid young boy-man, "I will make my own way—if fortune smile—to the islands that gave birth to me!"

"Right on," I whispered.

"You sir," said a testy old man's voice behind me. I spun around. Did he mean me? Sitting on an oriental rug placed on the grass as for a picnic. (It was fall, the leaves from the linden were falling.) "Look sharp," said he. "You'd be a scrivener?"

"Why yes, I guess so, your honor, if that's what's needed."

"Good boy," he nodded, indicating a quill, a bottle of India ink and a thick piece of paper placed conveniently on the rug beside him. I sat down cross-legged and leaned out over my knees so's I could keep the paper firm on the rug. A witty look of skepticism crossed his face. "Any experience?"

"No, your honor, but I'm prepared to do my best."

"Well said. We Jamaicans are a spunky breed. Now, take this down as I think it out. We'll make corrections later. Ahem . . ." I continued to hold the pen poised. He nodded. I dipped, and began to write as he spoke the following:

"I am heartily sorry, Sir, that the King's representative should be moved to so great a degree of warmth which I think must proceed from no other reason but by my giving my opinion in a court of which I was judge upon a point of law that came before me and in which I might be innocently mistaken (though I think I am not), for judges are no more infallible than their superiors are impeccable. . . . Am I speaking too fast?"

"O no, your honor, just the right speed."

". . . I may have been impertinent, for old men are often so, but rude or disrespectful—never. As to my integrity: my hands were never soiled by a bribe, nor am I conscious to myself that power or poverty hath been able to induce me to be partial in favor of either of them."

"I like that, your honor, it's very Libra."

"I'm glad, my dear boy; but remember, a scrivener is not usually entitled to his own opinion. Now, . . . I am neither afraid nor ashamed . . . I have served the public faithfully, and I dare and do appeal to it for my justification."

"There," he said, slapping his knee. "That'll lose me my judgeship. Delancy-of-the-mills, who stands upstream from me with the authorities, shall, I daresay, be appointed to the vacancy. No matter. One cannot but change one's life to advantage at my age. I shall," confiding this last to me with a whisper, "stand as candidate for the Assembly."

"Right on, your honor," I cried out with an enthusiasm that may have broken the connection, for the judge vanished as suddenly as the youth before him, and onto the dinted grass where the rug had been a very different sort of person, a thin, young man in soft-collared open shirt and dark green velvet jacket flung himself panting.

"You'll take cold," I said involuntarily. (The wind had come up, shaking the last few crinkled brown leaves from the linden.) "You're all over sweating. Here, take my coat."

"Never mind, my friend, we're not far from The Grange and will go in at once—soon as I've caught my breath. What's that you've got there? pen? paper?" Why so I had. The judge in vanishing, had forgotten them. He pulled himself up onto one elbow, grabbed the quill with his free hand, dipped and began hurriedly scribbling. "There," handing me the sheet. "What do you think of the first stanza?"

"I'd rather hear you read it."

"No need, I'll recite what's engraved upon my heart, listen."

I sat me down upon a green bankside,
Skirting the smooth edge of a gentle river
Whose waters seemed unwillingly to glide
Like parting friends who linger while they sever;
Enforced to go, yet seeming still unready,
Backward they wind their way in many a wistful eddy.

Tears filled my eyes. What an incredible coincidence!

"Don't Fritz." He patted my arm. "I'm the doctor, and I tell you it's no good. But for the future there *is* hope—of fame at least, and perhaps more. I haven't worked out the middle part yet, but the end came as I sat there recalling last summer's green." He rolled over onto his back and lay, head cradled in his hands, looking up at the gray wintry sky.

Yet I will look upon thy face again,
My own romantic Bronx and it will be
A face more pleasant than the face of men.
Thy waves are old companions; I shall see
A well-remembered form in each old tree
And hear a voice long loved in thy wild minstrelry.

"I sometimes wonder, Jo," I said, pouting, "who it is you love best anyhow, me–or the genius of the river. Well, haunt us both then, me while I live, your Bronx eternally. 'Blast not the hope that friendship hath conceived, but fill its measure high.' Let's to The Grange for hot rum punch! Here, lean on me; the way lies straight . . ."

". . . to the point of no return, I fear," said he, with a bitter laugh, "for who can prove immortality by staring all day at a river?" Pulling himself to his feet, he leaned against the tree and began to cough. I gripped his arm further to steady him until the spasms ceased. Then, with an energy of which I would not have thought his thin frame capable, he wrenched free of my grasp and started running across the field. Awkwardly, I staggered after.

I made it to the dusty road, but there the wind from off-shore began to force me back. It was like kite flying. The bony hand on the other end of the string could have tugged, I firmly believe, could have hauled me expertly in; but instead, the wind was allowed to have her way and I was played out, backward, until the string broke and I pitched forward onto an as-yet unpaved stretch of Hunt's Point Avenue.

"Hurt yourself?" A man in a red shirt and blue jeans was at the top of a ladder leaning against a telephone pole. Peering down at me, "Emergency call," he explained. "Trouble on the trunk line. Runs right under the river, on over to Flushing. Not that I mind, not me. I get time-and-a-half on Saturdays." Prying the lid off the box, he began to fiddle with the wires.

"Be careful!" I shouted.

"Same to you, brother. Me, I'm technical-trained. Some wind! Come up sudden—unforecasted. Let's hope the bulk of the storm holds off long enough for me to get this fixed and down off here!"

Ahead, through the swirling dust, I could see the swayback shingle roof of an old cottage. Of course, The Grange. Cautiously I pushed forward. Tea rose ran wild along the picket fence. The yard behind was given over, oddly, to corn ricks. The twin dormer windows were boarded up and the shed projecting from the stone end (nearest the street) was a caved-in wreckage of fence posts and rusted farm machinery. But wait, in the crenellated stone tower on the far end a soft light, probably kerosine, was burning.

I started to run. The dust had settled, and the wind now carried sea mist. Gathering all my strength into my shoulders, I flung myself forward, forcing the wind to give way. Too late. The old cottage, tower and all, had disappeared, and in its place—the familiar yellowish brown installations of the New York Department of Sanitation.

I ran to the breakwater, then leaped from stone to stone until I reached the bend that inconspicuously announces the merging of sweet waters with brackish. Which of the three was thus dissolving?

"No goddess nonsense," said a contemptuous voice. "Call it *Aquahung,* meaning high-banked-water-runs . . ."

". . . or flowing-through-high-places," said another, slightly huskier in tone, friendlier.

"We don't like to get too personal. We find *that* sort of familiarity offends the powers. On the contrary, we'd rather . . ."

"Hush, here he comes . . ."

And out of the water, black suit stiff with blacker mussels, a figure gaunt as a water-logged gull-perch appeared. His gray blond seaweed hair hung dank to his shoulders. To his tow beard clung a collection of tiny fishhooks, complete with broken lines and barnacles. His clear blue eyes flashed as he thundered, "Fools, O fools and slow of heart to believe all that our prophets have spoken!" That was all. Down he sank into the swell.

"Good riddance!" said the first voice, with a shudder.

"He comes on like this whenever there's a storm," the second voice explained. "Part of his penance."

"He claimed," said the first, "earth that was never ours to sell, even for a pittance, and upon waters that should only be witnessed with sight words, he bestowed the absurdity of his own name. Cursed be old Rough-thunder-throat . . ."

". . . or Rasping-strangle-croak."

"Cursed be the dismal Swede. . . ."

". . . Cursed be Johannes Bronck . . ."

". . . Bronck's name, Bronx, Bronx, Bronx; Ranaque . . ."

". . . and Tackamuch. . . ."

". . . have spoken."

Concha listened intently to everything I had to say about my first trip down the river. "So far so good. You sure saw a lot. And at last you've begun to speak to the dead. That judge is your guardian angel. He's going to help you every way he can. You must light a candle for him. And always a glass of water under your bed for that other one—the poet. He lives under the river, like he said. He wasn't, by any chance, black?"

"I'm afraid not."

"Anyhow, black or not, he's what we call your _conga_. He's going to warn you. Any jinx on your path, he'll head you off. Why do you think you crossed over the bridge? Or got off onto Edgewater Avenue?"

I couldn't say. "Just felt like it."

"You see?" she said triumphantly. "You should buy a puppet for him in the Botanica."

"How about a celluloid duck?" I asked, half-joking. "A bathtub toy. Then I could keep him always in his element."

She looked dubious. "We'll have to look it over."

Concha was particularly interested in the Indians, attributing far more importance to them than I, who thought they acted kind of funky. "What did they look like? Dwarfs?"

"I tell you I didn't see them at all, only heard their voices, but I supposed they were tall, shaved heads with porcupine quill roaches like the painted sachems you see in the Museum of Natural History."

"You're sure they didn't give you anything? A stone? A shell?"

"Only an interesting idea, good advice, and the name, of course—*Aquahung*."

"Are you sure it wasn't *Aka-kun*?"

"No, at least I *think* I got it right."

"Well next time, ask them to say it again. They'll be back," she assured me. "If you ever decide to go in for jinx yourself, they'll be a great help. There are ways of calling them up and tying them down. I'll teach you."

Although everything else that happened struck Concha in a positive way, even the man with the fix—that was Babalú, St. Lazarus—she didn't like the sound of the proprietor of the Cosy Corner. Not at all. "It's a good thing your conga kept you from eating that bran muffin," she said; "and who knows what she put in your coffee. That lady was, almost decidedly, a sorceress."

"But Concha, that's ridiculous. She was very nice to me. And it was she who sent me to the cemetery, after all."

"Makes no difference. You got to be careful. Might have ended up in a grave yourself. Look, Seraphina says she's a *mayombera*. That means what you call witch, or sorceress."

"Okay, so she's a witch. But—you've mentioned her before; just who is this Seraphina?"

Filling In

The river always led me back to Concha's place, and Concha (inadvertently, for she had no idea how I haunted it) to the river.

In order to have time alone with her, I'd have to be there very early Saturdays before her day got going. As soon as the phone began to ring (Unnnhunnn?), the spell would break, our suspended reality over. And when people actually started coming, I'd hang around a little just to be polite, then slip off on my wanderings.

Sometimes I'd knock at my usual 7:30, and prolonged barking would let me know she was out, or the dog's absence would tell me she was walking him. In either case, I'd run down the stairs and up Anthony Avenue to meet her—as far as Tremont Avenue if she'd already reached the little self-service open at that hour.

Unmistakably Concha: a block away, favoring her bunions. Pilgrim feet. I'd rush to take her shopping bag. On the way home we'd stop at the Spanish store for milk and the rolls, then mount the stairs in affectionate silence. She needed all of that she could get for breathing.

"Concha," I asked her once, "why don't you ask your daughter to do the shopping for you?" This daughter is an enormous, quiet, rather strange woman with a great sense of humor, who tends to stay—asleep mostly—in the back room off the kitchen. Awake, she's always pleasant to me, talks wittily of her fondness for cemeteries, of her infallible dream warnings.

"She doesn't buy what I like. You know, they don't care . . ." the only bitter remark I have ever heard from Concha—except on the subject of her godmother.

Because even Concha's grandson, if he was around, didn't get up till late, we always had the kitchen to ourselves. She'd make coffee while I put some of the groceries away and cleared a place on the oilcloth for butter, rolls and our cups and saucers. Then I sat down, for she liked to wait on me. And while we drank the coffee, we talked. Occasionally, at my prodding, Concha would recall snatches of her girlhood in Otoao, or she would decide to let me in on something; most often we just gossiped.

There's a Yoruba myth says, "In the beginning water." Then Obatala was sent down with a packet of black earth, seven pieces of iron and a chicken. Drunk on palm wine, Obatala didn't quite make it, but his ruthless elder brother came along, sprinkled the soil over the waters and loosed the chicken to scratch it into position. What the iron was used for, the myth doesn't say—at least Ferryman's version —but I imagine for something like—

When the City decided to move the wholesale market out to Hunt's Point, they simply extended the breakwater, set up dredges way offshore, and began to fill in. Bulldozers pushed the soil around, steamrollers flattened it.

Concha's story is like silt redeemed from the river bottom. Imagination is iron.

I

The next time Uncle Jochem came back to Otoao he brought my father a beautiful new set of butchering knives.

"These should lighten your work this busy season. The time will fly by, the money roll in, and you won't be missing your little Concha at all."

"Missing Concha?" My mother raised an eyebrow.

"That's right. Looks as though you'll have to do without your daughter's help in the kitchen," he announced. "I'm taking her to spend Christmas in Haiti."

"That pagan place? From all I hear, black cannibals, that's what they are. And besides, Jochem, you have no idea how ill Concha's been. She's only now getting back on her feet. To expose her to the excitement of such a trip would be foolhardy."

"But that's exactly what Concha and I have in common—foolhardiness. It's the only way to live. Come on, beautiful Dolores," my uncle said, getting up and giving her one of his hearty embraces. (Only Uncle Jochem dared kid my mother.) "You know you won't really mind. It'll do you good to have her off your hands for a while. And despite what you've heard, Haiti will do Concha good. A change of scene. A chance to ride horseback. We'll be staying out in the country. A lady friend of mine (my mother stiffened) —don't worry, seventy years old if she's a day—has invited us to her house. Madame Lorgnette LaPlace is her name. An important person, with a numerous family, so there'll be plenty of company for Concha, who oughtn't to spend so much time by herself. (This was a little dig at my mother who had become more strict than ever about my playing with the kids in the shacks.) Lots of bathing, good food. Why, she'll come home after two weeks fat as a partridge."

"Why not?" my father suddenly said. And so it was decided.

We spent the night in my uncle's shack on Rio Descala-brado beach. Early in the morning one of his men brought a boat inshore from Coffin-of-the-dead, where Uncle Jochem kept her ready for his island hoppings. We dropped the man back on that key—which I'd never seen up close before—then headed for Santo Domingo with the wind blowing from behind.

This was my first time sailing, and I learned a lot; but mostly I just sat enjoying the breeze, the speed. I never thought I'd feel such confidence. Across whitecaps I could hear salt-spray voices calling

"The sea is here, *baracoa,* and so are the sweet, sweet fishes, *itime, itime,*" over and over, until a deeper level answered them, "*Caracol,* shell kids, call up the trade winds, call hurricane and messenger, *whooo, swishhhh.*"

My uncle was an excellent sailor, and the little converted fishing boat was strong as an ox. Agwe, whom the Haitians worship as Master-of-the-sea, was the boat's name, painted on the hind end:

A G W E

C u r a ç a o

And to cheer us on, leaning against the bulwarks with the steering stick under his left arm, my uncle sang:

Agwe, Master Agwe
Don't you see me on the reef?
Mr. Cannon breaker,
Your tide's carrying me.
I've got my hand on the oar,
Too late to turn back now;
Master Agwe, don't you see me on the reef?

When, midmorning, the wind seemed to slacken, Uncle Jochem took a big conch shell out of his duffel bag, held it up to his lips—head thrown back as if he were drinking: *honk, wonk.*

He also had a wind string. Took it out of his pocket and showed me: three knots left to go. "Just in case you're becalmed and the conch won't work, you can cut off one of these. Should a storm come up, twirl till the worst dies down. An old Jamaican lady gave it to me. Very powerful."

He asked me to pour him a tin measure of white rum. I've never seen Uncle Jochem so happy. His crinkly beard gleamed in the sun, and his eyes, squinting up at the sail, were green with light as eels at play just beneath the surface.

We moored the boat at Jacmel and took a pony cart over to the mountain village where Madame LaPlace lived. That bumpy road was a continuous procession of the blackest people I had ever seen. I remember that blackness struck me more than anything. Then the pipes jutting out from under the brims of the straw hats of skinny men walking. They would stop and look at you as the cart passed by, as would the slim women walking with big bundles on their heads. Seraphina was delighted. What struck her was the whiteness of the dresses and head ties. "Like Africa, only sunbleached; and look," she said, "at the market!" The hardest part was the language. Those people all spoke French. I never did learn to speak but a few words: *mèci* (thanks) and *c'é moin* (it's me). But I learned a lot anyway. Sometimes Uncle Jochem was around to translate important things for me, but mostly he was off taking part in the men's activities, for he was highly thought of in Haiti, as everywhere in the islands. The songs? Ah, they were beautiful. Easy to pick up what's often repeated, and you bet I sang right along whether or not I got the whole meaning.

Madame had a big place in a clearing above terraced cane fields. Beyond, you could catch a glimpse of the sea. There were lots of small buildings. In the center was a long open shed supported by posts and propped by a center pole painted with stripes, all colors. Down this, during ceremonies, the orisha came—all the way from "Africa under the sea," for Madame LaPlace turned out to be a very important person indeed, the most powerful priestess—*Mambo* they call it there—in Haiti. Despite her years, she was busy and energetic. Good-looking, too. She wore beautiful gold earrings and her head tie was knotted up in a dozen directions. I suppose she had lots of things wound up working for her there. She had a nice smile (although she could get plenty mad when things went wrong or people didn't do what she said). Her eyes were quick-moving, didn't miss a trick. She made a big fuss over Uncle Jochem, as if he were the one person she wanted most to see that moment. She embraced me and called me "Ticaye," meaning "child of the house." After that everybody called me nothing but Ticaye, and I was permitted to call her Mama Nette.

They were all packed up to fetch new water from the spring and, luckily, we'd arrived just in time to go with them. It was like going on a picnic, everybody carrying hampers on their heads. Inside were food and drink and special gourds to be filled when we got there. Her "family," as Uncle Jochem had said, was indeed big—at least thirty-five persons, all ages, and we picked up more along the way. When we came to the place where a special path branched off to the spring, Mama Nette bent down. From a pouch pulled out of her bulgy dress, she sprinkled white cornmeal upon the ground, making a design already familiar to me, a circle with four crosses like the one Mama Titi drew in the cemetery, only fancier, like everything they do in Haiti. Then she lit a candle in the center and everyone began to sing:

> *Go, Papa (Eshu) Elegba*
> *Open the gate for me;*
> *Take away the barrier . . .*

You see? Same thing, with a difference.

When we got to the spring, she made another design, on a flat rock, of twisted snakes, heads facing each other. Again everybody began to sing, and this time Mama Nette got possessed—first time I'd ever seen it happen. Squirming and wriggling she threw herself in, and when she came up, began passing her muddy hands all over our arms and faces. I got gooseflesh. Others trembled violently.

> *Damballa Wedo*
> *Look at your children today, Heh!*
> *Look at your children today, Hoh!*
> *Damballa, Oh; Damballa, Eh.*
> *Look, Damballa what you done to me!*
> *Serpent in the water*
> *Serpent in the tree*
> *Damballa Wedo, look what you done to me!*

That's a special orisha those people have got, and how! On the way home we gathered herbs, some already known to me from the mountain.

Next evening after dark they began the ceremony of herb pounding. A huge mortar was set up in one corner of the shed. Drums in the other. We shredded them in, first roots, then bark, then leaves and as the drums began to play, two men stepped forward to pound, alternating: *whom-whum; whom-whum.* So strong were those herbs that we all began to sneeze! Some of the people began to dance—bent way over, jerking their shoulders back and forth, hands on thighs just above their squatting knees. Those Haitians really have strong legs. I've never seen such dancing!

> *Leaves, O leaves come save me*
> *From my (whom-whum) misery*
> *Leaves (whom-whum) (whom-whum) save me.*
> *Great Forest,*
> *Master underwater tree,*
> *I'm going to pick my leaves.*

So sad, I cannot weep,
Great Forest, from my sorrows,
O leaves save me.

Mama Nette again got possessed, and would you believe they lifted up that heavy mortar and put it on her back as she lay there panting. All the people lined up to take turns pounding. When they took the mortar off, she got up just as if nothing had happened and began ordering them to come forth with containers for the herbs. The mortar being all emptied out, she took a bottle of brandy, spit to the four directions and poured it in. Meanwhile, out in the yard a bonfire had been lighted. Someone rushed over with a flaming stick. *SSSSSSsss* the liquor went off, filling the mortar with flames, which we all rushed to dip our hands in, smearing that fire (which really didn't burn) all over our faces, shoulders.

And when those blue flames died down, we all trooped over to the bonfire and started dancing around. Some jumped right in. By now you could hardly turn around without seeing somebody stagger, fall into the arms of a friend and then start up dancing again in the character of the Loa who had mounted him. Loa, that's what they call orisha, and they think of people being ridden by them as if they were horses. They dress up the possessed the way we do, but again, fancier. Not just shawls—whole dresses, uniform jackets with epaulettes, giving them mirrors or swords to hold, whatever fits. Damballa mounted Mama Nette again, and this time she went all the way up into the crotch of a bougainvillaea tree that spread its purple branches over half the yard. There among the flaming blossoms she crouched, hissing, her tongue darting in and out—like this—until Uncle Jochem enticed her down with a raw egg cracked onto a plate of cornstarch.

Damballa OH, Damballa EH
Look what you've done to me;
Serpent in the water,

Serpent in the tree,
O Papa Damballa, Look what you've done to me!

Ogun, Ironmonger, O, Come with me!
I say Ogun, Red-eyed Warrior, Come with me!
Cannon can boom-boom; Pay no attention!
Gun can yaup-yaup; Pay no attention!
Ogun, O, Petro-leum, Come along with me.

Suddenly I felt a pair of strong arms lift me up. Round and round they swung me (O come, come along) closer and closer to the fire. It would have done no good to protest, so I held my breath. Right through the flames that son of Ogun passed me back and forth. Bell gongs bore into my chest. I heard clapping, the sound of whips cracking. A shrill whistle pierced my eardrum . . .

When I awoke, the party was over; the fire but coals. All around me people were stretched out on mats asleep. Some were snoring.

"Merry Christmas," said Seraphina brightly. "It's okay Concha, not a hair on your head was singed, and from now on you'll be able to pick up fire. Unlike your uncle!" She laughed. "You missed what happened to him, poor fellow. Agwe came down and swamped him; then he got too close to the fire and started to sweat salt, as though to dissolve. Mama Nette had to wrap him up quick in wet towels. Fire and water won't mix—no news to us, eh Concha? They really know how to do things over here in Haiti? Chaos I call it! Some fellow from the cemetery, weird-looking he was, with missionary frockcoat and dark glasses on, tried to sneak his hand up my skirts, but I fixed him. He can't stand fire no more than Agwe. Then some Indian warrior came along. We danced till I thought I'd shake inside out, but then I have always been partial to Indians . . ."

All day long we worked bottling the pounded herbs in Damballa's source water, Mama Nette handing out samples to anyone who dropped by. And many did, even people who hadn't been to the spring, or to the dance, or done anything whatsoever; but that's always the way it is—you got to be generous. Toward evening, we took our own private baths in the cement tub Mama Nette had built right into her Damballa shrine house. My rinse, I remember, smelled like jasmine. It was at that time she gave me my *paquét,* best anti-jinx in the world, I figure.

On the day of the Three Kings some of us were bathed again—this time in the pond behind the shed. Here and there in the crevices of rock, little double-jar offerings for the twins had been set. One by one we had to strip and stand on a stone to be cleansed. The men were told to behave themselves, and nobody peeked, I assure you. The last of us, a girl, maybe she was nervous, slipped. Her foot disturbed the water, and up rose an immense snake, big as this. And did she ever start screaming. Startled it back again. Then, one by one again, we had to lie face down by the edge while cuts —so small you couldn't see them afterward—were made in our backs with bits of glass. Herbs were rubbed in, then we had to stay very still ten minutes or so to see if any snakes would come up out of the water to give us extra strength. Sometimes they did, other times they didn't.

I kept my eyes tight shut, as they said I should. It was so quiet you could hear locusts singing out in the cane fields. Suddenly there was a sucking sound, as of drawing in breath. Shortly after, I felt a cold smoothness slither across my shoulders. Exerting the gentlest of pressures, no more than this, down my back those sleek fingertips slid. I could feel one of them coiling itself around my ankles. Softly Mama Nette began to sing a hymn.

> *O Damballa,*
> *Today let the twins, twins speak for me.*
> *Left my mother in Guin-ay,*
> *Twins, please speak for me;*
> *Left my whole fam'ly in Af-ri-ca,*

Twins, please speak for me.
Twins of the waters,
Twins of the rains,
Who's left over to pray for me
When the Kings come, please Damballa
Let the twins speak for me.

Then they all glided off into the water again, down under and over to Africa . . .

II

"And did you ever go back to Haiti?"

"No, Uncle Jochem might have taken me again, but he got involved in other things. The years went by. He dropped by now and again . . . Then, one day, we heard he was dead. And that was that . . .

"No, just old age, a natural death. He was a very powerful man . . .

"Sure. I could stop off sometime on my way to Puerto Rico; but what would be the point in it? All the old people are dead. My orisha would be good there, though, honored by them. I could attend all ceremonies . . .

"No, in those days there wasn't any real *Santería* in Puerto Rico. Just a bit of this and a bit of that, mostly on a part of the island where I didn't live. I didn't find out about the religion as it is until I got to America . . .

"Now that's a long story. I had relatives living on 112th Street, so I might have gone any time. I had money, as I told you, left by Jochem.

". . . Why? Well, the years went by, and strange to say, I was not discontented. They made me so strong in Haiti, I guess that was it, nothing could get me down. So for a long time I had no trouble. I helped Hermana Paquita out with her remedies, continued to keep in touch—no more than that—with Mama Titi, finished high school and got involved in politics. Also I worked the spirits with Doña Montoya and her group, my mother's friends mostly; but after a while I preferred to go to the dances held Saturday evenings at the schoolhouse, so I let that drop and my mother was just as glad as not, I guess.

"Don't get the wrong idea. We weren't allowed to fool around afterward. Parents called for their daughters at the door and took them right away home again. Which was okay by me, there was no one I liked in a special way until *he* came along. And *he* was the reason why, in the end, I decided to go to America . . .

"Handsome, I tell you. You'll never see anyone better-looking than that man . . . Carlos Gomez . . . Dark, much darker than me, but with good hair—straight as an Indian's. His was a well-connected family, lots of them politicians. His father owned a sugar plantation near Arecibo, and Carlos worked there—in a scientific way. He was bright. He'd been trained. He knew—how do you call it?—all about measuring the land exactly from a distance. Chemistry, too; for the refining process that's needed. . . .

"Times were hard for my father. The Americans took the best beef, and Don Montoya himself almost went broke. When a big shot from San Juan came out to set up a cigar factory, lots of men came into Otoao from the country to work there during the week. So my mother decided to open a boardinghouse. They could sleep in the building next door, which my father and his brother owned anyhow so that was no problem, and eat at our place. . . .

"In the parlor. My grandmother was by that time dead so my mother converted it into a big dining room—long tables, benches. My mother did the cooking and I helped a lot, serving mostly. We hired a neighbor woman, glad for the work, to help out. We were that busy. The house was full of clatter and joking. But if one of the men tried to get fresh, my mother would ask him not to come back. Weekends most of them went home to their own families anyway. Now, one day Carlos had business in Otoao. He heard that our board-

inghouse was a good place to eat, so he dropped in, saw me
—even if I wasn't much to look at—and that did it.

"He was a lot older, but he obeyed the rules, and since he
was from the Gomez family my mother let him come to call.
It was a long way from Arecibo and how did he get there?
Bought a bicycle and rode it over every Saturday. He'd stay
the night next door, and first thing in the morning he'd be on
our doorstep for coffee. Once we secretly arranged he'd come
over during the week. I met him where the Ponce road turns
off, then took him up to the mountain so we could tie our
footprints in the shadow of the blackwood. I wanted our love
to last forever. Foolish Concha. I can't give any credit to
Seraphina for warning me in this case. When it comes to men,
she's not to be trusted, at all. So, it was on my own, and quite
by chance, that I found out he already had a woman.

"She had come to Hermana Paquita for skin freshener.
Stopping by, as I often did, to deliver something from the
mountain Paquita needed, 'Imagine, Concha,' she greeted
me, 'this lady has come all the way from Arecibo. I'm getting
famous. Maybe we should go in for a mail-order patent-
medicine business.'

" 'Arecibo?' I said, 'pleased to meet you,' and then, fool-
heartedly, 'do you happen to know the Gomez family?'

" 'You might say I know *part* of the family very well.'

" 'Really? Which part?'

" 'Carlos Gomez is my man. The rest of them don't mean
a thing to me. If they don't care to look a fact in the face,
ain't nothing they can do about it now, can they?'

" 'Guess not,' I said, betraying nothing.

"The next time Carlos came over to Otoao I told him quits.
It wasn't me. It was the other one, her I'd seen. I just couldn't
have such a thing on my conscience. O he promised to give
her up, said he really didn't care for her in the least, that he
had wanted to marry me right away but was afraid of asking
my parents because my mother was so strict and I not yet
twenty. Now he must ask them. He refused to lose me. But I

couldn't accept his reasoning: she was there first, wasn't she? She cared, even if he didn't. That gave her a right. I just couldn't be responsible for taking him away from somebody. She might kill herself, and then where would we be? That was why I decided to go to America. He pleaded, said he'd kill himself before he'd see me go. But I said, nonsense, he would forget me.

"But he never did. When I came back to Otoao after my own marriage, I went to call on his mother. He was there and so was that woman, his wife by now, finally accepted by the family. They invited me to stay on for dinner. I stayed. He sat right down next to me. 'You go over and sit by your wife,' I reproved him.

" 'No. Never mind. It doesn't matter.' And it chilled my blood to hear her say right out in front of everyone that I was the only one he really loved, the only woman he would ever.

"When I put down my fork, he leaned over and ate everything left on my plate. Just like that. This frightened me even more.

" 'When I die,' he whispered, 'my spirit will haunt you. I have never given you up; and if I have to wait till I'm dead to be with you, then may I get life over quickly.'

"He was a strong man; but he died soon after—of tuberculosis, they said. And for fifteen years his spirit haunted me. Fifteen years, never left me in peace. I used to feel him crawl into bed beside me; he was that insistent. Finally, afraid of being driven out of my mind, I had to sacrifice a chicken to the dirt in his name, that is, to his shadow behind me, free his spirit and send him on his way. There was no other solution. Talk was never any use, nor had I any wish to turn that good man into something evil. His soul deserved purification.

"No, he hasn't bothered me since; but I shall never forget him."

"The man I married in America was a musician, from my hometown originally, although he left before we ever became formally acquainted. Too old for a schoolmate, too young to be one of my father's cronies, Ernesto, his name was; but everybody called him 'Losa' (Boulder) on account of his size. He left Puerto Rico before he was twenty, came to New York and got involved in the craze there was then for Latin music. He could play all sorts of instruments—trumpet, piano, guitar —but saxophone was his specialty. Eventually he formed a band of his own, Losax. I guess you're too young to have heard of it. Not that they were ever really famous. They made a few recordings, played the movie theaters downtown . . .

"I was living with my father's younger brother's family on 112th Street. There were two cousins about my age who did hand sewing, finishing, in a ready-to-wear factory. There was enough work for me, too, and because I had been taught well by my grandmother, I was able to do special orders for fancy things: beaded evening gowns, negligees, the fur and feather-trimmed kinds that were popular in those days. Eventually, I left the factory and did all my work at home. One of my cousins quit to help me. We had plenty of customers, made a lot of money, but it meant being indoors all day long, sewing.

"Sometimes Ernesto dropped in to see how the family was getting on. He asked my uncle to take us to hear him play, several times. And then, one Sunday afternoon on the front stoop he proposed to me . . .

"The first year was a lot of fun. You bet. I traveled everywhere with the band. They were getting out-of-town engagements almost every weekend. Then I got pregnant and that was that.

"My husband traveled more and more. They used to go to Florida for a couple of weeks' run at the Palm Inn. How they loved it down there! See, here's a picture of them then. How funny that old car looks! And here's a picture of the band set up (LOSAX on drum set and music stands). That's Ernesto on the tenor. I made all those ruffled shirts for them myself. Latin style was the thing. When they went out, they wore long white silk scarves (expensive!), fedoras with big brims . . .

"A few doors from where we lived an elderly woman held séances. Saturday nights, when the band was on the road, I got a neighbor girl to baby-sit and began working the spirits again. One evening a Cuban woman showed up. When the session was over, she came over to me and said she thought I might be interested in what was going on at her 'house.' She said it just that way, but the meaning was lost on me. Nonetheless, I went to see her out of curiosity, because I felt she had something.

" 'Watch out, good things sometimes come in rotton baskets.'

" 'Seraphina, if I didn't know you better, I'd say you were jealous of her white skin.'

"Pure Spanish, wealthy family. Her husband—I liked him right away—is different: very dark, brilliant. Very little of her snobbery has rubbed off on him. Just a bit. He's a *babalao*. They're all a bit uppity anyhow; but he with reason, I guess. No one can compare with him. From the beginning her possessiveness was all too clear to me, but only later did I come to realize why he put up with so much shit. It was she who discovered him, got him to go into the religion in the first place. She was Oshun, you see, and for her power to be complete she needed a diviner husband. So now she's got him. She encouraged him to quit whatever job he had then, financed his training. When he was all set, they came over to America —early—got themselves a nice apartment. Now that he's an enormous success, they've moved out to Flushing where he has plenty of clients among the better refugee crowd. They even call him down to Miami, pay for their round-trip tickets (she always goes with him) because something comes up and he's the only one who can handle it. . . .

"What she thought to get out of 'discovering' me, who knows? But I was equally eager to have her become my godmother. She took me back to Cuba for my initiation. In those days that's what everyone did. Very simple, no passport even, you just went: first to Havana, then back up into the hills, one of the villages. It's illegal now. If they caught you with your saints, they'd throw them into the sea. That's why those *santeros* who could manage have come to the States. But Fidel is a hypocrite—very well protected. I mean it. Why else do you suppose he's still alive and kicking?

"After that, I was pretty much on my own. It was more natural for me to start my own house rather than hang around hers, for lots of reasons. I don't know why she thought we'd ever get along. She never really taught me anything. Everything I know, seems as though I'd known it from the beginning, maybe in a different way, with different names. Seraphina has helped a lot, especially with the readings. And over the years I've gone here and there, watching carefully how things are done, most especially how they turn out!

"Maybe she's jealous. When she got sick, really bad, she blamed it on me. Told everybody I'd jinxed her. Can you imagine? My own godmother? She's sick all the time anyhow, lately. Hardly ever gets out of bed, except to go to Miami. And does he pamper her! Everything to her bedside. If something comes up, sometimes I call him on the phone. For, as I've said, he knows *a lot*. But I never go out there anymore. Just once. That was the time I got possessed and asked to be driven to Flushing, as I was in my bare feet, to get my godmother's blessing. They say I came up the sidewalk dancing; and before Obatala and my godsons, she had to do right by me. O she can be soft, sticky sweetness, but watch out, should you ever meet her, for that sting. As a matter of fact, I've been thinking . . . O Well, we'll see . . .

"He didn't object. Didn't go in for the religion himself, Ernesto, respected it though, you bet. Once he was threatened by the manager of a cheesy nightclub who wouldn't pay the band what was agreed on in the contract, and I said, 'Let me try a little jinx.' He said, 'Okay, let's see what happens.' Two days later the car that guy was riding in did a flip. Nobody hurt, but it sure gave him a good scare and he paid right up. Ernesto was impressed. When he was dying—he drank too much, that was the trouble with him, with all who led the kind of life they did—I put a set of Shango beads on him. He didn't object. 'Never hurts to take a chance,' he said. If I'd put them on earlier, maybe he'd have stopped drinking. But he didn't want that until it was too late.

"I worked over him, but couldn't bring him back to life. You see, his number was up. But a few times I *have* managed to do it. Once on the beach I revived a drowned girl; how, I still couldn't say. I just went into a trance and by the time I came out of it she was alive and breathing. They say I picked her up and danced in the waves with her body held high over my head. Calling on Yemaja, I must have been. And there have been other times, too. You have to know how; but, as I said, you can't overcome someone's destiny. For that there's no gift. . . .

"I have some wonderful godchildren. A few, the religion goes to their heads in the wrong way. They get the idea they're orisha in person. Then they won't listen to advice, go ahead and do crazy things, and get it in the end. I've actually seen Obatala strike somebody dead. You got to be careful. You never know what you might be in for. Right now Jamón's got me worried. He's left his wife. You wouldn't know her, but she's nice, a strong Oya person. Jamón won't look me in the eye these days. He spends more and more time at my godmother's house, of all places. He says he wants to learn everything he can from Jojo her husband; but doesn't realize she's giving him the glad eye and the swelled head on purpose. Jamón's going too fast and could do something we'd all regret.

"Everyone these days thinks he has the answer. All those kids running around wearing Moslem amulets on top of their beads, sacrificing here and there because they've read something somewhere, not because it's the way we do things. Apt to give us all a bad name, get us all into trouble. Not to mention jinx! There's no end to the dumb things people are doing. Only last week Mama Tele had the nerve to send one of her girls over here to my own street with some powder I was supposed to step on and it would kill me. We were coming down the steps. I saw her a block away hiding behind a mailbox. Thank god for my conga. When I stopped and told them, my godsons said, 'Go back in the house; we'll sweep it up.' But I said, 'No, you watch me. I'll show Mama Tele what I think of her jinx.' And with that I walked right down and started to dance on that powder in front of everyone. Don't think *that* didn't get back to the hen coop! What I got in Haiti hasn't run down yet so help me."

"But it might. I mean, Concha, you're strong. I realize you're well-protected, that no one can catch you off your guard. But that's just the hitch; there could come a time . . . I mean the accumulation of all those things that give you such authority. Those that are jealous, or scared will always try to put you down. So why not . . . Listen, Concha, I've got an idea. Why not go to the source for more of it? Haven't you ever dreamed of going to Africa? And I don't mean when you're dead. I mean now, living as you are. I'm sure you must have. Remember what you said about the knife in front of Pedro Cartero's? I know, you'll say you haven't the money, that Uncle Jochem's treasure got spent long ago; but if you really wanted to, and told Eshu, you'd win it! Wouldn't this be the answer to everything? And don't tell me you're too old. What was it the judge said? 'At my age one can only change one's life to advantage.' Besides, the elders who know the most, they're the one's you'd want to see and they aren't so young either! Suppose somehow or other we could arrange to have you invited as a VIP—Ambassador of *Santería,* Representative of the Yoruba Religion in America! Think of it, Concha! What a triumph!

"That man I know at the museum who goes over there all the time: I'm sure he knows everybody of importance —officials, priests. He's that sort of guy. Not easy to figure out, and not all that likable really; but what difference does that make. I think the idea of your going would appeal to him. He was a friend of my parents, feels somehow guilty, or maybe just responsible; anyhow, I think he just might do me one more favor. Shan't we try it, Concha, please?"

"Sure. What can we lose? Seraphina says go ahead, see what happens . . ."

Thornskyl
and Ferryman

"I will write," Mr. Thornskyl said, "to the Balogun of
Bonni, a remarkable man, chief of an ancient town near
the source of the Oshun River."

"Wow!" inadvertently escaped me. He paused. I shook
my head, "Nothing, please go on."

"Well then, the Balogun knows more about sacred
things than anyone in a comparable position, and his hos-
pitality, that of the town itself, is legendary. Moreover, it
just happens that the town's special protector is—Ogun."
Again he paused; but I refused to take him up, to acknowledge the link just visible, as it were, beneath the cuff of
his cable-knit sweater.

"O Concha will love that!" I exclaimed with eager neu-
trality. "She needs Ogun."

"Even more significant for her purposes, I imagine," he
went on, "is the fact that the high priest of Obatala in
Bonni, a man of extraordinary spiritual refinement, is uni-
versally acknowledged to be that divinity's earthly counter-

part: dissolution of the flesh—one phase of Obatala-in-person."

"Ah, so there really is that possibility! Concha worries about the illusion of it a lot. I mean the self-importance. I wonder what he'll think of her, if they do meet, what he'll see. She'd deny it to the ground, of course, be cross at me for even thinking so, but I have the idea that she herself, in her own way, might without knowing it be another case, if that's not blasphemy." I laughed, making it easy for him to discountenance the idea. But he took it solemnly into consideration.

"Could be. There is always, as you say, that rare possibility. So now." He smiled. "It is with even more than my originally intended warmth that I shall write to my friend proposing he sound out the high priest of Obatala about inviting her to live in that exceptional person's compound for a while, to participate in cult life there. How long, of course, would depend upon all sorts of things beyond . . ." he tightened his smile, drawing me closer in, "our power." I frowned slightly, prepared to stare him out of countenance if he went on like that. But he didn't. "Mainly, on how well she gets on with them."

"Do they," out of curiosity, "speak English?"

"The *Balogun*," he made it perfectly clear, "speaks better English than either of us—the king's," laughing a little at his own joke. "Should he agree to our plan, the Balogun will most certainly arrange an interpreter for her, initially. After that, the question would be, how much Yoruba does she?"

"I don't know, can't judge, really. My Spanish isn't good enough for me to tell, often, which is which. Obviously it's a mixture in the ceremonies. But it seems to me that after the first day or two if Concha gets on, as you say, she won't need much of anything verbal. That's not the way she picks things up. She got along fine enough without French in Haiti."

"Oh? She's been there, too, your Concha?"

"Years ago," I dismissed it, "when she was only a kid. Some songs have stuck with her, that's about all. She remembers them the way chants they sing have been remembered, partly Spanishified, from Africa."

"Mmmmhmmmm," rather impatiently. "Well, let us put down that your friend knows ritual Yoruba."

"Will that be news to them over there?" He didn't answer, for some reason or other, but went right on making plans.

"Now, with regard to the everyday. It would be an immense help if you could get a little phrase book for her. She ought to memorize a few greetings so that whatever she does or does not 'pick up,' she'll be able to get through the day with appropriate civility. Sounds strange to us, but over there such things are important. I certainly wish I could go along . . ." my heart sank, "to pave the way. But, as you see, I'm up to here . . . However," he said brightly, "one never knows the direction things may suddenly take."

With that I certainly agreed and began, in spite of myself, to fidget in my chair; for if I was afraid he was going to ask to meet Concha, I was equally uncomfortable in the position—after all his generosity—of not offering. I had had to make her interesting enough for him to make Concha's and my project his. This had proved easy, so perhaps I'd made her too interesting for even his uncanny reserve to resist. Clearly, I was taking advantage of him; and all that could continue to hold me aloof was the sense that at the least sign of my slackness he'd pull in. It occurred to me that somehow or other he had already done just that. But how? So far I'd promised nothing; and as far as meeting Concha was concerned, I'd hold off till the last. How I'd hate to have to pay that high a price for her salvation!

Dog-in-the-manger! Why, you well may ask, such a strange show of possessiveness? It isn't that, in a sense the very opposite, but awfully hard to explain. Her life goes on and out and everywhere past and present without me. Which is the beauty of it. But I can, or could, now, again and always tune in. How could I ever bear to forfeit even a taste of that privacy to someone from the outside like Thornskyl who, for all his (at least so I imagined them) "deep" affiliations, would clearly be unable to see Concha as she was. Sure, if he relied on my interpretation (already partly given so it was too late—even had I wanted—to put him to the test), he might on faith accept the extraordinary beneath the pixillated propriety, the minimal fuss with which she confronted the ordinary world, whose conventions she accepted when occasion warranted. But he would not have seen the ordinary as part and parcel of her. And this was not only a limitation of his; for unlike Ferryman, who always suggested the maximum of which he was capable, most probably Concha would in turn do her utmost to prevent any such recognition. Seraphina would put her finger to her lips and Concha's eyes, for all that her manner would continue courteous, would seal up. For just as she received, so she could turn off all vibes when she wished.

"One more thing," Thornskyl went on, obviously puzzled by my restlessness, verging on inattention, "while we're awaiting a reply from the Balogun, I suggest you go down to the Nigerian Consulate and begin paving the way for her visa." Did he really consider me equipped for this sort of thing? Ah, he would help me. "Come back tomorrow and my secretary will give you a letter of introduction—together with a summary of our 'case'—to the cultural officer, Chief Owolowo, an old acquaintance of mine. He is sure to be sympathetic. He and the Balogun are college chums and, more importantly, age mates. Between the two of them they may just be able to persuade the authorities in Lagos to arrange an 'official visit'—most likely through the Department of Antiquities." I laughed.

She would get a kick out of that: Old Concha! "But," he went on, "don't speak to anyone else at the consulate. I don't imagine you know much about the political situation over there these days, without anyone," he lowered his voice, "to clue you in. However, it is still tricky. Many of the wrong people remain in key positions, so one has to walk softly, like your friend the chameleon."

"No problem," I said, wondering at the timing of that last remark. "If you don't mind, I'd like to ask one more question. Do you suppose, I mean if it were to be an official visit, she would be met at the airport by somebody? She's not scared of flying alone, but is afraid, once she gets there, of feeling stranded. Even here she hardly ever goes out of her neighborhood alone. Concha does like to be accompanied."

"No problem," he imitated me in a friendly way. "If she goes at all she'll be suitably met. You can count on them to do things grandly: a delegation at the airport, a limousine to drive her up to Bonni, and when she reaches the gates of the Balogun's palace, talking drums to announce her arrival." He opened a tin box of carefully stacked cassettes, selected one and fit it into the tape recorder recessed in his desk. "The drummers will praise her age, praise the distance she's come, praise her wisdom in making such a journey. Listen . . ." He flipped the switch.

And she will enter the royal gates, I thought, dancing . . .

With the sound of *dun dun* drums in my ears, I took the elevator down to the first floor and walked into the Hall of Man in Africa. Paying a call on an old dream. I wondered how the place would strike me now. Would I recognize, at last, the inscrutable? Or would the exhibits seem ironically remote from my nitty-gritty encounters with those things of which they in their mute way tried, not only to hide, but—in case anyone could understand them —to speak?

There was another question. That this show was, after all, Thornskyl's—capstone of his reputation—had become of special interest to me. For here in this carpeted labyrinth of glass cases could be found, perhaps, some clue—not to his taste, for that was clear, but to his motivation, generally and with me. Again I wondered, why didn't he, overriding my puny resistance, come right out and ask to meet Concha? And why, come to think of it, had he never mentioned Ferryman again to me? Assuming that bond, by now hardly to be written off as mere suspicion, why did he keep his curiosity under such strict control? I knew myself to be a snake pit of questions. Wasn't, then, he? And what, at bottom, if not information, did he the anthropologist want of me?

No one was looking. I asked permission of Eshu-Laroye and greeted my iron warrior. Then I went on into the dark room, past life-sized boy initiates dancing in sisal suits fitted tight as banana skins before the place where masks of the dead hovered expectantly above an empty throne. What kind of face could I fashion for my judge out of stovepipe or flotsam fender?

An arrow pointed to a new exhibit: The Afro-American Heritage. I entered with some trepidation—one develops an instinct for these things. But what met me there could not have been more disastrous: a complete shrine to the orisha from Harlem, where, a notice smugly informed the public, "as a result of the slave trade (the shackles of which were exhibited directly opposite) there is probably a greater knowledge of the Yoruba religion than in Nigeria itself." Ridiculous. Lies. Lies. O, Ferryman, what a betrayal! I knew damned well who the "anonymous donor" had to be.

Tears of rage stung my eyes as I stared through plate glass at the shiny soup tureens. What was the matter with them? Oshun's golden lusterware seemed to be wilting its taudry pad of peacock feathers. Shango's battle ax leaned, sleepy-eyed, against his red chopping-bowl mortar. A rattle for bringing in the swish of the sea dozed, like some grandmotherly darning last, beside Yemaja's willow-patterned urn. Obatala's white-beaded walking stick blindly accompanied his ironstone pot into nothingness; and at the top of the staircase arrangement that had been made, Oya's cowtail switch—all tornado swooshed out of it—had been allowed to lapse across her sturdy baked-bean pot, all but obscuring the nine fighting tools she'd ripped off Ogun that time she left him.

All the other objects in the Hall were "antiquities." These, despite their flaccid disarray, were showcase new, as if available to anyone at bargain prices. And yet to me, who had seen them surrounded with offerings of fruit at a *bembe,* thus exposed, they suddenly became as remote as the secrets they were supposed to contain. Did not the case, the very room—discreetly lit, inexorably carpeted—resound with an anguished emptiness as old as Pook's Hill from which The People fled their belittling into elves and fairies? O Ferryman, how could you?

He unlocked the door. I burst into the room, shouted it right out, "How *could* you?" I hadn't called first. I had interrupted him at his work; but he hastily covered whatever it was with old newspapers and was disconcertingly gentle.

"Hold on, cool it, kid. Relax. Sit down and tell old Ferryman just what it is I've done now."

"Don't put me off. You know damn well. You can kill me with that dynamite you've got in the other room. Go ahead. I'm not afraid of you. I'm not afraid of anyone anymore. I bet you wouldn't want to put your little pots of poison on exhibition, would you? No, all you care about is saving up a little personal ammunition, right? Maybe this is just the first step in your master strategy of ruin. *Now* you're going to blow the whole city up. Well go ahead! Who's to stop you? Start lighting those fuses. Maybe it's high time to get rid . . .

"I notice you didn't put Agaju in the showcase. Well, he'll be the only one left, if that's any consolation to you. The others will refuse to be made superstars of. They'll go back to Africa for good. But not before they've made their final power play. They're going to stalk right through the museum on their stilt legs, Ogun in the forefront, Derrick-the-red, bashing the exhibits with those big-balled fists of his. And when they've finished with Thornskyl, they're going to come over here; so you'd better hurry, Ferryman. With a huff and a puff She'll blow your house in. Old Agaju will split his gasket; then Boom! and that will be the end of it, completely uninhabited. Come on, light those fuses. I dare you! . . ." Ferryman had slipped behind the partition. I covered my ears, half-expecting to hear a genuine explosion. But I fell to the floor instead and there was only . . .

Silence. The sound of a vacuum cleaner across the courtyard, the *rat-a-tat-tat* of a distant street drill. Everything seemed to have come to a halt in that bare sunny room, all creation reduced to the dance of dust motes.

I pulled myself up to a sitting position. "Ferryman?" There he was, cross-legged, leaning against the wall, watching me.

Reaching into his shirt pocket, he pulled out a pack of Marlboros.

"Smoke?"

"No thanks." He lit up.

"Okay, kid," he said. "Now we can talk. Do you often flip your lid like that? Better feed your head—take it from old Ferryman. You gotta cool way down." He paused, his forehead wrinkled, thoughtful. "Do you know what Ogun did when Oya stole his fighting tools?"

"No, what?"

"He made a pact with Oko (orisha of the farm), got a

contract to start making hoes. Oaths are sworn upon iron now; hoes ring out justice . . ."

"But Ferryman, I don't . . ." He waved me silent.

"See if you can't get some of those fighting words of yours down on paper. If I'd been half so articulate at your age, I wouldn't be brooding on a viper's nest of notes Thornskyl would give his wisdom teeth and ten thousand bucks to get his hands on . . ."

"So you let him have the orisha instead. Ferryman, don't you realize I've seen? I know! Why the hell do you think I came here like this? No, I don't often flip my lid, not since . . . but this time with reason. Please don't try to put me off. You owe me—owe all of us, in fact—an explanation. Someone besides me eventually will find out. The news will get around. I know you've got no use for any of them anymore, I mean even for Concha, Obalete. You've a right to be a loner, but you've got no right to betray something that belongs to everyone. The orisha aren't yours to sell out. How could you possibly have been *that* hard up?"

"You think the others don't profit?" he put in bitterly. "That just shows how little you know of the world."

"Well, maybe they do, in their own ways, some of them; but not one of them would ever dream of exposing the whole business to the public. The visitors who go there will get an absurd idea. And since they can't understand, their gawking will be offensive . . ."

"To a collection of empty pots?"

"Empty?"

"Sure, how dumb do you think old Ferryman is? The real stuff, all that counts, is right here in my apartment all wrapped up safe till I can afford to replace the containers."

"Well, I suppose that's some consolation, but all the same . . ." I wasn't convinced, yet couldn't get out the right

words fast enough to explain what I felt: that the museum
meant death. That's it, the museum was like a cemetery;
so it was already, despite anything I could have done or
might do, too damn late.

"You think a little publicity ever hurt the gods?" broke
in Ferryman, along the very lines—but the reverse—of
what I was thinking. "On the contrary. Did Venus cut off
her loving arms because someone dug her up and put her
in a museum?" And from there, I thought, right onto a
box of pencils. "No, indifference got her underground in the
first place. It was time buried her temple. The gods are not
human property, you're right there, kid. But they do depend on humans for their strength, and if nobody feeds
them, they get all broke up, or go to sleep. Maybe some
day human hunger will awaken them, and the old force
flow back into those funky stone faces. Scattered limbs
will be joined together again, torchlights go on in abandoned shrines and temples, drums and sistrums sound down
the mountains—or, as is more apt to be the case, men
will go right on destroying themselves, their gods, and the
rivers dry up, plants lose their medicine . . ."

"So you think a round of well-dressed applause will bring
Tinker Bell back?"

"What's that, kid?"

"O nothing, just something popped out suddenly from a
long time ago." Actually it was something my mother said,
not to me, but to the world, as we sat spellbound in the
theater. Matinee. My legs still dangling from the seat. How
old was I then? Five? Six? "Anyhow, Ferryman, whatever
you say, I just can't accept the *thing*."

"Look at it this way, kid; where would you be if you
hadn't dropped in and checked out Eshu-Laroye?" He
had me there. "That was, you might say, only a feeler, a
piece of bait, a sop to fend off Thornskyl for a while until
I could get my big show together."

"Well, you're honest enough about that. And I'll be honest enough with myself to react to your peep show the only honorable way I can. You carried me across, and I'll go on from there—the whole way. I suppose—and that must be what you meant by your speech—each additional *santero* counts, be he only one in . . ." and I had an image of those buses crowding into the parking lot, disgorging them, noisy and indifferent, strung along by their stupid teachers from every part of the city, the suburbs, even out of state. "But you told one lie that's still mysterious to me. Why on earth did you say more is known about the religion in Harlem, where neither you nor Concha live, than in Nigeria? Surely Thornskyl wouldn't go along with that unless you, and in what way I can't imagine, convinced him. Or has he really given up science completely? I've never been to Africa, but then neither have you; and even the little I've heard and read . . . After all, those blurbs under the other exhibits aren't in the past tense yet."

"Politics," Ferryman simply said. "Look, kid, all intentions are mixed. And lies have to be told now and then to keep things moving. That's how Eshu operates, by the way. Very important. Let's say I did what I did—for all the thanks I'll get—on behalf of my old pal Obalete. And even if the Yoruba Temple didn't exist, I'd have done it anyway. You seem to forget I'm a black man, Raymond, glad to have had a hand—after all the changes we've been through—in getting our power thing going again. Sure it's not quite so simple as the notice sounds. We had to pick up some stitches dropped off in Cuba; but we kept the knack. More than that—a little bit here, a lot more down there. I don't mean just tambourines to glory and all that shit. I remember my grandfather making me a toy I now know to be a bull-roarer, voice of avenging ancestors. And my aunt knew an old woman who still conjured with a medicine ball. So why not let the museum-traipsing kids from Harlem in on that much of our secret. And why not let them go on and think we've done the originals one better, that we're not just diluted Africans, but have got more than those we left behind, more zip and more knowledge."

"I get your point. I hadn't thought of *those* kids. No doubt there'll be two or three of them that'll ask the right questions. But I'm still not persuaded it's the wisest way to accomplish any of your objectives. Perhaps this sort of 'lie' is just what's wrong with *Santería* people themselves, why they go around with swelled heads playing orisha-in-person."

"Who taught you to say that?"

"Concha, do you know her?"

"She doesn't play Orisha, she plays Witch," sullenly.

"Well," I said cheerily, "I guess your notes are next."

"Are you kidding? That bread was just to pay off old debts. From now on I've got no more kicks for Thornskyl; he'll have to get them somewhere else. I didn't tell you? I got a job, kid, a bite off the establishment."

"You don't mean it! Where?"

"Second Chance, one of the city agencies—cures young addicts. They hired me, miserable as I am," he said proudly, "because I'm good with kids. Little do they know I'm going to start right out with the religion."

"Gee, Ferryman, what a great idea!"

"Well, I'm glad you approve of *that* at least. Now you'd better shove off. I've got something to finish before nine o'clock. Here's a pawn ticket. I want you to take it up to Benny's on 125th Street and claim my typewriter. Here's five bucks, all he'd give me; but it's worth a hell of a lot more. Now, when you've got it together on those keys, come by and read me something you've written. It can be all lies, the wilder the better, but I'll recognize the truth that's in it—if any—and give you credit both ways."

"Gee thanks, Ferryman. What a great present! I'm sorry

I was so hasty. I guess we just see things differently."
"More alike than you think. Wait and see, Mr. Innocence.
Now don't forget . . ."
"I won't, thanks again, take care."

On my way home from Ferryman's a really weird thing
happened, or, to be more exact, had happened already.

Five dollars in my pocket, I decided on impulse to stop
and pick up something for Oya I'd long had my eye on, a
cowtail switch displayed in the window of Ethiopian Im-
ports on Madison Avenue. I had almost the exact amount
saved up, only fifty cents short, so I wouldn't really be robbing Peter to pay Paul. Certainly there was no urgency
about the typewriter. Besides, there was no question of my
going all the way up there for that now.

Though I had nothing like a shrine in our apartment,
gradually over the weeks I'd been collecting things that
"belonged" to certain orisha. For example, from the Village, where Charlie, my sister and I occasionally went of a
Friday night to eat, I had brought back a peacock feather,
another time a brass banglet for Oshun. At the Botanica in
the Park Avenue market I'd come across 9 by 12 cardboard
placards printed up with prayers to Eshu and Shango in
three languages; at the Coney Island Aquarium shop, a
lovely piece of fan coral for Yemaja. Ogun was all too easy.
For him I'd constructed a mobile (attached to the central
light fixture in our living room) out of a horseshoe, buzz-saw
blade, bicycle chain, Honda hubcap and various other
items scavenged along the river. But for Oya I had nothing
but a locust pod. So when a beautiful black fly whisk appeared in the window of that shop, I determined to save
up and buy it.

Eventually. But now I wanted it right away, because of
all the orisha who ought to be placated for Ferryman's im-
piety, it was the one he'd made—in default of his own
Agaju—Queen of the Shrine exhibit that demanded it

most. His mother too? Or, come to think of it, did he at some level of cynicism see the museum as dead as I did?

The light changed. I ran across Madison. And stopped. The whisk was gone. A sort of coolie hat hung in its place. Bursting into the shop, "Hey Mister," I said to the neat young man behind the desk, "that cowtail switch, the black one with the thin handle; it isn't hanging there in the window anymore. That guy said he'd save it for me . . ."

"Let's have a look," the young man said pleasantly. "The boss is out right now, but I think I remember seeing . . ." He started toward the back wall. "Is this the one you mean?"

"Good grief what's happened to it? All lopped off—six inches at least. How horrible!"

"Hmmm, yes, I see what you mean," bringing over a white whisk for comparison, "rather odd, indeed . . ."

I had a sudden thought. "You must have a wastebasket."

"Why certainly." He pulled it out from under the desk and obligingly stood by while I rummaged.

"Black hair!" I cried triumphantly, "a whole hunk. That proves it; but why?"

The clerk, by now as mystified as I, pulled open the desk drawer. "Look here." On top of a neat pile of receipts lay a heavy pair of scissors. "Odd . . ." he mused, and then, in his slightly foreign voice, "I'm terribly sorry. I'll ask the boss when he comes in if he knows anything about this. We're about to close now. Perhaps you'd better drop in Monday. I'm sure he'll be able to get you another from the wholesalers," he added reassuringly.

But I wanted that one, already promised to Oya.

I did go back, right after school on Monday. The boss, a fortyish man with thick glasses, replied to my outrage with a dull, evasive look. "But why? why?" I persisted.

"I just felt like doing it, that's all. Thought it would look better. Wasn't selling as it was," he added.

"But you knew I, at least, figured on buying it."

"Perhaps you should have left a deposit."

"But you didn't tell me I needed to; you even promised to let me know if anyone else showed interest; you wrote down my phone number! Besides, I don't see how any of this gives you the right to disfigure a beautiful thing."

"If you want to buy another, please place your order," he replied stonily, "if not, will you leave at once. It's none of your business what I do with my own merchandise, now is it?"

From the back of the store the young man gave me an apologetic gesture as if to say, who knows what got into him? I think he's crazy.

Initiation

I

"Jinx"—the omni-word bag into which Concha stuffed the incident. By whom was not so clear. Granted the boss of the import store was mean, or even crazy; yet what he had done, didn't seem to have been his own idea. The impulse must have come from somewhere else: hence his grogginess.

"But that's exactly what *brujería* (witchcraft) is!" she declared.

And I replied, "Okay, so let's hope I never have another experience like that one!"

"Ferryman? You been seeing him lately?"

I said as a matter of fact I had been on my way home from his place when . . .

"Aha!" she pounced on this. "Reymundo, you *got* to be careful. I told you he's evil . . ."

". . . *and* crazy, I know," my usual way of mitigating the

charge. "There's a lot of hate in him, but not directed toward me. I'm sure of it. If I didn't think he wished *me* the best, I wouldn't go there, honestly Concha. Sure he does terrible things . . ." Ooops, I was hoping I wouldn't have to go into the business of the shrine at the museum; it would be much better if she found out *after* she got back from Africa . . .

"Seraphina," she suddenly remarked, "says it's the lady who runs the restaurant by the cemetery. You haven't been back *there* have you?"

"The Cosy Corner? No, but I can't say I haven't been tempted, on chilly days, by her coffee."

"O go on," she said, coquettishly pretending offense, "get out of here!"

"That was just a hint, Concha, honestly." With this crisis on our hands we'd neglected our usual routine.

It struck me, as I followed her into the kitchen, that for a second I'd been playing Jamón's part with her, and this made me realize how much she missed him.

"We got to talk to Oya," she said, easing onto the flimsy kitchen chair. Scant Formica seat becoming detached from aluminum tubing: I ought to ask her if there was such a thing as a screwdriver in the house.

". . . her fly whisk, after all. Maybe we offended her. Jamón got mad as hell at me when his wife had her three-year *ebo* and didn't give Oya a black goat. Went so far as to have my godmother's husband call up from Flushing; but I told him the reading come out all right without it. Maybe she changed her mind. Could be that goat is what she's after. If so, Jamón better give his wife some alimony to pay for it. Everybody talks how the price of meat is going up; are they kidding? Any higher and we got to start robbing the Bronx Zoo! Now this is going to take me some time, lots of preparation. You better wait in the front room. I'm going to take the phone off the hook, and if the doorbell rings, you call through the chain that I'm sick in bed with the virus."

I sat down over by the window, staring back at Seraphina, wishing she would talk to me . . . There was another possibility. Dare I convey to Concha the suspicion—as if I'd unwittingly tripped some lever and caused a short circuit—of my own responsibility? I remembered at the time of my visit to the Yoruba Temple feeling drawn by some invisible magnet. Well this situation had worsened, become more complicated, more magnets. As if at large in the world were supercharged thoughts that forced things to happen, and I was stuck in the ground like some telephone pole way out on Hunt's Point; my wires they'd rush through. And once in a while my own think box required to function as a transformer. Which is why the import man's loathsome gesture could have been directed by the very person it was meant to hurt. Self-*brujería,* boomeranging.

"It was a sign," Concha announced, emerging triumphantly from the bedroom, "that you got to make saint fast."

"I know," I said, very much relieved. "But why did the message come from Oya?"

"Because she says she's your mother. Now she's not going to fight for your head, like they sometimes do—you know, try to get the jump on each other at the last minute. She's going to let Ogun go right ahead; but you'll get her, too; and in exchange for a black goat, she's going to give you plenty! No more climbing over the fence into the cemetery, you hear? That's finished."

So far so good; but how to pay for everything—that was the problem. Apparently the ceremony for Ogun was much more elaborate than most, far more complicated than Shango's. And for Oya—even if she were going to take second place—Concha thought we ought to hold the rites for the dead required of her preferred children. My problem: the money, which, typically, didn't worry Concha. She was all taken up with getting the right people to officiate.

The mystical Ebo Jones, whose "year" had ended, would be my *yabona*—best man, sponsor. No difficulty there. But for days Concha toyed—tortured herself would be better—with the idea of attempting a reconciliation with her own godmother in order to secure the stellar services of Jo Jo as diviner. Finally she decided to make up for the inevitable recourse to Pedro Cartero by signing on Jamón as *italero*. For Jamón was willing, on account of his special fondness for me, to come back in this special capacity (that is, master of initiation ceremonies) for the occasion at least, which return Concha privately hoped would mark the beginning of the end of that painful estrangement. Lead drum would be played by Ogundoti, formerly of the Yoruba Temple. To "give" Ogun to me (since Concha didn't "have" him yet), someone I didn't know was being called in. A very strong Ogun. The gentleman was a friend of Jean-Claude's—did I mind? I probably wouldn't even see him. Very busy, the gentleman always arrived at the last minute, did his job and left right away—"like the surgeon who once operated my feet," said Concha.

"Gentleman? Why do you call him that? And if he does things right—let's hope better than that surgeon of yours— why should I? Who is this Jean-Claude, anyhow. Do I know him? . . . O the cake-eating Yemaja! Well what does his friend eat? Crowbars? People?"

So the crew was gradually shaping up; but not the money. Elaborate as things were going to be, the price, Concha insisted, would not go up. She even offered to give me the whole ceremony as a present, as if I were her grandson or nephew. But this I stoutly refused. No, I'd pay for it myself. Yet how could a cat like me possibly come up with

$2,000, just like that, without stealing it? "And even for stealing you need expertise," I said to Marty.

My sister, who had long since discovered all about Concha and had even been up for a reading, was all for telling my uncle that Miss Landaff thought my work would improve were I less distracted by matters that could doubtless be settled in a few sessions with a psychotherapist. My aunt and uncle would understand. Shrinks that generation approved of. Then we could use the money to pay Concha.

"Nonsense. A hairbrained scheme. Dishonest, particularly for a psych major, Marty."

"I know," she sighed. "Not really worthy of me. But how could we ever explain, beforehand at least, about your initiation? They insist on being broad-minded, almost radical. Even if it were a guru you wanted, maybe they'd consider withdrawing the money. Anything Indian—either kind—is respectably mystical. But Black Religion? You really must be mad, they'd say. Voodoo's regressive. Besides, haven't you heard? Integration's out; voluntary segregation is the thing. So where are we?"

"Politically, I guess it *is* nationalist all the way. But that has nothing really to do with the religion. Sure the orisha came originally from Africa, but they're here now, and I want to help them stay. Anyhow, if you want to talk ethnic, you'd have to say the business is mainly Spanish."

"But you're not Spanish," she said, giving me that annihilating look of hers. And we both laughed, thinking right away of the Levy's bread posters.

"Neither is Ferryman Spanish, nor Obalete and his crowd. Maybe—except for that lady whose child was a reborn spirit—I'm the only one like me. But, I tell you, where one's coming from is so much less important than where one's going. Think of the old-fashioned recruiting posters. Ogun wants me. And Oya wants Ogun to want me."

"All right, Raymond. I find it hard to believe, but then,

since I've met Concha I can't disbelieve in anything. Now don't get excited; this doesn't mean I'll ever go the whole way; but I will wear my Yemaja beads during exams." She laughed. "And I'll do the best I can to help you get there. O dear, how maudlin I sound," giving me a hug. "Mmm, where were we? You said Concha offered to do the job for nothing. That means she has the money—no visible signs of it, I grant you. Stashed away somewhere? Uncle Jochem's treasure—maybe it's a sort of magical hoard that's self-replenishing! So why don't you let her lend it, and you pay her back in installments. We could skimp a bit on household expenses. You could work for pay this summer up in Middlefield. I know you'd hate to give up your Saturday jaunts, but if you needed to, you could continue working on into next year—bus boy or something. How does that sound?"

"Marty, you're being awfully nice and helpful, but how can I explain that even a loan from Concha's no good. If she wanted to, she could win the money. But it has to come from me, or through me in a way that involves some personal sacrifice. *That* I'm sure of. I'd be afraid to have it any other way. Here's how I see it: If an orisha wants you it's like the reverse of being evicted. Sure, you can squat behind leaded-over windows for a while, sneak in and out of your tenement the back way. But eventually you've simply got to relocate. There's a nice furnished apartment with your name on the mailbox waiting for you. U-Haul, in you go. Well, imagine that—table's all set. So you start to eat. Shelves filled with books, so you start to read. Turn on the hi-fi. This could go on for weeks, even years. But one day, if you haven't already, comes a knock at the door: the landlord, 'pay up!'

"Like what happened to Doreen. Maybe I told you about her—the woman who got possessed and had to make Shango right away without even going home for her toothbrush. Since Doreen was broke, Concha paid the whole works; it seemed the only way. Well, Doreen killed herself three weeks ago. They found her hanging in a closet back of Ogundoti's studio. He's a drummer she'd worked for. She swore she wouldn't go back, but she did anyway. Maybe her other jobs didn't pan out. I do know she thought Shango would make her strong enough to take anything. He didn't. Ogundoti must have driven her too hard again and she couldn't take the pressure. I met Jamón one day on Tremont Avenue, and he told me all Concha's enemies are saying it was because she didn't do some little thing right at Doreen's initiation, skipped one of the ingredients. But that's not my theory."

"And what does Concha herself say?" asked my sister frowning.

"Her usual theme, and I'm sure in a sense she's right. It's so complicated, Marty, there never seems to be a single explanation for anything. Concha says Doreen got the idea she was more than just a human being. To be a priest is not to change places with divinity, but one by one people fall into that trap. Obalete, for example. He's really asking for it now. When I walked by the Yoruba Temple the other day, I found it all boarded up. 'What happened, Concha?' I asked her, 'did they bust him for bigamy?' 'No, he called me up to say good-bye, said someone had sold him a big piece of land cheap and he was going down South with all his people to form a black community. Can you imagine all of them working in the fields? Some begged off; Mama Tele, for example. But she proudly claims he's already bought himself a big white horse, just like Obatala when he was a banished king. Can you imagine what those white people down there will think? He'll be shot for sure, one of these days.' Frightening, isn't it, Marty? And the worst of it— why not? Given Obalete's personality, his scheme seems so logical. Why should someone so grand as he stay cooped up in Harlem? I'm tempted to say, more power to him! And, incidentally, what a joke on Ferryman! Gave the orisha away for nothing—except money."

"Raymond, you've got me really scared. How can I possibly allow you to get into such a business?"

"You can't and didn't allow anything, Marty. Sure it's dangerous; but I got into it, or it got into me, and now I've got to do the right thing, so *think*!"

"I can't anymore, but maybe I can help you to; listen, what do you know about iron?"

"Corrodes easily," I said, feeling pretty depressed.

"O dear. Wrong question, wrong answer. Try again. Suppose you were to give Ogun exactly what he wanted, would there be any money in it? Which is to say, to take the only gods I know anything about, if you were son of Ares, you should take up a martial art, win all by fighting. Or if a son of Hephaestus, make something. There's a lead; you're good with your hands. Or, of Apollo, take up your lyre, so to speak, or go hunting . . ."

"I get it. Okay. I'll play that game if you want. Let's see, Ogun's an explorer. I've done that. No money in it. Unless I go into the scrap-iron business. Craftsman—it's no use, Marty."

"Go on."

"The trouble is I can't think of these things except in the future. I really would like to learn the blacksmith's trade. Maybe in one of those restored colonial village scenes like Schuyler Mansion or that place out on Long Island we visited once when we were little. And then, I'd like to spend some summer working in a foundry, learn all there is to know about casting—big pieces. Welding also. Obalete has his dream, well here's mine: When I've learned all those things, something about engineering as well, then I'll march right down to City Hall and get myself a contract. No, first I'll have to form a company: the Bronx River Betterment Association. How's that for a title? Then I'll hire an army— no one over eighteen need apply—and together we'll scour the banks from Hunt's Point to 180th Street, cart everything away to a big lot for reconstituting. (The City will let us rent some of those marvelous machines.) Then from all those kids I'll choose a few apprentices, and we'll go to work peopling those clean shores with water spirits—some smallish, some fifteen-feet high like the stabile in front of Lincoln Center library. An old factory, the one that's a garage now, will be transformed into my studio. Think of it, Marty! And while some plant grass and willow trees, the rest will help make benches—in weird shapes, like sculptures, pleasing to the eye, where old people can come and sit, little children play. And there'll be trellises and footbridges here and there—frames through which to contemplate the river. And a special place to hold outdoor *bembes . . .*"

"Beautiful! . . ."

"O Marty, can't you see the problem with your game? Only Ogun can give me that power. I know that's what he wants—in the future. And yet, I'm very well aware of the difference between god and man, believe it! However, in the meantime, I've got neither the power, nor the direction; only a hint of who's in and who's out with him at the present moment. And that, I guess, is precisely what's been blocking my mind up. What does Ogun want now? Well, there's only one stone left to turn—the obvious. So I'm going to take the bit in my teeth and . . ."

"Raymond, what are you talking about and where are you going? You look awful."

"To see what it means in my case to sell out."

"What-do-I-want, not-that-you're-prepared-to-do-it, anyhow-what? Hmmm, quite a conundrum . . ." Here I, thinking I'd come to test the softness of the executioner's block, had apparently taken him by surprise.

He started to say something, then thought better of it. Stalled by lighting his pipe. "Well now, young man, you won't help me out? I can see you're in trouble. Wouldn't it be better for me to ask what you want?"

"Everything—and nothing. That's top and bottom of the box . . ."

". . . you're in?" I nodded. "They call it double bind, in our culture. I suspect you of being unnecessarily bound by the *quid pro quo* of mercantile convention. You don't owe me anything, if that's part of what's bothering you, until I ask for it. I thought you heroically considered me your friend. Besides, I'm just as interested in your Concha's trip as you are."

"I know; but you're also interested in more, in something I personally have to offer. I've felt it from the start—since you first sent me off to Ferryman's. Now does that help you out? I'm only asking you to come out with it now. And, as I said, I might refuse, throw the whole thing up—destroyed if I do, destroyed if I don't—but I haven't even that choice, have I? until I know exactly what's required."

"Ah, I think I am finally beginning to see. Perhaps you've been obscuring things by being somewhat less than honest with me. Cowardly words, the Yoruba say, are inappropriate from a hero; and yet you insist, if I may say so, on a noble view of yourself when in effect you are asking, correct me if I'm wrong, for nothing more nor less sordid than money—lots of it."

I nodded, too humiliated to say anything.

"Well, buck up, my boy. If I am indeed on the right track, the money you need will be transformed, as it leaves your hands, into something as spiritual as you could wish— matter into energy. Like antitoxin to the disease, it'll keep you from collapsing under the impact of that intangible 'everything' you're prepared to receive. But at this point you've simply got to take it for what it is—a check, nothing nearly so romantic as cowries." To my astonishment, having heard, I suppose, no denial from me, Thornskyl opened his desk drawer, groped for a block of checks, tore one off, made it out and handed it over. "I assume that's the going rate." A bit high, Ferryman must have told him.

"I don't need quite all that. And I wasn't asking you personally."

"Never mind, on either count. The museum will reimburse me, and you can put the rest in the bank for later. Things always come up. Now," going over to a polished cabinet, "I think what we both need is a drink. Then we'll discuss," he paused, to let it come out ironically, "your part of the bargain." He took out a bottle of white rum, poured a little on the floor—not by accident—then a couple of inches into each of two small glasses, handed me one, raised his—clink—together we drank it neat.

"For my part I shall be," settling back with a wry smile, "neither more nor less honest than our course of action requires, for we have chosen, you see, but one alternative. You know, Raymond, I'm not really the master strategist you seem determined to make me out. Indeed you often force me to think, as it were, on my feet. Be all this as it may, it *has* occurred to me that someday you might be in a position to perform a singular service, not only to the museum, but to the scholarly community of Africanists, to the growing science of urban anthropology, and perhaps to the larger public as well. So, if someday, why not—you being a rather precocious chap—immediately? We have money in our budget for such projects, and if I give you yours in anticipation, it is because I trust you to complete yours as faithfully as you can, of course, without betraying secrets neither you nor I would want betrayed."

Seeing me puzzled, he hastened to explain. "We publish a series of monographs on various things ranging from kingship rituals to calabash decoration, including now and again personal narratives of the sort one might call autobiographical anthropology. The best of these, Carla Krashnikov's firsthand account of witchcraft and fertility rites among the Nupe, was actually published commercially as a novel. You might read it—just to get an idea. For what I *want* from you within a year or so is simply this: a record of your experience among the orisha-worshipers here. Whatever you have to say will be of great interest, and will complement . . ."

"I know, Ferryman's exhibit. Written half of the examination. You're asking me to 'sing,' as they say of prisoners."

"In a way, yes, but your own song primarily, and of course you are free to refuse: simply tear up the check. Furthermore, should you decide to go ahead—with everything —then you are under no obligation, I must stress, to say anything you don't want to."

"But all sorts of people are involved; even you would have to come into it, sir, at least a little bit."

"No difficulty there; you simply change the names. Scramble the letters is one way. Let's see," he printed his own on a pad, "Thornskyl, *y* to *i* minus the *t* might come out Klingshorn, a magicianly name. I like that. Besides, you mustn't worry about giving me, as I'm afraid you will, adverse publicity. I shall insist on reading your," he paused to let it sound grand, "manuscript; but before it is published I shall probably be off to Africa."

"For good?" I felt it.

"Yes, for a long while now, I've felt my life here untenable. Whereas over there, well, perhaps someday you'll see. Before leaving the museum I wanted to make my section of it live. All the more reason for your 'doing your thing,' as they say, now—while I'm still around to sponsor it. And so, Raymond, good luck. We'll keep in touch. You know," he added, "something I thought when you first walked in— already captured by something you could only guess at through the glass—that boy, I thought, would make a splendid anthropologist."

II

That evening I went straight up to 125th Street from the museum, carried Ferryman's typewriter home on the crowded subway and then, next day, down to 86th to get it repaired. A Remington 17, cast-iron frame—can you believe? Must have already been antique when he hauled it into his wicked apartment. My sister bought me a method book, and in three weeks I was pounding blindfolded on my anvil. Charlie made a plywood traveling case for it.

He drove us up to Massachusetts in late June, spent the weekend, then he and Marty returned to the city where both had summer jobs—Charlie in an architect's office, she doing research at the Jungian Institute and taking an eight week's literature course on the side. She was thinking, she said, of switching her major.

My aunt and uncle were delighted to learn I'd decided to spend the summer writing. "It's never too soon to start being precocious," my aunt said. "A friend of mine at Sarah Lawrence had already published two books of poetry by the time she got to college."

"By the time I was sixteen," my uncle confessed, "I had already written my best novel—never published. Let's hope you have better luck than I've had. It's not easy to make a living writing what you *want* to write."

"I can't say I really want to write this, Uncle James, and all I hope to make, I've already got." Which mystified them, but I didn't feel like explaining—sell-out, the devil's parchment signed in blood. They'd only have congratulated me on my good luck. How galling!

By my physical appearance my aunt and uncle were stunned. I arrived only a couple of weeks after my initiation, looking, even my sister had to admit, rather like an inmate on the way out or, more precisely, like the odd fellow we used to see running around the reservoir in his undershorts, with rocks in his hands. I was just that thin. My head was shaven, but I wore a white cap covering it. White shirt (with beads tucked in), white shorts or Lees—such was my outfit, and will be until my "year" is up. "You mustn't ask him any questions," my sister said firmly. "Raymond's taken a sort of vow, is in what you might call a sacred state—you know how kids are nowadays."

My aunt was intrigued. "I know, into all sorts of weird religions—even James . . ."

"Shut up," my uncle interjected.

"Well then, one of my classmates . . ." She looked hurt, but chatted bravely on, "a perfectly ordinary girl from East Orange, is now a Sufi, of all things. Another converted to Islam and went off shooting films in Cairo. It's a shame you can't tell us anything, Raymond; you must be so full of interesting concepts."

"Just so long as drugs are no part of them," said my uncle gruffly.

"Nothing at all to worry about on that score," said my sister. "His high you can blame on river water."

"What fun!" said Aunt Marcia. "How resourceful." She always was good at puns.

Later, that night, when we took a swim in the pond, Uncle James admitted to having taken up Transcendental Meditation.

The place I went in: just above 180th Street falls. The time: night. Park: closed. We all climbed over the fence—except Jamón who kept watch on the sidewalk for the police.

They ripped my clothes off and let those scraps of my old life float away in the darkness to snag, perhaps, on some barbed wire bush or box spring hedge before sinking eventually into soft mud. "Reach down," Concha whispered, "feel around until you find something." Shivering I dove, exultant I came up with a slimy chunk of something which, wiped off and examined by candlelight, proved to be rock. "Not exactly a smooth stone," said Concha, "but it'll do. Good thing you didn't cut your hand on a rusty beer can or broken bottle. One of these days we're going to have to find another place farther upriver."

Pleased to have found anything at all within the limits of appropriateness, I carried my river's gift sloshing at the bottom of an earthenware jug balanced atop my head all the way to Jamón's delivery truck, standing in the back till we stopped at Hoe Street; then up the stairs, right on through Manuela's apartment into her vest-pocket backyard where, Ogun being beyond the pale, an out-of-doors-orisha, a thatched hut had been constructed to accommodate me for the solemn nights and days to follow.

So ended birth by water. There is a second cleansing in crushed herbs, and a final baptism in blood . . .

Throughout the central part of the ceremony, your eyes remain shut. After the herb bath, your hair is shorn by everyone present. Once upon a time—to judge from the aggression generated in the room—I'm sure there were lash strokes. I felt very much the victim. Then they sit you down, arrange your hands open-palmed on your knees, and what happens after seems to take an eternity. Up and down in my mind's darkness I went, gliding effortlessly along those ancient paths like a movie camera, always centering on the sunlit surface of the water . . .

(Hours later) I noticed it was becoming increasingly difficult to breathe. They'd thrown some sort of cloth over my head with a weight on top pressing my neck into my shoulders. *Chhh-chhh-shhh,* came the intimate rattlesnake sound of maracas . . .

Muffled, outside my tent, the continuous singing began to take on new urgency. Sweat stung my eyelids, but I couldn't wipe it off. More weight. I braced my spine to take it. *Chhh-chhh-shhh,* they came right on in like bad dreams under the covers. Closer, closer . . .

As if being forced down a deep tunnel, I gasped for what air was left. "That's it, baby, take deep breaths," Jamón en-

couraged me. But suffocation was descending like a solid
cloud. How could I possibly continue to cut through it?
The river, think of the river, my remaining willpower said;
and there she was, as if I were beholding her for the first
time: icy falls dissolving into steel-gray water.

Now like a blimp I floated up from my chair, coverlet and
all. Outside the singing mounted to an excited shriek.
Above thunderous handclapping, I could still make out the
dry crick of maracas and I kept my clogging ears focused on
them. *Ogun de, e arere.* I took a couple of steps. Then lightning struck the crest of the palm sprung up inside of me.
Sparks shot from my feet. "No!" I shouted in a voice so unlike my own that it startled me. Desperately, before that
tight incandescence should blow me out, I managed to raise
my right arm and fling one heavy, pockmarked stone into the
torrential joy of my awakening.

> *But now bring me a minstrel;*
> *(He brought me a rattle, a bell, three drums)*
> *And it came to pass when the minstrel played*
> *That the hand of the Lord came upon him—*

Said Ferryman, "Some parts of the ritual have been performed, you know, in all parts of the world from the Ice Age
on."

When I came back to the city (yellow leaves floating
on black pond up in the Berkshires), Concha being still
gone, there was no one to talk to except Ferryman, whom but
seldom I went to see. We didn't, couldn't, have the same easy
relationship anymore. And, when by chance I ran into him,
Jamón: "You think you're initiated, baby, and in a sense
that's right. You've begun to lead a new life. But so far
you've been allowed only a glimpse of the secret." In pursuit
of the whole of which, he still fools around out in Flushing.

It's true, when all's said and done, initiation doesn't mean what you anticipate—knowledge, a tremendous surge of power. To me it has brought—in the train of a deeper loneliness—the simple sly pleasure of belonging. And this for the first time in my life. Walking the streets I may meet, as in a mirror, another white-clad figure. Checking out each other's beads, he or she and I exchange stealthy greetings —fellow tribesman glimpsed in a bazaar—without touching (this being prohibited) or even speaking. Merely a gesture—one's own left hand to right shoulder, right hand to left shoulder, and the ancient acknowledgment of the eyes.

A *santero* in mufti may suddenly reveal himself in a crowd of people waiting for the light to change: *"E Yabo,"* in a teasing tone, meaning, "Hello, initiate." And as I move shyly through thronged corridors of the Spanish market, this new identity of mine, commonly recognized by this or that matronly smile, is always ratified by a quick nod from the salesman at the Botanica where you can buy anything from black-rag dolls to aerosol anti-jinx sprays and Florida water.

At school I'm considered something midway between a Jesus freak and a hairless Krishna type. Those who want to be mean call me "Doc" or "Bus Boy." That's all right by me. None of them have heard of *Santería*. Anyhow, I never mention it, or say what I'm about. Miss Landaff can't understand why I've suddenly become such an inspired student of American history. Little does she know of the revelations still made to me in the bathroom, or on the edge now of the cemetery. Never did have much problem with English. There's a new teacher for that, a bearded young fellow who supposedly gives revolutionary poetry readings in his West Side apartment. I'm tempted to go, maybe I will sometime; I'm also tempted to show him what I've been writing, but won't. So we discuss Victor Hernandez Cruz versus Felipe Luciano in the corridor, and leave it at that.

Weekends I take early morning walks, then work all day on this "personal narrative." Monograph sounds too fancy. Novel? Probably, since Concha plays so large a part in it. That's my price, the one I'm charging, for the double exposure. So, though maybe it's not exactly what Thornskyl had in mind, it should be of "interest," being fabulous and at the same time honest. A sword to brandish before thine enemies, Concha. Every Saturday I see something new out of my intravenous Africa. And every Saturday, if I'm tongue-tied, Eshu starts me rolling.

I wish Concha would come back, though, because until she does I don't see how I can bear to finish, this writing being my only way of keeping in touch. Were I to stop going over the ground we covered, I have the awful feeling it would swallow her up, leaving me stranded. So I think of the homey disorder of her room, the laundromat across the Expressway where we sit on the wide ledge inside the plate-glass window and discuss cockroaches, the Spanish grocery where we buy the hard rolls with soft insides, the bargain shops along Bathgate Avenue where she dickers for remnants to make into ritual costumes, the special weedy sites where she installs the sacred litter to placate gods who dwell with her in the Bronx as once and for all time in Africa.

Sometimes I take the D Train at River Road, walk along the ramp above the Expressway to the turnabout at the end of Anthony Avenue and stand beneath the wires dangling with Keds. Like the chameleon, Concha's empty window feeds on air, reflects the changing colors of the sky as the sun passes beneath a cloud of smoke from some sudden incineration.

I got one letter from her. I didn't expect that much. But here it is, tacked up above "the Anvil," and it says:

So far so good. The Balogun is very nice. So is the Obatala priest, very special. I'm staying on because they have decided to initiate me into the secret society of the elders, who perform ceremonies for the earth. They paid me a compliment, wrote me out a certificate saying, "Concepción Montoya y Rios is the only American who does orisha work as we know it." When Mama Télé sees this, she's going to kill me. But with all they've been doing to my head, I'll be so strong her jinx will go flying back where it came from before it even touches the ground. Also, you'll be glad to know I have the knife. The only trouble is with the food—too hot, like hell. But I've found a little supermarket that sells rice and am able to cook it, without offense. No good coffee, though. Kola makes me sick, but I try to be polite, so I take it every time and keep it in the back of my mouth without chewing. You bet it's bitter. Everything is very expensive, and the people here are poor, many kids running around ragged. So I'd appreciate your putting five dollars on my number for the lottery. Put the stub in your Eshu (tell him what you are doing). To send the money you'd better buy a postal order. Just as many thieves here as in New York, but no junkies. Take care of yourself.

Your loving godmother,
Concha

P.S. The Balogun, believe it or not, has twelve living wives. The Obatala has only one old, one young. The Babalu priest would like to marry me (!) but he's a dangerous old man, with sense of humor and wicked eyes.

She won, naturally; but she'd better come back soon. Without her, we have no house. There's heavy snow on the ground, though it's only twelve days after Christmas, and the trash cans are blossoming peonies.

Why This Book
Is Called Santería, Bronx

Santería is the name given by its followers to the Cuban
version of an ancient West African religion. Known as *Can-
domblé* in Brazil, this religion, which originated among the
Yoruba-speaking peoples of what is now Nigeria, is being
more and more extensively practiced in the United States
—most intensively in the Spanish-speaking quarters of New
York City where, for historical and ethnographic reasons, its
adherents far outnumber those of Haitian Voodoo, with
which the general public tends to confound it.

The Yoruba divinities, called orisha (*orișa*), followed
their worshipers across the Atlantic—some in the wake,
some settled right in the hold of the stinking slave ships.
Once arrived in Cuba, the orisha found it necessary for their
survival to conceal themselves behind the images of certain
Catholic saints (Santa Barbara and St. John the Baptist, for
example) and certain aspects of Christ and Our Lady. No
matter if the Christian worthies represented by the images
had little in common with the African powers who boldly

borrowed their likenesses. A tower, a sword, a golden crown, the rages of poverty and disease—one or two qualities in common, indeed the most superficial resemblances were enough: the Yoruba had found a coded way of keeping alive beliefs and rituals that in other places (where saints were not venerated, nor many Marías given homage) were suppressed, stamped out, forgotten.

All slaves were baptized in Cuba. Pious Catholics are entitled to veneration of the saints, "saints," which the Yoruba worshiped. Who could tell the difference?—especially where the slaves were permitted to celebrate holy occasions in their own way, with dancing and drumming, with songs in their own language.

By the time the descendants of the first Yoruba in Cuba had freedom enough to do their own thing in private, *santo* was firmly established, in their minds, as the Spanish equivalent of *orisha*. And as, over the years (until very recently) less and less concealment was required, not only did the name *santo* persist, but so, out of habit and cultural gratitude (for by this time most of the visual arts of Africa had been lost), did the images themselves—the statuettes and colored prints that still adorn believers' shrines and houses.

Those who practice this Cuban form of the Yoruba religion are called *santeros*. For according to the Spanish dictionary, a *santero* is:

(a) someone excessively devoted to the worship of the saints;

(b) the caretaker of a sanctuary;

(c) a seller, also a maker of images.

The abstract noun *santeros* give to their religion is not listed in the Spanish dictionary. They must have coined it themselves. But apart from its specific Afro-Cuban reference, we can easily construe *Santería* to mean established practice of the above activities. Stretch the meaning a little. Are not poets also *santeros*? Caretakers of sanctuaries, makers and vendors of images, excessively devoted?

Concha, heroine of this story, was born and raised in Puerto Rico. The earliest *santeros* in her memory are not the Cuban priests and priestesses she first encountered in New York; they are those of the dictionary definition, particularly the makers-of-images, vendors of beautifully carved wooden statuettes of such personages as Jesus of Nazareth and the Three Kings. The most important *santero* in the Bronx, Concha these days presides over the making of many saints of human clay. To "make saint" is a popular *Santería* way of saying "become initiated." Given certain signs that initiation would be desirable, even necessary, it is Concha's job to make a preliminary diagnosis—which "saint" wants to possess the candidate's head?—and thence to take charge of the performance of all rites and obligations involved in the "second birth" that initiation always is. Concha's ability as a saint-maker is reinforced by the nature of the orisha who owns *her* head—Obatala, "he who forms the child in the womb," patron saint of the harmonious creativity we call, after the Greek god, Apollonian.

One aspect of Santería that the handyman in me finds particularly attractive is the making-do with what-is. I have already discussed this in connection with the adoption of Catholic saints. But not only did the early *santeros* adapt other aspects of their masters' religion to their own purposes, they absorbed some beliefs and practices from their companions in misery: Africans from elsewhere, especially from the Congo Basin, and the fast-dying Indian aborigines. Later generations have borrowed from spiritists, from vendors of dream books to the dispossessed in New York City.

Tolerant of other religions, most *santeros* profess themselves Catholic; many attend séances as well as mass; and, careful of the distinction between white and black magic (with which *Santería* can have nothing to do), most willingly practice a little "jinx" on the side. All use herbs and chants for curing. But they are most conscious of orthodoxy in their religious procedures, critical of ceremonies conducted by rival priests. This insistence that things be done the right way has insured thrift in borrowing and kept *Santería* surprisingly "pure," close in all important respects to the way it must have been when first brought from Africa. Even the Yoruba language has been retained, in *Santería,* like Latin in the Catholic church, as ritual speech. Chanting and singing is still done in the African language, and there exists a Yoruba vocabulary, known to the initiated, for the conveying of information about medicines and other secret businesses of belief. Ritual costumes are quite different in the New World, but colors mean the same things. Some sacred ceremonial ingredients—foods, herbs and, most importantly, substances cut into the scalp during initiations, cannot be replaced, without loss of their magical powers, and must be included at any cost—imported if need be from Africa. In other cases, so long as the form remains, substitutions can be made: the porcelain soup tureen for the traditional clay pot.

Concha, a "character" in both senses of the word, is the mistress of ingenious solutions to ritual problems. Her intuitive grasp of the essence of the religion is so strong, her spiritual experience so broad and deep, her understanding of human nature so quick, that she feels free to take liberties in instances where other *santeros* tend to bind themselves hands and feet with "don'ts" often based on ignorance or panicky hearsay. I think Concha will understand, therefore, and hopefully forgive the substitutions I have made in this book, not only to preserve certain "secrets" of *Santería* and to disguise the identities of the priests, but also for artistic reasons. So, where want of information has been filled in by fantasy, I beg her to try and see the sense of such "authentic guesswork," despite the fact that she, an intensely practical person, has never had much use for poetry.

To me, finally, *Santería* suggests a turn of mind that takes off to sanctify intense experience generally, and to describe, in the inconsistent way of the Greek philosopher Heraclitus,

the same thing now as a god, now as a form of matter,
now as a rule of behavior or principle which (is)
nevertheless a physical constituent of things.

These words may seem difficult; let's hope the experience of *Santería, Bronx* will make the meaning clear. When such "descriptions" move into the real world, they become *santos, orisha.* In seeing the River Bronx as a goddess (which no doubt she is) and the lover who nightly lies along her banks as the marvel of human technology gone wrong, creativity turned to waste, I have been exploring the idea of *Santería* beyond the frontiers of its ordinary meanings. For such personalism, from the outskirts of orthodoxy I here make apology to the wisest guardians of the shrines.

Bronx: *place* in any animistic creed is of the utmost importance; therefore I have not changed the names of the streets, of the various locations in the city and along the river where the events occurred. For me these proper names —Hunt's Point, Hoe Street—carry charges of meaning beyond my powers of invention. Such are the mysterious workings of the "saints."

Raymond's Appendix

Where I'm coming from springtime is desolate. Not at all the way fancy poets describe it. By the time March rolls around Nature looks so beat up you wonder if she ever will recover. Where ball was played summer and autumn, now squats sullen mud. The bare trees have an exhausted, defeated look; and shrubbery hangs disheveled over the edges of the walks, twigs looking as if they'd sooner be broken off than put forth leaves. And there is no concealment of the rubbish. Do you suppose in the hinterland it's different? According to one traveler,

The scenery daily increased in beauty as we advanced up this noble stream. The ground teemed with exuberant vegetation, seeming often in the fantastic appearance of its wild growth to revel in its exemption from culture.

Could be. But though unexempt from ravages of culture, the part of the river I came to know last spring grew more beautiful the more I fastened on to it. They call this aptitude—when referring to college. Occasionally I went accompanied by my sister, to whom for the first time I had something important to offer. Which something we never dreamed of defining. That she was content to let me be in the course of our expeditions guide and conduit was enough. By now Marty knew Concha was a priestess, knew something about orisha, but rather than ply me with questions, as if playing a part in a different drama, Marty responded to the river not as my goddess, but in a way appropriate to the continuous problem with which she herself was preoccupied.

Not every place was appropriate for these joint explorations of ours. Below Lafayette Street, starting from the bakery, along the flats outside the parking lots and loading platforms of the market to the jetty that marks the end of Hunt's Point—this was our southern territory. Along the gray beach, exposed as if by perpetual low tides, various lengths of insulated wire—coiled tight at the top as bean sprouts—lie flush with rusty rockweed "as if part of the same embroidery, magnified," said Marty.

Our northern territory lay above 180th Street falls. As for the middle passage—tormented shores of dumpage, reefs of junk, the bolted clasp of girdered crossings—this dismayed and frightened her. Nor were the secret paths between briar bush and willow shrub below the viaduct hers to discover. Along these she was distracted by the possibility of muggers, with some justice. Neither her bit, therefore, nor her problem—thus to redeem that part of the river loved, lost and all but not quite forgotten.

Sometimes of a Sunday morning we took the White Plains line to Gunhill station and walked down through the park to the falls where there used to be a mill belonging to enemies of the judge, my guardian. Within these precincts of the Botanical Gardens, the riverbanks are high, rocky, very old; and hemlocks that grow along the ridge overlooking the gorge are all that's left, say Ranaque and Tackamuch, of virgin forest through which they and their forefathers once tracked antelope. In the clear space between two downward-sloping branches of one of these dignified old fellows, on one of our excursions, my sister saw an owl— scowling, poised, messenger from that part of time and space to which her soul belongs.

Farther on, where the moraine peters out, just above the forsaken beaver dams that mark the northern entrance to the zoo by water, as if recalling yet another phase of her remote existence, the river slowly separates into a maze of channels, creating islands—overrun with alders entangled in wild grape, all overlaid with fallen tree trunks—that look like giant birds' nests afloat upon sultry primeval waters. I looked for a white egret, or gray parrot, but saw no migrating messenger from the regions my soul calls home. "Never mind, all's as it should be anyhow. Some day I'd like to go to the source," said Marty.

It was my turn to deliver a paper (five pages, longhand) to the ninth-grade world-history class of the Walton School, Miss Landaff presiding.

"Ladies and gentlemen," I began, "of the objects of inquiry most engaging of our attention, there is none that the learned and unlearned so equally wish to investigate as those blanks in the map hitherto unexplored, unexploited.

"Notwithstanding the progress already made in the discovery of certain private parts of darkest Africa . . ."

Titters. "Mmmmmmmm," from Miss Landaff.

". . . the course of the Niger, even its existence as a separate stream, has not yet been determined. How shameful, therefore, must seem our equivalent ignorance of the Bronx: the place of whose rise remains unregarded, its lower reaches neglected, depths unfathomed, narrows unappreciated.

("Here! Here!" interjected no one.)

". . . Resolved, therefore," said I, upon clearing my throat, "by a certain band of stalwarts, no matter what the exertions, tribulations and malarias, to ascend on foot (unassisted by native bearers) the course of said River Bronx from Hunt's Point to hidden origins whence they should afterward feel at liberty to return (from the nearest station) by train to New York City."

A long pause. "The above expedition having already been successfully completed, there follows a brief documentation in the form of photographs by Charles Jessamon, captions by (Captain) Raymond Hunt of the Royal River Bronx Society, Ltd."

"Is that all?" from Miss Landaff. And then, "You mean to say that you didn't even take your own photographs, Raymond?"

"Of course not. How could I? I haven't got a camera. Charlie, that's my sister's boyfriend, has a good one. He needs it for the sort of work he does. I helped him develop them in our bathroom, and sometimes we got some weird effects—reflections and such—that we hadn't counted on."

"We'll see," said Miss Landaff, "if the captions—together with your introduction—add up to five pages."

The trouble was . . . I mean what we discovered was much too simple and at the same time too complicated to write up. No more can words do justice to a happening. Hence the photographs. These you either get or not, far better without captions.

The idea had come, of course, from that chance remark of Marty's; but the form it took came as a kind of defiance of Miss Landaff's assignment: to write, during spring vacation, a research paper on some topic having to do with the Age of Imperialism.

"Which is far from over," my sister remarked, while Charlie wound up to deliver one of his radical speeches. We were sitting over a late breakfast the day school let out, making a list of things that ought to be done, like cleaning out closets, planting nasturtium seeds in our window boxes and going to the library. We both had papers, Marty and I, hers a psychoanalysis of some Greek myth. "I don't think it has anything to do with politics," she insisted quietly. "The reason historical forces don't run down, as the textbooks pretend, like watches, is because the personality structures that give rise to them are constants."

"Exactly," I put in. "I don't understand a word you're saying, but I am convinced of the truth. Isn't it only insofar as things are always the same that we can understand them? That we can pick up messages from the past? Now the only part of the history we're studying that really interests me is the exploring. What if I were to do this research myself?"

"Who else?" put in my sister dryly.

"I mean do in the sense of act, the way we did in kindergarten when we made pemmican on the radiator. Why has all that gone out? Why not, instead of sitting with the shades down working my way through somebody else's 'Narrative of Exploration,' conduct my own expedition to the hinterland? Get to the headwaters, not of the Nile, nor of the great, gray, greasy, but of the only river in the world that really matters to me . . ."

"Raymond!" she exclaimed, "you're fine! It's a shame you don't do better in school. If I were your teacher . . ."

"Thank God you're not; tough luck Miss Landaff is; but who cares? This will really be fun. We'll all go. Charlie, it's about time we introduced you to the Bronx. You can be official photographer. And . . ." I hesitated. "Melissa. I'd like to ask her to come along as botanist. Is that okay with you?" For some reason I was afraid she might be jealous.

Melissa Wohnung is a girl who looks about my age, though actually she's Marty's. Now she's upstate, where she comes from, working up results on the water-lily buds she dove for all last summer from a boat on a pond, while this old professor in a canvas hat collected the specimens in bottles. She sent me a wonderful drawing of the whole scene. But when we met Melissa last spring, a month or so before the expedition, she was a dropout with no home but a rucksack stuffed with little pouches of organic grains (which she mostly ate raw, but sometimes cooked in a little aluminum pot she had with her), an old fashioned flute with silver fittings (kept in a hard, velvet-lined case), a sketchbook, bottle of India ink, a couple of books which doubled as leaf-pressers, sleeping bag, tarpaulin, and that was all.

Melissa was camped, when we ran into her, in a toolshed she'd managed to pry her way into on the east shore of Agassiz Lake between the beaver dam and the 180th Street falls. We asked her wasn't she afraid of bums or junkies, alone at night in the zoo, and she said they were probably afraid of her. Then she asked us what we were into; and when she heard, said she wouldn't mind joining us for a while, but couldn't leave her stuff, so we waited while she packed up, which didn't take too long, and she went the rest of the way downriver with us, came back to our place afterward, camped in our living room a week, then took off promising to keep in touch.

Just the night before Melissa had called from a commune on Staten Island. She'd been making perfume from magnolia petals picked off the ground out there. Maybe Marty would like some . . .

"Sure," said my sister. "Don't be so defensive."

That settled it. I called Melissa at the commune.

A glance at the road map Charlie brought over that night told us it would take about three days to get from Hunt's Point to Kenisco Dam, a big blue blot fed, I presumed, by tributaries. Which (we couldn't see any on the map) would be longest? "We'll know instinctively," I said, "when we get there. Explorers' luck." (I planned to strew some black beans on the path for Ogun, just to make sure. "If I were going, I'd kill a white cock at dawn," said Ferryman. "*Don't* try it.") Melissa suggested we take sterilized spice jars along to sample how far up the river was polluted. "Good. Charlie's photographs ought to document the same process." My sister, fortunately, put herself in charge of supplies and cooking. I went so far as to buy a speckled logbook. At the last minute, Charlie produced an inflatable life raft which belonged to a fishing friend of his divorced father. "Don't worry," he assured us cheerfully, "I'll carry it; you never know what'll come in handy."

So, all preparations accomplished in twenty-four hours, we set off from Hunt's Point about ten o'clock on April fifth, spent the first night in Woodlawn Cemetery and arrived in Scarsdale close to 4:00 the second afternoon. Our pace—leisurely. We walked close to the river along paths the local kids used, but saw almost no one. Two motorcyclists encountered in the stone tunnel below Gunhill Road were an exception of major psychological importance. Roaring arrogantly through mud pools on the path, they forced us back against the iron piping of the balustrade. DRAGONS loomed in spray can letters overhead. "This, their private portal," my sister remarked, moving very close to Charlie. Below the curved ramp, on the murky marrow into which was here transformed all but the deepest layer of water, picked bones of a bedstead floated beside three half-sunk whorls of tires.

From there on all signs of civilization began to peter out. Only an occasional up-wheeled carcass of a tricycle or supermarket cart served to remind us that all was not equally beautiful and calm beneath the surface. "In search of springs," I noted in the plural, and the season, as we pushed northward, seemed, despite the increasing (you could hardly call it exuberance of) vegetation, to be steadily withdrawing, as if sucked back up into that unknown source the river was flowing out of.

Among the dry leaves of the hardwood forest below Scarsdale, Marty suddenly spied an outcrop of Dutchman's-breeches
dancing upon their pliant stalks above dark-green leaf platforms
"like little stubby-armed ghosties." And she stood, herself rooted
to the spot, with a strange half-humorous look on her face that
warned us not to prod. Then she saw bloodroot, "plump, white
stars in a cornflake sky," she said, bending down to examine
them more closely.

"I wonder what's got into her," whispered Charlie. And since
no answer was forthcoming, he busied himself changing lenses
for closeup shots of the flowers. Feeling rather at a loss myself,
I eyed him sharply. No, Charlie was not my enemy. Nobody's.
It was even difficult not to be fond of him.

Down at the swampy edge of the river, Melissa was gathering
skunk cabbage. "Makes a wonderful spice for soups, if you let
it dry first," she said, looking up with her solemn, yet pixilated
expression. "Three months is usually long enough. I'll put these
in something airy like burlap and you can hang it up meanwhile."

"Sure," I said, "in the kitchen window."

All the way up we'd seen various concrete pores and conduits
seeping, gushing evil-smelling sludge into the resolute felicity of
the river. But at Scarsdale this process suddenly reverses itself.
Valves hidden in the steep rock of a channel worn as long ago
as the Ice Age opened to let little freshlets contribute the modest
clarity of their underground experiences, their inaccessible organic decencies. And the river, acknowledging their entrances as
human flesh assents to music—cold shivers beneath her languor-
ous surface, continued, O how well I knew, as far as the murky
Turning Basin, all the way to Hunt's Point, in little hidden swirls
of reminiscence to sound their clear pitched voices.

Below the Kenisco Dam—which we never did visit—a thin
stream branches off to the left toward a town (remarkably
named), Valhalla—and proceeds, or rather recedes—past a series
of cemeteries to abut eventually upon a stone wall, which backs
the stream up into an ornamental lake called (together with
burial grounds along the left shore) Gate of Heaven.

"No kidding! How marvelous!" exclaimed my sister. "Swans
and all! Do you suppose if we counted we'd come up with

nine and fifty?" While the three of us ran along clipped, dry lawn bordered with laurel and rhododendron, Charlie stayed behind to inflate the lifeboat.

Breathless, we came to the rustic stone dike, climbed up and looked on the other side: no river.

"So that's where she disappears!"

"Or comes out again, Marty, depending on which way you're facing. Suppose this was where we had started—or from farther up, where that sign points (TO MOUNT PLEASANT), then life would have a different orientation, wouldn't it?"

"O come off it, Raymond-the-preacher," Marty sighed. That hurt my feelings, but it shouldn't have, knowing she thought, really, at that moment the same beginnings as I.

"The source is underneath, though," said Melissa, "from up top we can't possibly see it. Raymond, hold my legs, will you; sit on them . . . there, that's right." With which she acrobatically stretched herself over the edge until her head was level with the miniature cave from which we could see silver water trickle.

"The surface of the rocks, so far as I can reach, is covered with moss," Melissa reported, "and, from the feel of them, miniscule ferns. Shall I break one off? . . ." she hesitated.

"No thanks, unless you want them as specimens," replied Marty. "Anything else?"

"Sorry; nothing more I can stretch to. Want to try, Marty? Raymond?" Swinging herself back up. My sister shook her head.

"I will. Here, both of you, hold on," and I let myself over slow and easy.

Dark, couldn't see anything at first and then, in a shallow depression no bigger than the palm of my hand, bedrock upon which grew no fuzz of algae—nothing, the merest film, damp beginnings of water. "Hey Marty, bend down." And I touched first her eyes, with that knowledge.

Among the sprouting narcissus at the water's edge, Charlie stood ready with the life raft. "How funny it looks," cried my sister, running to hug him, "like a giant yellow duck."

"Drake!" I corrected her.

"Come on girls, you try it first," said Charlie, "there's room for you both." They flopped hilariously in, first Marty, who weighs more, then Melissa.

"Wait a second!" A bizarre thought struck me. "Keep hold of the rope a bit longer, Charlie." And I dashed across the paved walk that discreetly distances idyllic park from low-rise city of tombstones.

There must have been a drunken funeral the night before, high winds, or else a sloppy gardener, for the ground in front of the graves was littered with half-broken wreaths, lush white dahlias, loose peonies and garlands of dark-leaved camellias. I scooped up as much as I could carry, ran back to the lake and plumped them in Melissa's lap. This wild bouquet hid everything in the boat but the girls' pale faces and one of Melissa's bare feet.

"Cast off!" I cried. Charlie threw the painter into the midst of the flowers and the little boat began to drift with the current out to the center and then, gathering speed, down to the concrete sluice—where we caught them. On impulse Marty heaved the flowers on over. "Gifts from Persephone," she said, "who is really her mother's ghost, it being Persephone, you see, who went in search of Demeter—not the other way around. I'm sure that's the deeper meaning!" I don't think any of us grasped the point she was, obviously so brilliantly, making; but with deferential O-Wow! we solemnly watched the flowers continue through the breach onto the rocky beginnings of the stream bed underneath. How far would they get, those bruised dahlias, tattered stemless peonies, white petals of camellias?

"Too bad the river's too shallow here for navigation," said Charlie as I helped him deflate, the life raft, fold then ease the neat square into his rucksack. "Another time we'll have to try it farther down." Then Marty gave us each an arm; I grabbed Melissa's; and juvenile we skipped off toward Valhalla station to catch—only ingoing train that afternoon—the 5:57.